COMFORT AND J

India Knight is a bestselling writer and columnist for *The Sunday Times* in London, where she lives with her three children.

Comfort and Joy

INDIA KNIGHT

PENGUIN BOOKS

PENGUIN BOOKS

Published by the Penguin Group
Penguin Group (USA) Inc., 375 Hudson Street, New York, New York 10014, U.S.A.
Penguin Group (Canada), 90 Eglinton Avenue East, Suite 700, Toronto,
Ontario, Canada M4P 2Y3 (a division of Pearson Penguin Canada Inc.)
Penguin Books Ltd, 80 Strand, London WC2R 0RL, England
Penguin Ireland, 25 St Stephen's Green, Dublin 2, Ireland (a division of Penguin Books Ltd)
Penguin Group (Australia), 250 Camberwell Road, Camberwell,
Victoria 3124, Australia (a division of Pearson Australia Group Pty Ltd)
Penguin Books India Pvt Ltd, 11 Community Centre, Panchsheel Park, New Delhi – 110 017, India
Penguin Group (NZ), 67 Apollo Drive, Rosedale, Auckland 0632,
New Zealand (a division of Pearson New Zealand Ltd)
Penguin Books (South Africa) (Pty) Ltd, 24 Sturdee Avenue,
Rosebank, Johannesburg 2196, South Africa

Penguin Books Ltd, Registered Offices:
80 Strand, London WC2R 0RL, England

First published in Great Britain by Penguin Books (UK), a member of Penguin Group Inc. 2010
Published in Penguin Books (USA) 2011

1 3 5 7 9 10 8 6 4 2

ISBN 978-0-14-311981-4
CIP data available

Printed in the United States of America

For Lynn Barber, with love and admiration

Everything is collapsing, dear
All moral sense has gone
And it's just history repeating itself
And babe, you turn me on
Like an idea, babe
Like an atom bomb.

– From 'Babe, You Turn Me On' by Nick Cave

PART ONE

I

23 December 2009, 4 p.m.

So I'm walking down Oxford Street, sodden by the sheeting rain, like I walk down Oxford Street sodden by the sheeting rain every single bastarding Christmas. Well, I say Christmas – I mean 'festive period' (which always makes me think of menstruation, except while wearing a jaunty paper hat and blowing a tooter, for fun. Poot poot!). It's not actually Christmas Day – that would be tragic or, come to think of it, maybe quite refreshing: just me and the odd tramp and our cozy cider, rather than me and my sixteen or so, um, loved ones.

No, it's the 23rd and I'm picking up a few last-minute bits and bobs. Quite why I've left these bits and bobs so late is a mystery, but again, it's an annual ritual. If you didn't know any better you would think – fancy! – that there are people I subconsciously don't especially enjoy buying presents for, people who pop right out of my head until 23 December every year, when I remember not only that they exist but that they are coming to spend Christmas at my house, yay and wahoo.

I couldn't possibly comment, except to point out that the incredibly annoying and pointless thing about my approach – you'd think I'd have figured this out by now, since it happens every year – is that, in the last-minute panic, I end up spending far more money on the bits-and-bobby presents for the bits-and-bobby people than I do on presents for people I really love. Take this grotesque china cat with boogly eyes and improbable eyelashes, the one I am holding in my hand right now (I've come out of the rain and into John Lewis – as, apparently, has half of London). Perfect for my mother-in-law. £200, you say?

Well, my goodness. I stare at the sales assistant in disbelief. Has she looked at the china cat? It's eye-bleedingly hideous, it's not very big, and here she is, saying '£200' with a straight face. Also, 'collector's item'. Yeah, maybe, if you're mad. I'd rather collect those dried white dog turds you never see anymore (why? Where have they gone?). No, not really. I wouldn't like to collect dog turds at all, obviously. I'm just becoming bad-tempered, which always makes me go a bit Internal Tourette's. It's just – it's so much money. Having glared, I smile penitently at the sales assistant and gingerly hand the cat back.

But then I go trawling off round to the bath salts and 'novelty gifts' bit of John Lewis, and there are so many people, and having been cold fifteen minutes ago in my parka, despite the fact that it is designed to withstand temperatures down to −20 degrees, I am now boiling hot, and I think I can't give her bath salts again, or soaps – it's got to the stage where it looks like I'm making a point about personal hygiene – and she doesn't read books and she doesn't listen to music and she has no hobbies except collecting cats, so . . . off I return to the china animal concession, sweating lightly, forcing a smile that probably looks more like a death rictus. £200. £200! The financial markets are falling apart, Sam keeps muttering darkly that our mortgage is about to do something terrible, I'm wearing frankly shabby underwear that I'd like to replace, and I've just spent £200 on a china cat that looks like it came via a full-page ad in a Sunday supplement: *Pretty Lady Pusscat needs a home. Look at her pleading eyes and feel your heart give way. Fashioned from the finest porcelain by skilled craftsmen, Lady Pusscat will be your cherished friend . . .*

It gives me a lurch in my stomach to think of the cost, on top of which I'm now paranoid about dropping Lady Pusscat. I'm going to tell Pat, my mother-in-law, that this is what it's called. I know exactly what she'll say: 'Oh, isn't that grand.

Lady Pusscat! What a beautiful name. Isn't that grand.' Pat likes to sandwich normal speech between two expressions. The thought of it makes me smile to myself with a mixture of love and irritation. This is more than I spend on my own mother, I note, as I hand over my credit card. Well, more than I *initially* spend on my own mother.

But at least Pat will be really pleased with the cat. She'll appreciate it and say thank you nicely, and put it on her special cat shelf, and possibly get a little piece of card and write LADY PUSSCAT on it in her best handwriting, and place it reverently underneath. The problem with Kate, my esteemed mama, isn't that she's on the list of people I can't be bothered to buy presents for until the last minute. And neither – ha! – is she a person that I forget exists. The problem with Kate is that she has all the stuff she could conceivably want. She's on a list of her own, called 'People Who Have Everything' (mind you, she doesn't have a Lady Pusscat. Now there's a thought. Maybe I could mix things up a bit and get her a Lord Puppy). There is nothing I can buy her, though obviously I'm going to have to buy her something.

The thing is – you wouldn't think it from this rant, even though it's true – I really love giving people presents. It gives me pleasure. I put a lot of thought into it. I start early, even if I do finish on the 23rd. And I've yet, in adult life, to give Kate something that provokes the kind of reaction I'm after: the gasp of delight, the genuine grin of pleasure that makes you think the whole flipping Christmas faff is worth it. She liked a clay ashtray I made at school when I was six. She still has it on her desk, all beaten up and manky and poignant in about ten different ways. It's nice that she's kept it, but I haven't been able to match that present in the intervening thirty-four years.

What happens with Kate is I throw money at the problem. I think, if it costs enough, she'll like it. This is a fatally stupid approach – it doesn't work, and all that happens is that when she glances at her present, murmurs her thanks and then leaves it behind, I feel incensed and want to run after her telling her how much it cost. I did this once, to my shame. I'd bought her this amazing, hand-stitched sequined stole – beautiful, dull-gold proper sequins, not brash plasticky ones. It cost a fortune: I was still paying for it months later; in fact, if I remember correctly, there was an unpleasant episode with a red bill that I'd shoved in a drawer to make it magic itself away. She unwrapped the stole and said, 'How sweet,' and then she put it on the sofa next to her, never to be glanced at again. I couldn't help myself: I said, 'It's by this amazing new designer. I had it commissioned for you. It, um, it cost . . .' and I told her what it had cost. Kate put down her glass of champagne, closed her eyes as though in an agony of pain, and said, 'Clara. I beg you. Please don't be vulgar.'

I said I knew it was *quite* vulgar, but that I hoped she liked it because I'd had it made especially and . . .

'Don't, darling. And you shouldn't spend that sort of money on me. I'm a simple person. I'd have been just as happy with a candle.'

'A candle? What do you mean, a candle? Like, a scented candle?'

'A beeswax candle.'

'A beeswax candle?'

'Don't repeat everything I say, Clara, it makes you sound dim.'

'But I'm just checking. That's what you'd like for your present, ideally? One beeswax candle?'

'Yes. Beautiful and useful, as William Morris said.'

'Gosh. Well, I'll know for next time.'

'Quite. Pass me a blini, would you?'

What I should really do this year is go wild and buy her one lone stupid waxy candle and see what happens. 'Here you go,

Mother. Don't burn it all at once!' But I won't, because I want Kate to love my present. I want her to love me for buying it for her. I want the present to say everything that we don't say. That's the thing about presents, isn't it? Especially Christmas ones. The judiciously chosen present, the perfect gift, is offered up in the spirit of atonement and regeneration. It says, 'Look, I know I don't call as often as I should, and I know you think I'm grumpy and short-tempered' – insert your own personal failings here; I'm merely précising mine – 'but the thing is, I know you so well and I love you so much that I have bought you the perfect thing. And so now everything's okay, at least for today.' Which is all very lovely but a great deal easier said than done, and which is why I can feel the hair at the back of my neck curling with heat and stress. For a present to be eloquent, it's got to be just right, and everything I've seen so far is wrong to the point of mutedom.

I'm back on Oxford Street now, headed for Selfridges, sharing the pavement with one billion people and a mere million arsing pigeons. Can I just say, about pigeons? a) Why aren't they in their creepy old mank-nests, sheltering from the cold rather than festooning the streets with guano? Also, more urgently, b) Why do they walk along the pavement in straight lines, as though they were human? This has bothered me for years, and I find myself thinking about it once again as I slowly shuffle my way west, with one pigeon keeping pace on either side of me. We are walking three abreast, like a posse. The pigeons are my bitches: here come the girls. It is so, so wrong. But it always happens because, alone of all the birds, pigeons don't just alight, strut about for a few seconds and take off again. No, they walk for miles. They follow the invisible horizontal for a freakishly long amount of time, pretty much keeping up with us. *Pigeons think they're people*. It does my head in. It also explains why you see them on the Tube, pottering up and down the platform before walking into the carriage, calm as you like. In London, pigeons mostly walk – they only fly if you run after them. It's bloody odd, is what it is. I don't like it. Birds should fly.

Here we are. Even my temporarily unseasonal heart gladdens a little bit at the sight of Selfridges' Christmas windows, a stunning exercise in glitter and luxe. They've done fairy tales this year, but subverted them a bit, so that bosomy Goldilocks is looking minxy in boned Vivienne Westwood and the three bears give the impression that never mind the porridge, come and sit on our laps (even the baby, disconcertingly. I'm not mad about the idea of Baby Bear with a boner). Little Red Riding Hood is wearing fuchsia silk underwear under her billowing cloak, which has fallen open for the wolf's delectation. So much sex, I think, as I watch an exhausted-looking couple and their two small children staring at the displays. Sex everywhere. The children practically have their noses pressed up against the glass, mouths open in amazement and delight. I suppose it goes above their heads, the fact that everyone looks like they're about to ravish everybody else. (I find myself wondering how they pick the fairy tales at the window-display meetings. Does someone clear their throat and point out that yes, you could technically put the Little Match Girl in sexy knickers but that it wouldn't necessarily add to the joyous Christmas vibe when she dies, broken and alone?)

They've done a nice thing with 'The Ugly Duckling', though: the Mother Duck is old-school glamorous; and the Ugly Duckling is new-school nerdy, with fabulous clothes that look like a beautiful mess and big black glasses. She looks good, the Ugly Duckling. She makes the Mother Duck look like she's trying a bit too hard. I expect the Mother Duck spent the Ugly Duckling's childhood trying to wean her out of vintage – then called second-hand – and into Laura Ashley. And I bet the Mother Duck didn't like the Ugly Duckling's boyfriends, because they weren't called Rupert or Jeremy. The jewels glitter on the Mother Duck's hands; the Ugly Duckling is wearing a plastic necklace. I realize that I, too, practically have my nose pressed up against the glass, and that my mouth is slightly open.

God, Christmas. It makes my brain melt. Because – I've finished over-identifying with the Duckling and am now, appropriately enough, in the beauty hall – I love it so much, and I want it to be so lovely, so redemptive, so right. There's no point in doing it craply, is there? I know people who do do it craply, sitting there miserably with their substandard presents and their overcooked titchy bird, but that's not how I roll. The idea of that kind of Christmas makes me want to cry: I can't bear even to watch pretend people doing it on television. It's not that I want it to be perfect in the Martha Stewart sense – I don't even own any matching crockery. I just want it to be . . . nice. Warm. Loving. Joyous. All those things. Christmassy.

My feet lead me to the Chanel counter, for Kate. They have these fantastically expensive – of course – special scents, called things like Coromandel, which I start spraying on thick, heavy paper strips. Why am I not able to roll that way? Why can't I just go, 'Eh, Christmas, it's just another day – more food, more stuff, but it's just a day, a mere day, one lone day that in the great scheme of things doesn't matter very much'? I don't know. If I knew, I would fix myself. I just know that I want it to be right, absolutely exactly minutely right, and that people who bang on about the pressures of commercialism – she said, from the beauty department of a luxury store – are missing something. That's not what the day's about – well, not entirely. It's about love, and family, and, like I said, redemption. If I didn't want to run the risk of sounding like the king of the wankers, I'd say Christmas was about hope. Yeah. Hope. And optimism. It's like the fairy tales in the window: for families, every Christmas is a new opportunity for Happy Ever After.

No pressure, then.

So Kate now has the scent – it's called '31 rue Cambon' and they package it in a thick black box with a fabric magnolia inserted behind the grosgrain ribbon, and I feel temporarily reassured, because it really does smell delicious and will be perfect on her skin. But then, as I head toward Jewelry – crammed with men emergency-buying stuff for their wives without really looking at it properly – I think: I can't just give my mother one lone bottle of scent, even if it is super-scent. I'm veering dangerously into shout-out-the-price territory again ('I'd have been just as happy with a rose petal'). I need to get her a couple of other things. Small things. And pick up something for Jake. And I need to bump up Sam's present. Sam's present is too small, because I've been annoyed with him recently. And he with me. But it's Christmas. And while I'm at it, I could have a quick look for things to add to the children's stockings. Maisy's (I know: I did actually name my daughter after a cartoon mouse whose face is only ever seen in profile) is done, because she's five and it's easy, but my boys are teenagers and when you're a teenager and the only things you're into are bands and techy stuff, your stocking suffers. An iTunes card barely fills the toe; a DVD lies there all flat, making the stocking look tragic. And again, brain-melt: I am whooshed back through time to my own teenage years, at home with my own much younger sisters, Flo and Evie, clocking their fat, bursting-at-the-seams stockings and looking down at my own considerably thinner one.

Kate was married to Julian at the time – he is my sisters' dad. And my mini-stocking was always fabulous: earrings and lipsticks and thoughtful, hand-picked little books of poetry and suchlike. There was absolutely nothing, nada, zero, to complain about. But I felt – jealous isn't quite the right word. I didn't want more or better stuff. Envious, then. Envious of my sisters' fat, teddy-stuffed stockings and everything they symbolized: their childhood, with two parents who were their parents, two parents who loved each other living under the same roof; the ordinariness of the teddies and little games; the absolute safe, cozy, family-ness of it.

And now, oddly – or not oddly at all, depending on your viewpoint – my own children are in the same situation, with a stepfather, and a much younger sibling (just the one) who lives, utterly secure, at home with a mummy and daddy under one roof; a sibling whose fat, teddy-stuffed stocking may present an emotional contrast that kind of harshes their Christmas morning mellow. Or not. They're happier than I was by miles, but still – I'm taking no chances. I hurtle down a floor, to the HMV concession, to stock up on Xbox games.

It all gets done, eventually. It always does – I don't know why I get myself in such a flap. Unless I've miscalculated, I've now got presents for everybody – enough presents, good presents, the gifts that will bring joy to the family home and would cause the Baby Jesus to kick His legs and coo with pleasure if His crib were in our kitchen. I take out my tattered list and double-check: yes, all done, though I'm not sure about the fluorescent underpants for Jake, which seemed a good – well, a comical – idea at the time. Still, too late now. I'll do a last-minute supermarket dash tomorrow – this might finally be the year that we don't run out of bay leaves – and try to get the bulk of the wrapping done tonight after dinner. I'm laughing, basically. All that fuss, and here I am, sorted, good to go, like some marvelous housewife in a magazine. Things are looking up.

The crowds have thinned out a bit – it's just before 6 p.m. – and even the pigeons no longer seem that keen to walk alongside me. Maisy's at home with her granny, Sam's mum – mine doesn't do babysitting – who said earlier she'd actively like to look after her and put her to bed. 'Take as long as you like, love. It's what I'm here for,' she said, in her martyred but kind way. I have time – ample time – for a coffee and a sit-down.

It suddenly occurs to me that I can probably do better than that. I don't really want to donkey my parcels and bags around in the rain only to squeeze myself into an overcrowded, over-heated coffee shop, and besides they start shutting at about this time. A light bulb goes on up above my head: I could go and have a drink somewhere really nice. Somewhere I could leave my parcels with a matronly guardian, and where someone would take my coat and bring me, I don't know, a giant Martini. And some olives. And some nuts. Maybe those little Parmesan biscuit things. Because actually I'm starving. Yes. Who does those things? Who cocoons you in that way? Why, a hotel. I've perked up massively by now: under the giant wet hood of my Arctic parka, I am smiling in the rain. I'm going to take myself to a glamorous hotel, for a pre-Christmas drink by myself. How festive is that? Just the one drink (don't want to spend a fortune), and then home within a couple of hours tops, in time to cook supper.

If I'm going to do this, I might as well do it properly. I don't want to sit in the bar of a sad hotel, with sad men from out of town who've come to London to see their children before heading off again to spend Christmas all by their lonely, divorced, broken selves. This leads me to quickly count my blessings, an old hobby that I've never quite managed to give up. Chief among them, tonight: I am not a sad man whose ex-wife only lets him see his children for a couple of hours on 23 December, while she sits silently in a corner, bristling with resentment and old woundage and he thinks, 'This used to be my home.' No. I may be divorced but I am not sad. Or a man. Also, I'm really good at being divorced. I'm a gold medallist.

I'm an Olympian. Robert, the boys' father, remains my excellent friend, as evidenced by the fact that he *and* his parents are coming to Christmas, as they do every year. Pat on the head, Clara. (Everyone thinks I'm awfully clever to be good at divorce, and I smile and look positively crammed with the wisdom of the ancients, but actually there's nothing to it. Put it this way: if you've been the child of serially divorced parents yourself, you become very, very skilled at How Not To Do It.)

The Connaught, then. Ha! Why not? The Con-bloody-naught, so chic and refined. I haven't been in there for years. It's exactly the sort of place where a person might go and have a drink and be left in peace and feel like a lady in a hat in an old-fashioned novel, plus it's barely a ten-minute walk away. Worry: do I look smart enough under my polar-explorer coat? Why, yes, for once: I had coffee with my editor this morning and thought I'd better make an effort, so I am wearing an actual dress. A silk dress, since you ask, nicely cut to emphasize the good bits and minimize the bad (stomach, chiefly. We'll speak no more of it). And I have proper shoes on, and makeup in my handbag. No problemo: Connaught here I come. It is fated.

I'm walking through Grosvenor Square now, past the American Embassy, which it is impossible to get near because of all the anti-terrorist barricades. People huddle past, braced against the rain, which hasn't let up since eleven this morning; hundreds of outsize Christmas lights glisten from the enormous trees lining the square. Two cars nearly splash me a little, but I don't care: I feel elated. I never do anything like this – take myself off to hotels, I mean. Once your default setting is switched to domestic, as mine has been for nearly two decades, you don't spend an awful lot of time on your own doing randomly fun, extravagant-seeming stuff. You only have minutes a day on your own doing non-homey, non-worky stuff, if you're lucky and all your children are at school and it's not the holidays. Some people must really like it, I guess, and I like it too, the whole big bustling family thing, but I also really like my own company and sometimes I miss it. What's that awful expression that makes me gag? 'Me-time'. That's what I'm having. Perfect timing: me-time before the onslaught of Christmas Day.

Slight left, and here's Carlos Place, and here's the Connaught, shining in the dark with that yellowy light, like a house in a book, like a beacon of possibilities. A uniformed doorman outside is seeing someone into a Bentley: the scene is the definition of old-fashioned glamour. I wish I wasn't wearing the stupid parka, but anyway. In I go. Yes, madam would love to leave her parcels. Yes, do take madam's coat. No, I think I remember where the bar is, thanks, and anyway I'm just going to nip into the Ladies first to put on some makeup. Which is just as well, because when I look in the mirror I see the rain has washed all of mine away, leaving only two smudged black circles around my eyes: I look like I've been crying. New face, back out down the corridor, and yes – air-punch of a yes – here it is.

Here is my me-time bar. There's a fire, and dim lighting, and old-fashioned sofas and leathery club chairs and a polished walnut table just for me, with puffy, monogrammed paper coasters awaiting my drink. I sink into the chair, which seems to sigh with pleasure upon receiving my bottom, and I unfurl like a flag. Begone, stupidly expensive china animals! Shoo, pointless panic about presents! All is well with the world, and here's my waiter, and it's two days to Christmas and oh man, this is nice. This is *so nice*. A champagne cocktail, I think, rather than a Martini – I have a vague notion that it won't be as strong. I don't want to be drunk: my tolerance for alcohol has decreased tragically with age, and these days my hangovers can last up to forty-eight hours. I wouldn't mind, but they're so seldom worth it.

The white-jacketed cocktail man catches my eye and smiles as he makes my drink, and I am filled with love for humanity. This is so . . . civilized, so old-fashioned, so *wonderful*, such a rare treat. The waiter brings an assortment of snacks, and having taken a sip of my drink, I peer round with interest at my fellow humans. It is as I thought: smart couples of a certain age, the odd patrician-looking, pinstriped businessman of the kind that has offices in St James's, two elderly ladies with stonking jewels and too much face powder, hooting with laughter. I imagine this is their annual ritual, that they are old friends who still meet for their Christmas drink, like they have done for decades. I hope me and Tamsin are like that, when we're really old. I can just see us.

Arse. Tamsin. My oldest and dearest friend. Tamsin is coming to Christmas and I haven't gotten her a flipping present. How did that happen? She always comes to Christmas and I've never forgotten before. I got her boyfriend a present and not her: how crap. I rack my brain, trying to picture the contents of my emergency present closet, which is where I store gifts that need to be recycled because they're not my bag, or stuff I get sent by PR people (advantage of working for a glossy magazine). But Tamsin likes the same stuff as me, so if it's in the closet it won't be her bag either. And she can always tell if I palm her off with some freebie. Crap. Crap. Crapadoodledo. Wasn't she on the list? I dig around in my handbag and find she wasn't. Terrible oversight, of the kind that makes me worry about getting Alzheimer's. I take another sip of my cocktail, surprised to note that it's nearly finished. The thing is, now Tam's finally hooked up with someone, the pressure to give her a fantastic present isn't as massive as it used to be during her (prolonged, eternal-seeming, much moaned-about) single years, when I felt it was my duty as friend-in-chief to buy her the kind of thing that a) she could never afford (she's a schoolteacher) and b) a boyfriend might give her. And now, hallelujah, she has a boyfriend, a proper one, Jake – they've been together nearly a year. He is incredibly old and sometimes they use Viagra (again, I worry fleetingly about having bought him pants: aside from anything else, does it make it obvious that Sam and I have discussed his aged loins?), but we needn't dwell on that – the point is that as far as I remember he usually buys her nice presents. He gives good gift. So it's not so bad. I'll just make a note to nip to the . . .

'Is this seat taken?'

I glance up briefly. There's one of those interchangeable men in suits standing there, pointing at the club chair opposite mine.

'No, no – have it,' I say, looking down at my present list again. They had really nice stripy cashmere scarves at the shop down the road from home – I'll get her one of those in the morning. And some books. And maybe some pants, so Jake doesn't feel victimized. 'I'm not expecting anyone.'

'You don't mind?'

'Not at all,' I say, still looking at my lap and scribbling 'T – scarf + pants' on my list. 'I'm going in a minute, anyway.'

'I'm grateful. It's very busy in here,' the man says. 'May I get you another drink?'

'No, thank you. I think I'd better . . .' I look up properly for the first time. 'Oh.'

He is raising his eyebrows, and smiling.

It feels like about twenty minutes go by, in slow motion. I am looking at the man. He is looking at me. Nobody is speaking. I can hear the old ladies laughing, though they sound very far away.

'Another drink?' he repeats.

I realize that, for the second time today, my mouth is slightly open. I snap it shut, only to open it again. 'I, er. I. No. I have to go. I can't. I. Yes. NO!' is what comes out, humiliatingly. I can literally feel the blood rising to the surface of my skin. I am about to become puce.

'Have one more. For Christmas,' he laughs. 'Same again? I promise I'll leave you alone with your, ah, paperwork.'

I say 'Okay' in a weird squeaky voice.

To me, the man is the most attractive man I have ever seen. I don't know what else to say: it's a simple statement of fact. I, Clara Dunphy née Hutt, have literally, in my life, never seen anyone so handsome. It's subjective, of course. But . . . it's not just handsomeness. I know handsomeness, from interviewing the odd film star and so on for work: it takes you aback initially, but you adjust to it very quickly and just feel annoyed when you go back into the real world and find everyone walking about with their plain old faces. You don't, as I do now, feel like you've been winded, punched, jacked out of time. And that little stab in my stomach. I know what that is. That's not good. That's not supposed to happen to the old-lady wife and mother. I mean, it's been *years*. How weird.

'He's bringing them over,' the man says, coming back and sitting down. And then, gesturing to my ratty little list, 'Please. Don't let me put you off.'

'It's just my list, you know, for presents,' I say, pretending to write something important down on it. What I actually write is 'HELP', not in letters so large that he could see them from across the table, but as a useful aide-memoire to myself.

'Ah yes. I've been doing some of that too.'

'I was in Oxford Street,' I volunteer pointlessly, and then, as if that piece of banality wasn't enough, I add, 'I had two pigeons walking on either side of me. We were like a gang.'

He looks mildly surprised by this, as well he might. Surprised doesn't even begin to cover how I'm feeling. A little voice in my head says, 'Leave. Go home. It was fun, the drink in the Connaught, but it's over now.'

'I went to New Bond Street,' he says. He has been smiling at me ever since he sat down. It's a knowing sort of smile, and I know what it means. If I were a different sort of person – one to whom these things happened, one who didn't find anything odd about being winded by strangers in hotel bars – I would smile back at him in exactly the same way. I'd be wearing stockings under my dress, instead of M&S tights and flesh-colored Pants of Steel, and the whole stranger-in-a-hotel-bar scenario would be almost drearily familiar to me. But I am not a different sort of person, so I frown and blush and frown and stare, until it occurs to me that it might be an idea to compose my face, which is, as predicted, a fetching shade of scarlet.

'Bobond Street,' I say. 'I hope it was less crowded. Bond, I mean, not Bobo . . . Bobond.' I am sounding like a nutter. I have never stammered in my life. 'I'm sorry,' I say. 'Bond Street, you were saying.'

'It was hideous.'

'Yes. Will you excuse me?'

I have to leave the table. I wish I could explain it properly. To be succinct: if the man, whose name I don't know and whom I met maybe four minutes ago, said, 'Let's go round the back and do it against the garbage cans,' I'd say yes. This disturbs me profoundly. I feel like someone's flicked a switch in my head; lobbed a bomb into my little world of domesticity and special Christmas-treat drinks. Actually, I feel like I've had a brain transplant. No – like zombies ate my brain. Because I can truthfully say that it has never happened to me before. I understand the concept of lust, obviously – I had entire relationships based on lust, when I was younger – hot monkey sex with someone who you knew was a bit pointless, if exceedingly hot.

But this isn't normal lust. This is . . . filmic. Surreal. Another thing altogether.

I go back to the ladies' room. They have armchairs in there, and I plonk myself down on one. Am I drunk? Surely not from one cocktail and a quarter.

Other hand: maybe I've got completely the wrong end of the stick. Maybe this man is smiling and looking at me like that because he feels sorry for me, all alone in a bar two days before Christmas, clutching my scrappy little piece of paper and wittering on about pigeons, with a face so red it looks like it's been boiled. His heart goes out to my speech impediment. He's just being kind. Christ! He's probably waiting for someone. His former-supermodel wife and nine exquisite children, I expect. I need to get a grip. 'Get a grip, Clara,' I say to myself out loud. I am in a bar, someone has sat down at my table, they are incredibly, amazingly, inhumanly attractive, and that's that. So what? I am an adult, and quite a responsible one. I have self-control. I am also a biped, who can – and will – stand up and leave whenever I like, using my two stout feet to propel me homeward. The world is full of attractive people: there's no need to flip out like a weirdo because one talks to you. Deep breaths. Wash hands. Be normal. That stab in the stomach isn't necessarily desire: it could be hunger. Go back, eat the nuts, finish the drink, say thank you, go home. Not rocket science, by a long chalk.

The problem is, I wasn't always a person of the flesh-colored pants variety. There was a time, many centuries ago, when triceratopses frolicked playfully across the plains with diplodocuses, when I was acquainted with the woman in the stockings. Well, not the actual stockings – they're so ooh-saucy, someone's-feeling-lucky – but the general 'Here we are: anything could happen' thing. But it was a very, very long time ago. Happily for me, I don't find that many people attractive, plus my propensity for bad behavior has been napalmed into extinction by years and years of marriage, children, supermarkets, laundry, bills, school, work, all of that stuff. And, I tell myself again, I have probably got the absolutely wrong end of the stick.

But I know, when I sit down again. The air is heavy, like syrup. Even the molecules in the air seem charged. And I smile back at him and lean forward in my chair.

No, we didn't do it against the garbage cans. But, all the same, there exists, it turns out, an accelerated and dizzying kind of intimacy that is so intense and overwhelming, it feels not a million – or even a hundred – miles from infidelity: while you could certainly state that 'nothing happened', this would only be true if you were an emotional imbecile and your heart was dead. What I learned tonight is that it is possible for nothing and everything to happen in the same breath. I push the thought – confusing, exciting, disabling, impossible – out of my head and try to calm myself, and in the taxi home I make myself think about Sam. Sam, Sam, only Sam.

To be perfectly honest with you, and if I'm to be *completely realistic*, Sam and I are no longer at the passionately romantic stage. Not by any means. It pains me to say this. It actually makes me feel prickly in my armpits, that sort of shame-guilt prickle you get. And it makes me feel sad. Because, why? Some people go on forever, happy as two happy clams at the bottom of the happy sea, for decades and decades until death do them part, and even then they probably fly around heaven chastely kissing each other and having joint hobbies. I see them in Sainsbury's sometimes, ancient old couples holding hands. They make me want to cry. I'm not just saying that: they literally make my eyes fill with tears. Sometimes I follow them around for a couple of aisles, until I can't bear it anymore.

What's so wrong with me and Sam, with us – well, with me mostly – that I know we won't be buying cheap ham together holding hands when we're eighty-two? And why do I assume the fading of romance – the perfectly normal fading of romance – is somehow fatal, against ham? I bet most of these old couples went through some rough patches. Like, you know, loved ones dying in wars, like the Blitz, not just some low-level pissed-offness. So actually there is no reason why we shouldn't buy cheap ham in our time of decrepitude. I want to buy cheap ham with Sam. Sam's my man, for ham.

But anyway: it's true. The passionate, easy tiger, grr-grr bit is petering out. There's a bit of tiger and a bit of grr, but – how can this be? – I don't get that ache of longing anymore. I just think, 'Oh look, there's Sam.' Occasionally I think, 'Oh look, there's Sam, who is quite easy on the eye.' Or, 'There's Sam, who makes me laugh, which I find attractive.' Or, 'Sam has said an intelligent thing, and that appeals to me.' And then I carry on with whatever I'm doing. This seems really pretty incredible, considering the longing I used to feel for him. I used to watch him when he didn't know I was there – coming up the stairs at a party, once – and feel dizzy. I used to think, 'Oh my God, that's my boyfriend. That man – that clever, funny, charming, talented man, whom I fancy to the point of giddiness – has chosen me. Me! Out of all the gazillions of women in the whole gigantic universe. Me!' And then I'd want to laugh wildly, hahahahahaha, to roll around the floor kicking my legs in the air and whooping with incredulous, delighted joy. I didn't, obviously. But I wanted to. Inside, I whooped. I whooped on our wedding day; and when Maisy was born, I cried with happiness and whooped some more.

And then, slowly, the petering. Oh, it kills me. On so many levels, really. But mostly because it's so sad. I'm like Kate: I believe in romance. But I don't want to be like Kate and show the strength of my belief by marrying four different men – at the last count, though I think she's pretty settled with Max. Two should suffice, which means I've run out of options: it's the end of the line. (My friend Amber sang that at our wedding – 'The Trolley Song' from *Meet Me in St. Louis*, which ends, 'And it was grand just to stand with his hand holding mine / To the end of the line.' Everyone thought it was a sweet, camp choice, but I knew.)

I also know perfectly well – I've read the books, and as I keep saying, I am an adult – that the kind of romance I believe in is silly, unrealistic, schoolgirl, Emma Bovary-ish. Penny novella, cheapo stuff, with *coups de foudre* and manly chests and sweepings into arms and elopements and never any boredom or nappy-changing or sleepless nights or wee on the toilet seat. I *know*. I know I'm silly. But it slays me. It pierces me that the early bits are always the best bits, that you go from falling into bed every hour on the hour to being lucky if you feel like it once a fortnight. I don't mean just sex – I mean that feeling of being transported, of your stomach plummeting three storeys when he gives you a call. The first time I found Sam's wee on the toilet seat, I stared at it reverentially. I thought, 'That is His wee, on my lowly toilet seat,' and I felt privileged.

And anyway, there are things you can do. I can't guarantee that Sam and I will be buying ham when we are tiny, withered old people, but I do know how to maximize our chances. I know – I have observed – that the secret to a happy marriage, apart from the obvious stuff like saintly patience and award-winning acting skills, the ability to cope with disappointment, and a dramatic lowering of expectations, is to put out regularly. Oh yes. You may frown, and I'll grant you the concept doesn't exactly thrill my good feminist heart, but it's true. Put out regularly, seem extraordinarily eager for the mighty husbandly front bottom, and you're improving the chances of your marriage succeeding – whatever that means – by about 300 percent. Do the whiny thing about being tired and how you were up half the night with X or Y child, and you're doomed. The whiny thing, which starts off as a temporary measure based on the simple fact that you are, actually, broken with child-exhaustion and cracked-nipple agony, segues seamlessly, over the months and years, into 'We are lovely friends'. It's insidious. When you are lovely friends – and it's lovely to be lovely friends, I'm not knocking it – sex slips down the list of stuff to do. And there is no man alive who wouldn't like more sex. Ergo, there is no man alive who would like less. So. Put out. I know it sounds simplistic, but I'm not making this stuff up: I learned it from my first marriage and from all of my girlfriends. It's very crude and very effective.

The thing is, even if you give a good impression of being permanently up for it – if you came top of the class at RADA, say – the petering usually comes along anyway. It does for me, at any rate. I don't see how it can't. Perhaps it's different if you don't have children. But I have children: three of the blighters. I love them to pieces, but children do stuff to relationships, or maybe just to mine – there's no point in pretending that once they sleep through the night or start getting their own breakfasts, or going to school, you slip magically back to where you were to start off with: madly in love and dizzy with longing. You don't. You reinvent the relationship to incorporate Mr. Muscle and cooking and nits and arguments and in-laws, and all the claustrophobia that brings with it. And because you're an adult, you crash through it. You say to yourself, 'It's like this for pretty much every married couple in the world. You get through it. I love him. He loves me. It's fine.'

And it *is* fine. It's more than fine, and besides there are compensations. Many, many compensations, which it behoves me to remember. You may no longer live with Mr. Take Me Now, but you've acquired a new best friend, someone who knows you intimately in the way that your girlfriends never could, someone who truly loves you, warts and all, though hopefully not literally. You never have to do anything on your own again. You have a permanent ally, someone who's always going to be on your side, someone who winks at you at parties and whisks you home, lying about babysitters, because he knows you're not enjoying yourself. Someone to cook for (I love cooking) and save up your jokes for, someone to communicate with in shorthand, someone to laugh with and hug and sleep with – that lovely comforting sleep, like two peas in a pod, all cozy. Someone, more to the point, who loves the children you have together as insanely much as you do. That's no small thing, is it? That's maybe the most important thing of all. There are literally hundreds of compensations for the death of passion. Thousands. Millions, I expect. It's just a question of persuading yourself, as other people seem to have no difficulty doing, that this bit – companionship – is in fact *better* than what came before it. And I'm a horrible person, because I want both. I want companionship – obviously, who doesn't? – and passion. And I don't think it's possible for them to coexist. I'm forty: I don't want just passion, like some sort of super-slag, hopping about for the hot rumpo for all eternity. On balance, I'd rather have companionship. And I do, plus the hottish rumpo as often as I like. So. I don't really know what I'm moaning about. Except, you know a really beautiful, huge roaring fire? I wouldn't trade the beautiful roaring fire for cozy central heating in every room. I'd rather be cold, and then go and sit in front of the amazing, blazing fire in all its glory. That is my problem. I don't want my children to die of hypothermia, so I'm grateful for the central heating. But.

Sam was a dancer when I met him, though now he's a much-esteemed, manageably famous choreographer. He's fit, in both senses. He is extremely attractive. But you see, even with that – I lie in bed and watch him getting dressed and I think, 'He's extremely attractive,' but I think it like one might think, 'What a sweet dog,' or, 'I really like what the Browns have done to their spare room.' It's become objective. I would prefer it if I had the thought and then felt compelled to remove his pants with my teeth.

Do I sound sex-obsessed? It's to do with my age. Eleven years ago, when my older children were small, it was pretty far removed from my mind. Everything was removed from my mind, really, and not only because when you have young children you basically lose a decade – a large part of the nineties, in my case. I existed in them, obviously, but I'd have a hard time telling you much about them beyond the basics – Britpop, Blair, opaque tights, my discovery that avocado humus existed. And then my marriage to Robert was breaking up, though Sam and I got together pretty quickly afterward. And then Maisy came along, and the children grew up, and I hit forty and realized that my prime was pretty much behind me. I mean, I'm okay, I'm in good nick, I look all right, but I'm never going to see twenty-one again, obviously. And what I really don't fancy very much at all is spending the next twenty or thirty – or forty – years pootling about all filled with *companionship*, like an old lady, like a bloody *nan*. To tell you the absolute truth, the idea of it kind of freaks me out. I repeat: what's wrong with me?

Anyway. Sam's annoyed because I said we couldn't have his entire family to stay for Christmas. There are so many of them: he has four brothers, who all have wives and children. We have one spare room, which Pat, his mother, is in this week. He said that his family didn't mind, that they could all bunk down on the floor (kids) and sofas (adults), but the idea filled me with distress. I don't want to be stepping over bodies on Christmas morning, you know? I don't want my painstakingly decorated tree to be surrounded by teenagers' worn socks and the debris of their lives – bags of chips, cans of fizzy drinks, general crap. I just don't. Not at any time, really, unless someone wants to buy me a twelve-bedroomed mansion, but especially not at Christmas. I suggested we put them up in a nice B&B I know locally, but that was like suggesting we round them up and slaughter them like pigs. I'm still not quite sure why it was like that, but it was. Something to do with the Celtic concept of families, I'm guessing – Sam's Irish. I said they could come to our house from breakfast to bedtime, but sleep elsewhere. No go. Apparently they have to do their actual snoring under our roof, otherwise it doesn't count as hospitality. I used to think this kind of thing was charming – amusing cultural differences and all that. Now I'm not so sure: it just seems stupid, and a stupid thing to be arguing over. But it's okay. I'm going to fix it. It's Christmas.

All of this works, I must tell you. My marriage works. There is nothing the matter with it. I just wish that marriage wasn't predicated on everything being perfectly balanced, positioned just so. It's like a stack of cans in a supermarket: it only works if every can is in the right place. And we both, consciously or not, work very hard at moving the cans back into place when they start to slip out of position and threaten the structure of the whole edifice: it's become second nature. It's just what you do, when you're in a long-term relationship – keep shoving the cans back into place, like a couple moonlighting as shelf-stackers in their sleep. Of course, all of that presupposes that a wrecking ball doesn't swing in out of nowhere and demolish the pyramid in three nanoseconds.

Home, to the known universe, and where my love does not lie waiting silently for me. Maisy's in bed already and Pat is kindly tidying the kitchen, Jack and Charlie having made themselves and a couple of their mates supper – spaghetti with butter and cheese, by the looks of things: to think there was a time when I imagined them whipping me up little snacks for treats; I even taught them how to cook.

'You shouldn't tidy up after them, Pat,' I say, bending to kiss her hello. 'They're perfectly capable of using the dishwasher.' This is a lie: the dishwasher exists, their dirty plates exist, and never the twain shall meet, unless you make dire threats involving either gating or pocket money – and even then, they don't rinse them first and the filter gets clogged up with disgusting bits of old food. 'It's no trouble,' Pat says sweetly. 'And Maisy was good as gold.'

We've known each other for six years, Pat and I, and she's never been anything but lovely to me. Well, you know. 'Lovely' in the mother-in-law sense, where the word is elastic enough to encompass a high degree of competitiveness, some jealousy, plenty of resentment, and more childrearing advice than the Old Woman Who Lived in a Shoe would know what to do with. This latter is especially bold considering her own – how shall we put it? – complicated relationship with her children. Pat, like so many former matriarchs, now sees herself as a martyr, a sort of Mater Dolorosa who has been abandoned by her ingrate offspring; it seems never to have occurred to her that her children demonstrably love her but are a) a bit busy, what with work and families and children of their own, and b) wary (justifiably, frankly) of giving up a weekend to go and stay with her and be told, tearfully, what complete disappointments they are to their mammy. Happily, Pat doesn't find me disappointing – just perplexing, as though I were a different species, which I suppose I am. Pat is originally from County Tyrone and has worked hard all her life, first in factories and then as a shop assistant in a bakery; I am from west London, privileged and spoiled. The difference used to thrill us in the beginning: I was, in those early months and years, fantastically excited by her modest origins, her salt-of-the-earthness, her council flat with its china cats and artificial flowers. Here, I would think, sipping vodka on her unfeasibly plump, immaculate sofa, was proof that we were all the same. We weren't: I was just pissed and filled with hippie-love for all of mankind. But I know she liked my accent, and the way I knew how to order in restaurants – the way I took her to restaurants in the first place, or to shops, and was, unlike her, never made to feel small by a maître d' or snooty sales assistant. I have my uses. Also, I make her laugh, and she me.

'Tamsin called to say she was on her way over,' Pat says. 'She's bringing Jake. Is he the oul' fella you told me about?'

I am torn between loyalty to my friend and wanting to know what Pat, who is despite everything quite wise about stuff other than her family, makes of the age discrepancy.

'He's a bit older than her, yes,' I say, with princely understatement.

'Ah, it's a shame,' says Pat, looking fantastically – disproportionately, really – downcast and wiping down the table for the third time. 'A dirty oul' fella like that, with a young girl.'

'She's hardly a young girl, Pat,' I say, wanting to laugh hysterically at her description. 'We're practically the same age. We're middle-aged women.'

'All the same,' she sniffs. 'It's not right, fellas like that playing the goat. And she should know better. A beautiful girl like that!'

'But she loves him, Pat.'

'Love!' Pat says, quite forcefully.

'Pat. Did I tell you about my friend Fay?'

'Does she have an oul' fella as well?' Pat says, quite waspishly.

'No, she has a very young fella. Er, man. Boyfriend. Husband.' And therein lies a tale, which I am about to share with Pat, except that Sam and the boys burst into the kitchen.

'Is dinner ready? I'm starving,' says Jack.

'You've just had spaghetti!'

'Yeah, but that was only a snack,' says Charlie, who is, incredibly considering the amount he eats, not clinically obese.

'I thought you'd eaten,' I say. 'Lay two more places then. It'll be ready in about half an hour.'

'Oh man,' says Charlie, clutching his flat stomach. 'I'm so fucking hungry.'

'Charlie! For God's sake. Please don't swear.'

'Mum?' says Jack. 'I think Charlie has worms. Seriously. He eats like a freak. He never stops.'

'I don't have worms, you twat,' says Charlie. 'You have worms in your brain. And if I did have worms, I'd get them all together and put them in your bed.'

'Whatever,' says Jack. 'And if you did that, I'd crap on your head while you were asleep.'

'Please don't be revolting,' I say, pointlessly. Such are the joys of boys, especially twelve- and fourteen-year-old ones. 'And do your friends want to stay and eat? And could you do me a favor and go back upstairs and stay there until supper's ready?'

'They're going home in a minute. Don't you love us?' says Charlie, making a comedy sad-face.

'Sometimes,' I say.

'Cool. See ya,' they say, blurring into one, and galumphing back upstairs.

'Hello, babe,' says Sam.

2

23 December 2009, 8 p.m.

We have drinks in the drawing room, which is a complete mess of presents, wrapping paper, scissors, packs of batteries, teenage boys, used plates, gift-containing carrier bags, Scotch tape, empty mugs, one laptop opened to MySpace, Maisy's sizeable pig-pink pop-up tent, which she has ignored all year and chosen to erect 'for Christmas' as a cool place for the reindeer to relax in for a while, a couple of school projects, half-started, and this morning's newspapers, not in an orderly stack.

Treading gingerly over these – Pat immediately sets about tidying up, until I tell her to leave it – we arrange ourselves in a little huddle near the tree, which is nine feet tall and shining like a beacon, bedecked with white Christmas lights, the red baubles I bought when I left home and lugged about with me from house to house over the years, and a manageably scant number of child-made decorations (sweet but often hideous, let's be frank). The tree is beautiful. It's blazing magnificently by the window, with an obscene pile of presents already underneath. The sight of these presents – they cascade all the way around the room because no under-tree is roomy enough to contain them – would be enough to cause any sane person to denounce capitalism and join Class War on the spot, but there are only so many because there are so many of us: sixteen on the day, plus all the friends and relatives who've sent the children gifts.

We're eight to supper, not counting the boys, who have now decided to eat on their laps in front of the telly, all the better to add to the chaos of the room. There's me and Sam and Pat, Tamsin and Jake, my friend Hope, who was going to come with 'this amazing man I met', except the amazing man seems to have been mislaid en route and now Hope's running late, and Sophie and Tim, who are that strange species: parent-friends from your child's school. They're very ostentatiously happily married and have three small children aged five and under; we know each other vaguely from morning drop-off and a year's worth of quiz nights and school concerts. Their raison d'être seems to be to disprove my theory about marriage and children doing things to relationships: they are almost provocatively happy together, and consequently not un-smug. I kind of have the feeling Tamsin and Sophie aren't exactly hitting it off, but I'm going on body language so I may be wrong.

'All done, then?' Tamsin says to me.

'Pretty much. I had a last-minute burst this afternoon. I went to Oxford Street.'

'That's madness.'

'I know. But I needed to.'

'I'm surprised you're looking so unstressed,' Tamsin says. 'Oxford Street on the 23rd would kill me. I'm going tomorrow. It's practically deserted on Christmas Eve.'

'You have nerves of steel.'

'Clara went for a drink, didn't you, babe? To the *Connaught*,' Sam says. Everyone looks at me as though this were the most earth-shattering piece of news.

'The Connaught?' says Sophie. 'But what about the children?'

'I'd say it was more of a question of "The children? But what about the Connaught?"' says Tamsin dryly.

'What about them?' I say. 'They were here. Pat looked after Maisy. Sam was around. I just had the one drink.' More or less.

'Goodness,' says Tim. 'A mother, drinking alone in a hotel.' He says this much as one might say, 'Goodness, a man, legs akimbo, self-fellating.'

I force a smile and point out to Tim that it's 2009, and that a shop-weary person – a woman, even one who has procreated – might find themselves liking the idea of a little light refreshment, especially if that person is in the middle of organizing Christmas for sixteen people.

'Sure, sure,' says Tim, whose manner is quite annoying. 'Roger rog. Even so . . . would you go for a drink by yourself to a strange hotel, Soph?'

'It's not a strange hotel,' says loyal Tamsin. 'It's the Connaught. It's the Queen Mother of hotels.'

'Of course not, Timboleeno,' laughs Sophie. 'If I wanted a drink, I'd come home and have it with you. And the kids.'

'I hate my kids,' says Jake, which is startling enough to move the conversation on, though 'Timboleeno' worked for me. 'Bloody little buggers. I'd hole up in the Connaught and not come out for a week.' He squeezes my arm. 'Good on you, Clara. Hope you got good and pissed.'

'You can't mean that,' says Sophie, looking absolutely appalled. 'About . . . about hating your kids.'

'Fuckers, every one,' Jake says, downing the rest of his red wine in one.

'Jake's children are grown up,' Tamsin explains. 'He doesn't hate, like, toddlers. Or babies. Or Cassie.' Cassie is her six-year-old daughter, the product of a one-night stand with a man called David, who, I happen to know, had a micro-penis (called Little Dave – true fact) and who, immediately after sex, did the most enormous poo in her toilet. 'If only his tool had been as large as his stool,' Tamsin had said, disgustedly, at the time.

'I imagine they're about our age,' says Tim, 'Jake's kids, I mean.' Tim is, it now strikes me, one of those men who doesn't self-edit, causing you to wonder whether he is on the socially crippled end of the autistic spectrum. I asked them to supper because they'd asked us so many times and we kept saying no, and on the last day of term I rashly felt I should make amends and have them round to ours. But why two days before Christmas? Mistake.

'Older,' says Sophie, smiling at Sam, whom she clearly fancies. 'They must be older than us, surely.' The missus is clearly 'on the spectrum' too. Result. I also have the feeling she is my least favorite of things, a mummy-wife, who mothers her husband as well as her children. There are an awful lot of them about. I bet she lays out his clothes for him the night before.

'So,' says Tim. 'So she – I'm sorry, I've forgotten your name . . .'

'Tamsin,' says Tamsin, not exuding festive spirit.

'Right,' says Tim, looking at Jake. 'Tamsin. So Tamsin isn't your daughter?'

Jake's response to this is to hand Sam his empty glass, turn to Tamsin, put both his hands on her bottom, knead her buttocks vigorously and rhythmically – it's quite hypnotic – and then stick his tongue down her throat. Tamsin snogs him back enthusiastically.

'Whoa,' says Charlie from the sofa. 'Get a room, grandpa.'

'That's disgusting,' says Jack.

'I don't do this with my daughter,' says Jake, still wet-lipped. 'Do you?'

'Well, would you look at that,' Pat says, with fascinated, almost anthropological interest. 'Now that's a cuddle.' She is smiling approvingly, her earlier repulsion at the oul' fella nowhere in evidence. 'Oh, it's nice to see a proper cuddle.'

Sophie and Tim stare at Jake and Tamsin in utter, appalled silence, though whether it was the snog or the suggestion of incest that shut them up is unclear; I'm guessing both. Sam catches my eye and winks. I feel a well of hysteria rising in my stomach, and whereas if I'd had less to drink I'd have somehow managed to control it, it now comes out in the form of an inelegant, snorting guffaw. This is what's so nice about

Sam – well, one of the things. If I'd been hosting this dinner on my own, I'd be mortified by now, desperate to smooth things over before we all sat down. But Sam and I are allies. He'll make it okay – he's professionally charming – and he sees all of it: the funniness of his mother, the hilarity of the geronto-lurch, the comic aspect of our poor neighbors' distaste.

'I'd better go and check on supper,' I say, still giggling as the doorbell rings. 'Ah, perfect timing – and let Hope in. Come down in ten minutes, would you?'

'Roger rog,' Sam says, staring straight at me and absolutely po-faced. 'Now, who wants another drink?'

Hope is crying at the dinner table, wearing a Father Christmas hat and being watched over by a protective Tim. It's about a man. It's always about a man. Men, if you believe what Hope says, are uniquely badly behaved toward her. Within Hope's vicinity, men – all men – reach an outlandish level of bastard-ishness that has to be heard to be believed. Sometimes I make her swear that such and such an outrage really has happened and that she played no part in provoking it, because I simply can't get my head around the level of dreadfulness. This one – the formerly 'amazing man' she mislaid on the way to supper at our house – is no exception. And here she is, sobbing. She looks good crying. She weeps well. Just as well, in the circs.

I met Hope at yoga. I did yoga for three weeks when I was pregnant with Maisy, thinking that given how geriatric I was – thirty-four – I'd better adjust my being-pregnant method, which with the boys had mostly consisted of lying on the sofa eating rose and violet creams. Pregnancy yoga and I didn't get on especially brilliantly, mostly – but not exclusively – because all those pregnant women farting like billy-o as they contorted themselves used to disable me with laughter. This was frowned upon, but it really was pretty funny, especially around here: the women in question were yummy types, with perma-tans and very expensive highlights and banker husbands; the kind of women who hate being pregnant because it makes them feel 'fat', i.e. not a size four. I loved that they farted uncontrollably – it used to literally make my day: I'd get up in the morning and laugh in pleasurable anticipation. But a couple of them complained about my constant howling with mirth, and I wasn't really sure how the classes would help my labor in terms of, you know, actual human anatomy, so I stopped going. Before that, though, I met Hope in the changing rooms. She wasn't pregnant – she was doing some class that would improve her tantric abilities, she said, because she liked having sex 'for four or five hours'. She was crying – obviously – over some man or other and we went for a coffee. It turned out we had a couple of friends in common, and I liked her immediately: calamities aside, there's something enormously engaging and big-hearted about her.

That was just over five years ago, in which period of time Hope hasn't had a single relationship that hasn't ended in abject disaster. There have been a couple of lying, cheating married men, but they're really nursery level. Hope has a PhD in this stuff. One was an illegal immigrant who wanted to marry her. Anybody else would have worked out the visa thing – he clearly had no personal interest in her, and the photographs in his wallet clearly weren't of his 'nephews and nieces' – but not Hope. I tried to tell her several times, only to be informed that I didn't understand the undemonstrative, downright sullen demeanor of Nigerian people who are madly in love. When I said that Nigerian people seemed perfectly cheerful to me, in love or otherwise, and that maybe something was just up with her Mr. Right, she didn't speak to me for a couple of weeks. They got married at Chelsea Town Hall, had a small party – paid for by her – afterward; he went to the bathroom halfway through the speeches and never came back. Mobile dead, no response from his alleged workplace – the whole lot. Then there was the Polish builder, who combined the renovation of her basement with – well, actually, with the renovation of her basement, if you know what I mean. He went back to Poland to become a priest. I know – it must have been *crushing*: 'After this relationship with you, I vow never to sleep with a woman again.' But there's more: Hope's also a magnet for men with addictions, emotional sadists, men with unusual sexual fetishes, and men who seem to hate women – or maybe just Hope – to a pathological extent. Hope's quite suggestible. But she has a good heart, and I find something endearing about the chaos of her life: eventually she blows her nose, washes her face and – cheerfully – just keeps going, optimism intact.

Hope runs her own company and is in charge of 300 people. She's very good at her job. It's just the men thing. And the men thing is becoming quite urgent, because she really wants to have children. She doesn't, as has been suggested by several of her friends, want to get pregnant and bang one out before she becomes peri-menopausal, and nor does she wish to be a single mother. She wants the whole shebang. She's aggressively on the hunt for the father of her child, who will also be her bridegroom, which may have something to do with the string of failed relationships – but that's another thing I'm not allowed to say on pain of banishment. 'They *can't* smell the desperation, Clara. That's a horrible thing to say.'

'And then he just said . . .' she gulps. 'Pass me the wine, would you, Sam? He said . . .' At this point tears spurt out of her cornflower-blue eyes. Tim inches his chair slightly closer to hers and proffers paper towels. She smiles, blows her nose. 'He said I was too needy. Me! Needy! Me! I'm all about other people, Tim. Ask Clara.'

'Um, yes. You are. In a way,' I say.

'I'm an independent woman. I'm a brilliant catch. I'm loaded, for a start. I don't think that's a bad thing to say. I mean, it's just true. You should see my house.'

'Right,' says Tim, nodding. 'That's not at all a bad thing to say.'

'Money doesn't buy happiness,' says Pat, whose entire emotional vocabulary is based on a) soap opera and b) platitudinous 'wise' sayings she's overheard here and there, or read in those magazines that are printed on toilet paper. She can only respond to stuff in the way she has seen demonstrated on *EastEnders* or *Corrie*, which can make her exceedingly melodramatic, and also sound like she's occasionally possessed by spirits. She once told Sam that he was 'doing my head in, babe', in a pitch-perfect, ventriloquial impersonation of the late Frank Butcher.

'I know it doesn't, Pat,' Hope wails. 'I'm living proof.'

'And neither do fake breasts,' Sophie murmurs to me. Hope does have a pretty spectacular rack, which cost £8,000 from the Lister Hospital and came about at the request of yet another Mr. Wrong, who, Hope claims, said she would be his ideal woman if only she weren't so flat-chested. Now – you'd pack your bags and say bye-bye, wouldn't you? Maybe sew some prawns into the curtain linings while you were at it. Not Hope. I think he hung around for about three weeks after the bandages came off.

Encouraged by Hope's soap-operatic wail of misery, Pat tries out another one of her helpful mottoes:

'What's for you won't go by you,' she says, wisely.

'But Pat, darling, what was for me is on his way back to Kensal Green in a black cab as we speak.' Pat and Hope get on very well. They bonded – this is absolutely true – when they discovered that one of Hope's ancestors was directly responsible for the terrible famine that decimated Pat's home village. 'Grand to have a wee bit of common ground,' Pat had said, looking pleased.

'He'll be back, so he will. Sure as eggs is eggs.'

Hope sniffs – Tim hands her more paper towels – and gazes limpidly at Pat before taking a huge glug of wine. 'Do you really think so?'

'Sure he will.'

'He's a Scorpio. I think that's part of the problem, you know. They have such a dark side.'

'Their wee tails,' Pat says, nodding.

'Right,' says Tamsin, whose patience has visibly been tried to the limit by this exchange and for whom the mention of astrology is a deal-breaker. 'That's enough of that. Delicious prawn curry, Clara. What have you got Maisy for Christmas?'

'Various bits and pieces, you know – pink stuff. And a doll's house, a really nice wooden one.'

'I got her this fantastic makeup set,' Tamsin says. 'She's going to love it.'

'We don't let Honora wear makeup,' Sophie says.

'Well, it's not really *wearing* makeup, is it?' I say, wearily. 'It's more playing with it. She's not nipping down to the pub in it in her high heels.'

'It's an extension of face paint,' Tamsin says tersely. 'It's a child's makeup set, not an adult's.'

'That's cool,' Hope says, 'because I got her this bumper pack of mini nail polishes. Our presents match.' She smiles at Tamsin.

'Sophie and I feel . . .' Tim begins to say.

'We are very much opposed to the sexualization of young children,' Sophie finishes.

'Lucky I didn't get her the crotchless panties, then,' mutters Tamsin.

'I don't think,' Sam says, in an even-tempered way – the thing about his accent is that he makes nearly everything sound friendly – 'that anyone is *for* the sexualization of young children.'

'But the things you can buy in the shops, Sam!' Sophie says. 'Have you seen them? Awful lingerie for little girls! High heels for toddlers!'

'It's not quite that bad,' says Tamsin, who is, let us not forget, a primary-school teacher. 'We had a Year 6 girl come in wearing a T-shirt that said "porn star" a couple of years ago, but apart from that . . .'

'It's just so *inappropriate*,' Sophie says tearfully, her mouth set defiantly, as though the whole of the table were likely to rise as one and shout at her that, on the contrary, children dressed like hookers gave us all the most disabling horn.

'You tell them, Soph,' says Tim, looking proud. I mean, really – what kind of people do they think we are?

'Anyway,' I say, making really quite a big effort. 'What about you? What are you giving Honora?'

'Well,' Sophie says, having the good grace to look faintly embarrassed. 'The thing is, we don't like giving her any pink stuff either.'

'There's an awful lot of it, isn't there?' This is Sam, being conciliatory. 'We don't like it much, but what can you do?'

'What you can do, Sam,' says Tim, pouring himself another glass and topping up Hope's, 'is resist. Put your hands up and say, "No. No go. Not in my name."'

'What kinds of girls are we raising?' asks Sophie rhetorically, looking agonized. 'Girls who love pink. Girls who are obsessed with makeup. Girls who'll clearly grow up into . . .'

'Absolute tarts,' says Tim, who must, I note, be on his fourth or fifth glass. 'Ab-so-lute . . .'

'Steady on,' says Tamsin. 'Aren't we talking about five-year-olds?'

'I love pink,' says Hope, who is indeed wearing a very low-cut pink dress that clings to her wiry, toned yoga-body. 'Cheers, Tim. Chin-chin!'

'Not quite *tarts*, Timby,' Sophie says, throwing him a surprisingly irritated look. She is drinking water. 'Just . . . silly little girls. I mean, I didn't get a First from Oxford –' here Sophie pauses very slightly, so we may swoon '– by playing with pink stuff.'

Always nice, isn't it, to be in your late thirties and remind people of where you went to university and how you graduated. Any minute now Sophie is going to say 'at my public school'.

'And before that, at my public school,' Sophie says, 'we were encouraged to read and play music and involve ourselves with societies and things. That's the kind of upbringing I'd like for my girls.'

'Well, yes,' I say. 'But – they're awfully small for the debating society, aren't they?' She has a five-year-old, a three-year-old and a six-month-old. 'Do you really think the odd piece of pink plastic is going to make that much difference?'

At this point, I let my mind wander. The thing here is, I don't care about the answer. I don't give a toss. It's boring. All this child stuff is boring. I didn't find it particularly boring the first or second time around – or especially gripping, to be honest, but at least it didn't make me want to go to sleep. But now – and with such a big age gap between Maisy and her brothers – I know for a fact that the following are demonstrably true, unless of course a child is born with disabilities:

a. it doesn't matter if you're breast- or bottle-fed, or born naturally or by Caesarean
b. everybody learns to walk
c. everybody learns to talk
d. everybody learns to pee and poo in a lavatory
e. and wipe their own bottom
f. everybody learns to read and write
g. nobody gives a crap about when any of this happens.

Nobody goes around as an adult saying 'I learned to walk when I was barely one' or 'I was potty-trained exceptionally early.' (Some people do say 'I was reading fluently by the age of three,' admittedly, which pinnacle of achievement kind of tells you everything you need to know about them.)

h. it's okay to have sweets or bad additives every now and then
i. giving your son a toy sword isn't going to turn him into a serial killer; giving your daughter a dolly doesn't mean she'll never read Proust
j. it's okay to ignore your children on occasion, if you're busy and they're safe but merely a bit bored
k. in fact, occasional boredom is good for children: it makes them self-reliant
l. children usually turn out fine, unless of course their parents become demented with all of the above
m. it is impossible to say any of this to people whose children are younger than yours without sounding unattractively like Old Mother Time, so there's no point in even trying
n. which is fine by me, because *it's boring.*

God, I think, idly observing Tim stare at Hope's amazing bosoms out of the corner of his eye while he is pretending to talk to Sam about the school play. It's such a waste of time, all this lunacy about what they play with, or *how* they play, or how well they do or don't do at 'homework' when they are five, or how many activities they do after school, or how early they learn to ride their bike without traning wheels, or how they have dried fruit for treats because it has been decreed that chocolate shall never pass their lips. How it bores me to the point of actual despair. It makes me want to tear off my ears and throw them on the floor in disgust so that I don't have to hear. These children – mine, Sophie and Tim's – will always be fine. They are lucky, loved, wanted, privileged children. The end. Everything else is bourgeois hysteria. Sophie is still droning on about the pink girly stuff, as if it were the end of the world rather than mildly irritating.

'Have some more,' I say quickly, largely to stop myself saying 'Oh, do stop talking.' I also kick Hope lightly under the table and raise my eyebrows at her. She takes her cue immediately and starts asking Tim what he does (something to do with futures, apparently. Good luck to her, with that). 'And have some raita.'

'Did you make the yogurt?' asks Sophie.

'No. But I did grate the cucumber.'

'We make our own yogurt,' says Tim, quite slurrily, from across the table. 'Well, Soph does.'

'Why?' says Tamsin.

'Why do I make yogurt? Well, you know – it's nice to be self-sufficient, even if it's only yogurt and bread and growing a few vegetables,' Sophie says. 'It's empowering. And the children love it. Tim and I are great *gourmets*, you see.' She pronounces the word with a strong French accent. 'We really *mind* about what we eat. We mind passionately. And the kids eat everything we do.'

'Yeah,' says Tim, rather pointlessly. 'They do.' He's quite red, old Timboleeno. He's drunk.

'That's great,' I say, which it is.

'My boys were the same,' Pat says. 'They ate everything we did. Fries, mostly.'

She hoots with laughter, but I can see Sam practically twitching at the direction the conversation has taken. He is, to all effects and purposes, middle class these days, and he has no issues with most of the aspects of middle-class existence – niggles, yes, but nothing that really tips him over the edge. Except for this one thing: there is a certain kind of approach to eating that sends him absolutely round the bend and that, to him, works as perfect shorthand for everything that is vomit-makingly wanky about the social class he now finds himself occupying. Triggers include: people who say 'leaves' instead of salad (see also 'fizz', 'vino' and every permutation thereof); people who extol the virtues of X or Y cheese for more than one minute, particularly where they say 'chèvre' instead of 'goat's cheese' or specify the variety – sourdough, baguette, focaccia – instead of just saying 'have some bread'; people who have ninety-five different kinds of vinegar but never the one that you'd want on your fries; people who call fries 'frites'; people who won't drink tap water, or – worse – people who will only drink one brand of bottled, because they only like the taste of that one; people with 'allergies' who are really on diets; people who order off-menu in restaurants; and any kind of over-thought-out, over-fussy arrangement on a plate. He can't stand wine bores, on the basis that nobody normal can tell the difference between a £10 and a £20 bottle of wine, ergo they're just pretending to, like the bourgeois ponces they are. His particular bugbear is people who make too much of the fact that their children are omnivores.

Once, in Italy, we were sitting in a restaurant next to an English couple – overconfident, entitled-seeming, red with sunburn, foghorn voices booming over everyone else's conversation – who said to their toddler, 'Try it, darling, for num-nums. It's called Parmigiano. Par-mee-gee-ah-no. That's right! Come on, try it. You'll like it. It's only a tiny bit stronger than Grana Padano, and you loved that, didn't you? And do you remember the name of the greens you liked yesterday?'

'Puntarelle,' the child said.

Sam grabbed the table, his knuckles white like in a story, and started swearing under his breath – 'Get me away from the cunts, Clara, or kill me. Just kill me.' He's so good-natured normally that it was quite amusing to see, and I wasn't as incensed by the display as he was – actually I was rather impressed with the baby's command of language. But I know what Sam means: there comes a point, with foodie-ism, where you think, 'These people are just fetishists,' especially when they see food as the echt signifier of class and social place. There's a certain kind of eating that basically says, 'This is what *we* do, because we are special and unlike the herd. We are not proles. We make pesto out of ferns and acorns: that's how evolved we are.' Sometimes we both pine for the days of casseroles and fondue sets, which were a great deal easier to get your head around when you were eating at someone's house than having to admire people's perfect, fantastically elaborate recreations of restaurant food – and not just any old restaurant, but 'fine dining', if you please. Besides, as Sam points out, he developed his own athlete's body on a childhood diet of potatoes, canned food, mayonnaise and fluorescent fizzy drinks.

'Wouldn't eat this, though.' Tim points out helpfully. 'Spicy. Hot. Hot and spicy.' He leers at Hope as he says this. I silently push the water pitcher in his direction, trying to catch Hope's eye, only to find that she's just as blotto as he is.

'Nice curry,' says Jake. 'Quite authentic. I lived in India, you know. For a couple of years, back in the sixties. Man, what a country. What a place.'

'I didn't know that,' says Tamsin, smiling at him. 'How cool. You've done such cool stuff, Jake.'

'I know,' says Jake. I suppose when you get to his stage – he must be in his late sixties, though we've never been given a straight answer to the question of his exact age – there isn't much point in modesty or self-deprecation. 'I'm rock 'n' roll, baby.' This is also true: he is wearing leather trousers, for starters. They're quite nice, as it happens. Worn in, not all stiff, a description that could, from what I hear, also apply to Jake.

'We should go,' Jake says, putting his hand on Tam's thigh. 'To India. Me, you and Cassie. Take her out of school for a bit. Let her travel. See the world.'

'Broadens the mind,' says Pat, who has traveled to England, Greece (once, with us), Calais and to the bits of Spain where you can get a Full English.

'Exactly, Pat,' says Jake. 'Broadens the mind. Very good for children.'

Pat beams at him. 'India!' she says. 'It's that far away. Mind, you'd have to watch out for the monkeys.'

'How long would you take your daughter out of school for?' This is, of course, Sophie.

'I don't know – what do you think, Jake? Three months or so?'

'Three months,' nods Jake. 'And if we liked it we could stay longer. Or move on somewhere. Go with the flow, you know.' He is beaming too now, his lined, weathered face split into a leathery, trouser-matching grin. Have I mentioned Jake's teeth? He has the most improbable gnashers, a full set of crazy, blindingly white, immaculate veneers, purchased at vast expense and a great deal of discomfort shortly after he met Tamsin. It's like a bathroom showroom every time he smiles – white porcelain as far as the eye can see.

'Three months!' says Sophie.

'No point going for less,' says Jake. 'Maybe we should go for longer, Tam. Maybe we should go for, like, a year. Hang out.'

'Cassie'll turn into a little monkey herself, so she will,' says Pat fondly. 'A little brown monkey, like a watchamacallit, a gibbon.'

I'm not sure I entirely love the juxtaposition of Indian people and monkeys, but I know from long experience that this is a losing battle. There aren't any brown or black people where Pat comes from, and she marvels every time she takes Maisy to school with me at the multiculturalism on display. Or, as she puts it, the number of 'darkies'. We had our first row about this, many eons ago. 'Don't mind me,' Pat had said. 'I don't mean any harm.' And she doesn't. However.

'I don't think gibbons are little brown monkeys,' says Tamsin.

'What are the wee brown ones called?' Pat asks.

'Marmosets?' Sophie suggests, looking confused by the turn the conversation has taken.

'No,' Pat says, frowning. 'Ah, come on, the wee brown ones. Agile, like. They always remind me,' Pat starts, chuckling affectionately, 'of Clara's friend . . .'

'Sam!' I shout across the table in despair. 'Sam. Darling. Please.' I flick my eyes to Pat.

'So,' Sam says, bang on cue. 'Who's coming to see my show on the 27th? I've offered you all tickets, right?'

'He was a lovely wee dancer when he was a boy,' Pat says to nobody in particular, her mind having – mercifully – wandered away from primates. She takes a genteel sip of her vodka and lemonade. 'Loved it. Absolutely loved it. His da and I used to joke that he was a pansy, didn't we? Oops,' she laughs. 'Not a pansy. Oh, it's that hard to keep up with how you talk in this house. What would you say – a gay? We used to think he was a gay.'

'So you did,' says Sam. 'And I've always thought you'd secretly like it if I had been.'

'Ooh *yes*,' says Pat, nodding violently. 'I'd have *loved* it. Well, not then – I'd have been that ashamed. I wouldn't have been able to show my face. Oh, I'd have died. It was bad enough having to take you to dance classes – I used to cry about it sometimes. The shame, you know.' Sam rolls his eyes, having heard this all his life, though the other people round the table look mildly astonished. 'But I'd love it now. Like in *Sex and the City*! All the gays. Oh, they have fun, don't they? They have great fun. They're that colorful.'

'Do you know anyone gay, Pat?' asks Tamsin.

'No, my darling, I don't,' Pat says, looking pretty cut up about it. And then, seamlessly, 'You'd like a gay, wouldn't you?' she asks Sophie. 'One of your kiddies. I can tell. A wee mammy's boy. A wee gay dote.'

'I . . .' says Sophie. 'Good Lord, what an extraordinary thing to say. I wouldn't mind a . . . gay. A gay child. I wouldn't mind at all. But that's not to say . . .'

'Aye,' Pat says. 'I knew it. For company.' As I was saying, Pat occasionally has piercingly acute flashes of insight. This particular one has the welcome effect of temporarily silencing Sophie. Tim, meanwhile, is now howling with laughter – an oddly feminine sound – at something Hope, whose breasts are falling out of her dress, has said, and I feel the first twinge of pity for Sophie. The horrible truth of the matter is, you can home-make all the yogurt you want, but it's not going to stop your husband's eye from wandering.

'Have we finished eating?' asks Jake. 'Because I think it's time for a little smoke. A little doobie. A little blow. Mind if I skin up, Clara?'

I don't know what's happened to my supper. It sounded perfectly normal in my head: a few friends round, a couple of acquaintances, us, pot luck in the kitchen, two days before Christmas, everyone out by about eleven. Instead, this. It's not quite the easy, relaxing evening I had in mind. Good practice for the 25th, I suppose, but still. And now Tim and Sophie, both very active in the PTA, are going to go back to all the Reception parents and share the glad tidings that we adore makeup and heels on small girls and like nothing more than a bit of skunk after supper. Though I suppose I could always come back with the news that Tim likes his wine by the pint.

'Um,' I say, inclining my head toward Sophie, and then swiveling it around and indicating Pat. 'The boys are upstairs. I don't want them to come down and find people smoking.'

'Maybe now's not a good time, Jake,' Tamsin says, putting her hand on his; the effect is of marble next to papyrus. But Jake's already on his feet and marching up the stairs, trousers squeaking, to see what Jack and Charlie are up to. He comes down triumphantly a minute later. 'They're not there,' he says. 'They must have gone to bed.'

'Ooh, let's have a smoke,' says Hope.

'Ganja,' says Tim, in his idea of a Jamaican accent. 'GANJA! Yah mon. Takes me back. Takes me back, Hope.'

'I don't know,' I say lamely, 'that this is quite the night for it, Jake.'

'I know what cannabis is,' Sophie says indignantly. 'I'm not that square.'

'Well, none for me, thanks – but suit yourself, Jake,' I say. 'Though open the window, would you?'

'Is that drugs?' says Pat.

'Medicinal,' Jake says, pulling a gigantic packet of grass out of his jacket pocket (denim: the leather and denim combo reminds me of the Fonz). 'Relaxes me, that's all. Soothes away the aches and pains. So that I can concentrate on the important stuff,' he adds, giving Tam's thigh a squeeze. 'Right, babe?'

'Right,' says Tam enthusiastically.

'Drugs!' Pat says. 'Well, I never.' She picks up Jake's bag and has a good sniff. 'Smells nice,' she says. And then, after a pause, 'What kinds of aches and pains?'

'Oh, just the usual,' Jake says, swiftly constructing an enormous joint. 'The aches and pains of age, Pat. Though you're only as young as the woman you feel, eh?'

'I know all about those.' Pat nods. She's looking more interested than I'm entirely comfortable with: I'd sort of have preferred it if she'd expressed abject disapproval. I catch Sam's eye and wince: it seems to me that neither of us is entirely in control of the situation, but he just shrugs at me and leans back in his chair.

'You must have smoked, Pat,' Jake says. 'At some point in your life. Everyone smoked in the sixties.'

'No,' Pat says. 'That was only on the telly, and we didn't get one of those till 1969. Dollybirds and parties in London. Such fun, they looked, the swinging sixties. We liked Val Doonican.' She does a little dancing motion with her arms.

'Ah, of course. You're Irish. No Pill for you,' Jake says, succinctly. He lights up. 'I forgot.'

'I have four kiddies,' Pat says, laughing. 'No Pill for me, no. No parties or miniskirts either, mind.'

'You can make up for it now, Mum,' Sam says fondly.

'I'd maybe leave the miniskirts,' says Tamsin, eyeing Pat's small, rotund form. 'That ship has sailed. And Pat's probably okay on the contraception front.'

'Ooh yes,' Pat laughs, winking – yowsers – at Jake. 'My cuddling days are over.'

'You're only sixty-five, Ma,' Sam says. 'You never know. But I didn't mean miniskirts. I meant, have a smoke.'

'Did you? Right you are,' says Pat cheerfully. 'I will, so.'

See, this is what happens. This is the man I live with – my husband – and he still occasionally has the power to absolutely astonish me. I mean, he's encouraging his mother to smoke weed. What is he doing, and why?

Sam and his mother's relationship occasionally takes me aback. They're not close in any obvious way; they never say anything especially nice to each other. They love each other, obviously (though *is* it obvious? Do we all *obviously* love each other through the goodness of genes?), but they're not particularly physically demonstrative, and they don't stand around saying lovely things to each other. But then, sometimes, you find that they are closer than you'd ever imagined. Once, I came home to find them both in front of *Sex and the City*, this being Pat's absolutely favorite program in the world. Pat was red with mirth and howling with laughter, Sam only marginally less so. 'Oh, you have to see this, Clara,' Pat had said, breathless with giggling. 'It's that funny.'

I'd seen the episode in question before: it was the one where Samantha has a boyfriend whose sperm tastes bad. 'Funky', if I remember rightly. Now. The idea of watching this with my own mother doesn't bear thinking about, and my mother is a metropolitan, much-married, wised-up sort. The idea of Sam watching it with his totally blew my mind. There they were, huddled companionably together, honking with laughter at sperm-in-the-mouth jokes. I don't especially think of myself as a blushing flower, but I felt so embarrassed that I went downstairs and tidied the kitchen. When I asked Sam about it later, in bed, he said that Pat was laughing at the alien campness of the program generally, at the hilarious (to her) out-thereness of the women, rather than at bad-tasting sperm *specifically*. But I wasn't so sure. Pat has had four children and, presumably, an active sex life before her widowhood. I couldn't really take the conversation forward beyond that without causing myself to visualize Pat administering oral sex, so I didn't. But still. I don't think she's quite as unworldly as Sam believes her to be.

I don't know what manner of blow Jake's brought along to my supper party, but everyone's completely wasted by the time I dole out pudding, including – incredibly – Sophie, who took several deep puffs to prove, I suspect, that she was as game as Hope, who offered Tim a blowback (enthusiastically accepted) and who is now being stared at by him with unabashed, red-faced, drunken longing. This has the effect of making me cross with Hope and making me feel sorry for Sophie for the second time tonight, and so I engage her in a safe-territory conversation about schools and nurseries and local babysitters. We've been chatting amiably enough for five minutes or so – about baby slings, and whether one exists that doesn't hurt your back – when Sophie suddenly says, 'Did you like being pregnant?'

'I loved it. It's my ideal state.'

'I hated it,' Sophie says in a quiet voice, looking straight at Tim, who is not looking back at her. 'I was so ill, all three times.'

'Poor you,' I say, meaning it. Her face looks smaller than it did ten minutes ago, more vulnerable, and also more stoned. Across the table, Tim is still drunkenly gibbering at Hope; I notice Sam has poured him more water and is now offering coffee.

'Constant morning sickness,' Sophie says, laughing mirthlessly. 'It never really went away. Pretty much twenty-four hours a day. The first time round was dealable with, but when you have toddlers running about and you need to throw up three times an hour . . .'

'But Tim helped, I'm sure?'

'He was working,' Sophie says.

'But . . . but so were you. And you were ill. Looking after children is work too, you know.'

'Mm,' says Sophie. 'So people keep telling me. It's hardly the same thing as going in to the City at the crack of dawn every morning.'

'It's much worse,' I say.

Sophie smiles at this, unexpectedly. 'Can I ask you another thing?' she says. 'It's . . . it's quite personal. I wouldn't dream of asking normally, I don't know what's wrong with me.'

'Ask away,' I say. 'And it's Jake's blow.'

'It's about sex,' Sophie says.

'What about it?'

'Did you . . . After Maisy. Because with me, I'm just . . . I'm just so tired. So tired,' she says, closing her eyes.

'You have three small children,' I say. 'Of course you're tired. You're exhausted. Maybe stop baking bread and making yogurt?'

'But Tim . . . Tim has needs, you know.'

'Nobody needs yogurt to that extent, Sophie.'

She smiles again. 'No, not that. He says that if we let our sex life fall by the wayside now, it'll be the thin edge of the wedge. And that we must get back in the saddle properly. Gosh, I'm speaking like your mother-in-law. And I am willing, it's not that. The body is willing, but the spirit is weak. The spirit is just *so tired.*'

I don't think this is the time to share my theory about putting out with Sophie. And besides, it's all becoming clear now. Sophie has turned herself into some kind of domestic goddess to compensate for the fact that she needs to be asleep by 9 p.m.; Tim is drooling all over Hope because he's sexually frustrated and pleased to have someone flirt with him: it means he's perceived as more than Dad Man. Hope is letting Tim drool on her because she thinks it means she's more attractive than his wife, and that's the kind of reassurance she needs, because she's Needy McNeedpants. Hope would kill for Sophie's marriage and three children: it's all she wants. Sophie would kill for a bit of me-time and to have her job back and for Hope's wardrobe and enviably flat stomach. Everybody wants what they can't have: it's the dance of early middle age, and we're all doing it. What freaks me out is that I don't see any way out: everybody's going to keep on doing it until they either drop dead or admit defeat. And even then – admitting defeat only means trying again later, with somebody else and no guarantees that anything is ever going to pan out differently.

Jake, who has smoked most of the joint, seems the least stoned. He now turns his attention to Hope, staring rather off-puttingly at her giggling with Tim, until she senses his gaze and is forced to look him in the eye.

'Hope, darling,' Jake says, conversationally. 'Why are you flirting with this poor woman's husband?'

It's one of those moments when every conversation taking place around the table coincidentally ends at the same time, and Jake's words ring out as loudly and clearly as a bell, except it's more gloomy tolling than jaunty peals.

'Not flirting,' says Hope. 'Being friendly. I'm just being myself, Jake.'

'Why don't we swap places,' I say. 'Hope, come and sit next to Tamsin.'

'Don't want to change places,' says Tim. 'Want to stay here with the sexy lady . . .'

He is interrupted by the ringing of Sophie's phone. 'Damn,' she says, looking at the screen. 'Babysitter.' A quick conversation establishes that our neighbors need to get home to attend to their youngest child, who has woken up and is refusing to go back to sleep.

'Why don't you go, Tim?' Sophie says, with a glint in her eye that wasn't there before. 'I'll be along in a while.'

'What?' says Tim.

'Why don't you go? Pay her – here, I've got cash – and sort Bee out and I'll come home in half an hour or so.'

'Me?' says Tim.

'Yes,' says Sophie. 'You.'

'But . . . why?' says Tim.

'Because your daughter's awake, and one of us needs to get home.' She says this very calmly.

'You,' says Tim.

'Not tonight, Tim. Not me. You.'

'I don't want to,' says Tim. 'Drunk.'

'You'll be fine. She's not ill. I'll be home soon. All you have to do is lie down with Bee for a while. Take her into our bed.'

'Might squash her. Squashed baby!'

'Go and look after your daughter,' says Tamsin. 'We'll miss you, obviously. But . . .'

'Are you a feminist?' says Tim. 'Yes, you are. A big scary feminist lady. Brr! Hoo!' He takes a gulp of the fresh cup of coffee Sam has placed in front of him, and winces. 'Sophie,' he wails. 'Soph.'

'Do you know how long it's been since I've been out to dinner with new people?' Sophie asks her husband in the same calm voice, rhetorically as it turns out. 'Five months. Five months, Tim. And those new people were septagenarian friends of your parents.'

'Poor Soph,' says Tim. 'Poor Sophie-woo.'

'Ah, you big gobshite,' says Pat. We all turn to stare at her, but having gotten this off her chest, she looks around the table smiling the serenest of smiles and gets up to clear the plates.

'I should go,' says Hope.

'And do you know,' Sophie continues, 'how long it's been since I've had an alcoholic drink? Last summer. Last summer was the last time. And do you know what that drink was? One sip of champagne in the hospital, when Bee was born.'

'Here,' I say, passing a bottle over. 'Have some wine.'

'And I don't mind any of these things,' Sophie says, to nobody in particular and with her gaze fixed on the middle distance. 'I honestly don't mind. Except. Except. That . . . sometimes I do. I really, really do.'

'I'm sorry,' says Hope in a small voice, 'if I upset you. I can't help myself. I have issues. I'm working on them with my therapists. I didn't mean to . . . to upset you,' she peters out feebly.

'You?' Sophie says witheringly. 'You haven't upset me. I'm not upset. I'm just explaining a couple of things to Tim.'

Tim, who has been listening to all of this with his head bent, in a position that suggests contrition, now looks up again.

'You never want me to be happy,' he says, forming the words slowly and precisely, so that he sounds almost sober. 'You hate me being happy. You hate me having a nice time or having any fun. You . . . you *kill joy*. You're a killjoy. Because so what,' he continues, 'so *what* if I want to have a drink? So bloody what? It's two days before bloody Christmas. I get up at the crack of dawn and I come home late and I work hard and I earn all the money and it's two days before bloody Christmas and so what if I have a drink? So fucking what, Soph?'

There is an awful, laden sort of silence.

'I'll go,' says Sophie. 'Thanks for a lovely evening, Clara. Thanks, Sam. Very nice to meet you all,' she says to everyone else around the table. Her face is flushed and she is somewhere – somewhere uniquely feminine – between tears and absolute rage. 'And happy Christmas.'

'I'll put you in a taxi,' says Tamsin. 'I know you're only local, but you shouldn't walk on your own.'

'Thanks, but I'll be fine.'

'I insist,' says Tamsin, getting up.

'Bye, love,' says Pat, scooting round the table to give Sophie a hug. 'You take care, now. Don't let the bastards grind you down, eh?'

'Thanks,' says Sophie.

'Say it with me,' says Pat. 'Come on, love. Say it with me.'

'I'd rather just . . .'

'DON'T LET THE BASTARDS GRIND YOU DOWN,' Pat shouts, making a small resistance fist, before smiling pleasantly and getting on with her tidying.

'Your mum's completely stoned,' Tamsin says to Sam. 'Come on, Sophie, let's go.'

'There you go,' says Tim. 'That not-fun one is going to get you a taxi.'

'I really should go home too,' says Hope, in the way that she does – the way that expects six people to cry, 'Oh no, please don't.' But even Tim seems to have lost interest. He says nothing, though he turns to look at her, glassy-eyed, his expression unreadable save for the tiniest flicker of contempt. This does not go unnoticed by Hope, whose eyes well up as she stumbles away to get her coat.

'You too, Hope,' shouts Tamsin from the hall. 'Come on. I'll put you in a taxi as well.' And they are gone.

'Shall I skin up again?' asks Jake.

'Absolutely-tootly,' says Tim. 'You betcha.'

'They didn't have any effect on me at all, those drugs,' says Pat, who, yelling aside, has been smoothing down the same tea-towel for ten minutes with a blissed-out look on her face. 'Ooh, hello love,' she says to Tamsin when she comes back in five minutes later. 'That's funny. You were sitting right here a minute ago.'

'I was just putting Sophie and Hope in a cab,' says Tamsin. 'There was one right on the corner.'

'I'm sorry about my wife,' Tim says. 'I don't know what got into her.'

'Life got into her,' says Jake, shaking his head. 'It gets into all of them eventually.'

'Them?' says Tamsin. 'Them? Who's "them"?'

'Women,' says Jake.

'But . . . what do you mean, "Life gets into them"? Doesn't life get into men too?'

'Babe,' says Jake. 'It's not the same. We're not the same. Take my second wife. Gorgeous girl, just gorgeous. Real beauty. Tits like torpedoes.'

'Right,' says Tamsin.

'She was the best fun ever. Oh, we had such a laugh. Everything was great. I actually *liked* her, you know? Properly liked her, not just fancying. Though I fancied her like mad too, of course. We were always at it. Couple of rabbits. But she was my mate as well.'

'Right,' says Tamsin, looking at me and making a 'what the fuck?' face. My own face has been set to 'what the fuck?' for the past twenty minutes.

'So. Get hitched to make her happy. Get her up the duff to make her happy – I had a couple of kids already. Everything hunky-dory. We're as happy as Larry. And then what happens? She goes mad overnight. She goes mental.'

'What do you mean, she goes mad?' This is me, wondering how literal Jake is being.

'I mean, she goes mad. She looks different, for a start.'

'That great indicator of insanity,' says Tamsin, whose body language does not bode well for Jake's nocturnal needs.

'Well, you know. She piles a few pounds on. I'm not a monster. I know chicks do that when they're pregnant. I don't really get why they do it after, but anyway. I roll with it, you know? Even though fat chicks – not my bag.'

'Right,' I say, sighing.

'But it's not just the poundage. She used to have her hair done and stuff. Eyelashes. Dresses. Sexy underwear. Laughing. All gone. Now she's mooching around with leaky tits, grumbling at me when I get in late. And I do get in late. I get in later and later, because I don't like her standing there fucking leaking and moaning at me.'

'Jesus, Jake,' I say. 'What about the children. Your children with her?'

'Yeah, yeah – they were cute. Cute little kids. But I didn't marry to have more cute little kids. I married because I fancied my missus and she was my mate, and she wanted to get married and I thought I'd be nice.'

'Good of you,' says Tamsin, looking like she's just had lemon juice squeezed in her eyes. 'Princely. So then what happened?'

'Ah, long story. But I slept with one bird too many. Got caught. Legged it. Bit of a relief, to be honest.'

'I don't know what to say,' says Tamsin. 'Pass me that bottle, would you, Sam?'

'Oh, it's different with you, my love,' says Jake. 'Water under the bridge, all that old stuff. Wouldn't do that now. Badly behaved. Bit shabby,' he says, and laughs.

'You live and learn,' says Pat. 'Aye, so you do.'

'So, Jake,' says Tamsin. 'When you said she went mad? You meant, you meant –' she takes a big gulp of wine '– that, basically, she let herself go? Wasn't sexy enough? Wasn't hot enough? Didn't want to shag you enough?'

'Got it in one, babe,' says Jake happily.

'And that this was insane behavior on her part?'

'Yep,' says Jake. 'If you think I'm hot now, you should have seen me then.'

'It wouldn't have registered,' says Tamsin, her voice like ice. 'I would have been about nine years old.'

Jake winces at this – the first angry words I have ever heard Tamsin address to him – and carries on rolling his joint.

'That's exactly what's happened to Sophie,' Tim says. 'It's exactly as you describe.'

'My God,' I say. 'This is unbelievable. It's a wonder we're not all lesbians. It's a wonder the human race didn't die out years ago.'

'Heh-heh,' says Jake, fiddling with the roach. 'A bit of girl-on-girl. Nothing to beat it.'

'I mean it,' I say.

God, do I mean it. *Do I mean it*. Well, not so much about lesbians, but about the unbelievableness. About the absolute fucking miracle of the eternal human capacity for hope. We think everyone's going to be different, that things change, that people evolve. Pfft. There's more than thirty years between Jake and Tim, and they're exactly the same. 'Oh look, my wife's gone mad. Put on a bit of weight, knackered all the time, not what you'd call gagging to fuck my brains out. What a nutter. Where's the exit?' The thing I need to remember is that at least Sam . . .

'It's not unbelievable, Clara,' Sam says. 'It's just true.'

I'm actually winded, so I can't say anything for twenty seconds. When I get my breath back, I say, 'Which bit? Which bit is true?'

'All of it,' says Sam. 'Tim, Jake, all of it. Not put in the best way, but true.'

'I can't believe . . .'

'I'm not expecting you to like it,' he says with a sad smile. 'I'm just saying, it's true. It's what most men think.'

'It's nice to keep yourself nice,' says Pat. 'Sure it is.'

'Oh my God,' says Tamsin.

'You know,' says Sam. 'Why shouldn't he have a drink? Why shouldn't Tim here have a drink? He's right: he works hard and it's two days before Christmas.'

'Thank you,' says Tim. 'Exactamundo, Samundo.'

'Nobody's saying he shouldn't have a drink,' says Tamsin.

'Well, you lot are,' says Sam, drawing on Jake's new joint. 'You're sitting there like a row of fucking harpies . . .'

'What?' I say.

'You heard. Like a row of fucking harpies, sitting in judgment on some poor bloke whose only crime . . .'

'Whose *only* crime,' Tim echoes.

'. . . is to get pissed at a dinner party and maybe flirt a little. With a woman who flirts for a living. You know? What's with the disapproval? You were pissed when I first met you, Clara. And you had two young kids. And you flirted with me. I didn't judge you. I thought it was funny. You were charming.'

'I wasn't roaming the streets of London pissed, Sam. My children were safely in the care of somebody else. And I . . .' I want to say 'I'm still charming,' but – oh God – I suddenly feel like I might cry if I say it out loud. It's so pathetic. Nobody should have to point that kind of thing out about themselves to the man who's supposed to be in love with them.

'Of course they were,' Sam says. 'I wasn't suggesting you'd left them to fend for themselves.' I am ridiculously, pitifully grateful that he has said this, and then – a fraction of a second later – irate, *incensed* by my own gratitude.

'The fact remains,' Sam continues, 'that there is nothing wrong with a man going out of an evening and getting a bit pissed and eyeing up some flirty woman. Even if that man is married. Even if that man has a family.'

'Oh Sam,' says Tamsin. 'Nobody was saying there was. The point is . . .'

'I get the point,' says Sam.

'What is it, then, in your view?' I say, trying to keep my voice steady. 'Apart from me and my friends being fucking harpies.'

'My point,' says Sam, speaking weirdly slowly, 'is that you – women – have kids and then go into this mode, this pretendy grown-up, adult mode, and you start hating us. You . . .'

'I have three children, Sam. One of them is yours. And I'm forty. It's not pretendy.'

But he isn't hearing me. 'You start hating everything you used to like. And you hate it with that sort of convert's zeal, like an ex-smoker hates cigarettes . . .'

'Similes now,' I say nastily.

'You're not the only one with a brain, Clara. I was saying, you hate everything you used to love. The things you found funny aren't funny anymore. The fun you used to have stops being fun. Just like that. Overnight. You have a baby and you become different people. And we get no warning. Nothing at all. We wake up one morning and there you are – the charming girl who used to like cocktails, berating some poor bloke because he's had a couple too many, and siding with his self-pitying wife.'

'You thought Sophie was *self-pitying*? Sophie who never goes out? Sophie who doesn't get enough sleep and makes yogurt and bread?'

'She was, darling,' Jake says in a reasonable voice. 'Riddled with self-pity. It's just a fact. They get like that.'

'No man likes to see that,' says Sam. 'It's emasculating, for a start.'

'So . . . let me get this right. Telling a man something that is simply a fact is somehow the same as cutting off his balls?'

'There's no need to be melodramatic, babe.'

'Don't,' I say, my voice rising uncontrollably, '*don't* call me babe.'

'Suit yourself.' Sam shrugs.

'We should go,' says Tamsin. 'Well, I should go. I'm going.'

'One more drink,' says Jake.

'As many more drinks as you like,' says Tamsin. 'I'm going.'

'Where?' says Jake. 'Where are you going, darling?'

'I don't know,' says Tamsin, getting her phone out. 'I'm going to text my sister Tara and go back to hers, I think.'

There are tears in Tamsin's eyes, as there are in mine. 'It's fine,' I say, giving her a hug. 'Say goodnight to her from me, and see you both at Christmas.'

'See you at Christmas,' says Tamsin. She blows Pat a kiss but doesn't look at Sam or Jake.

'What's happening, Clara?' she whispers as I show her out. 'Why has everything become horrible?'

'It'll be fine,' I say, like the world's best liar.

I should leave it. I should give Pat a hand with the last bits of the tidying up and say goodnight and go to bed. It's too late to do any wrapping, and for the second time inside of five minutes I feel myself on the verge of tears. Wrapping is nice. Wrapping is soothing. Wrapping is exactly what I need right now. But I ignore the voice in my head and go back into the kitchen. I sit back down at the table with Jake and Sam. Tim is now slumped across it, his floppy, posh-boy hair being wiped around by Pat and her eternal J-cloth.

'Please leave it, Pat,' I say. 'You're an angel to have tidied, but stop now. Come and sit down. You're not the bloody cleaning lady. I'll make you a cup of tea.'

'Ah, it's no trouble,' says Pat. 'I like to feel useful.'

'All the same. Sit down.'

'I think I'll go up to bed,' Pat says. 'It's getting late. Would you mind if I took up a wee snack? A wee cake. I don't know why, but I'm famished.'

I make her a plate of Christmas cake – a fine achievement by Maisy and me, if I do say so myself – and cookies to go with her tea and three sugars. Pat is fearless in the face of encroaching diabetes, I'll give her that. She hugs me tightly as she says goodnight and shuffles off to bed.

So now it's just the four of us and a bottle of whisky that Sam's unearthed from somewhere (without much difficulty). If you're Irish, or indeed Scots, and people don't know what to give you for Christmas, they always go for whisky. Sam gets about twelve bottles a year from various people he works with.

'Well, that was jolly,' I say, pouring myself a couple of inches. And then I don't say anything at all, because I want Sam to apologize to me, or to somehow convey regret, by his face or by something he does with his hands, or even by sighing sadly and contritely. But he doesn't. His expression is absolutely serene.

'Tim,' I say. 'Tim! Wake up.'

'Awake,' says Tim.

'I think he should sleep on the sofa,' says Sam. What the fuck is it with him and people sleeping on sofas?

'He only lives ten minutes' walk away. Can't you walk him round? The fresh air would probably do him good.'

'I'm fine,' says Tim, shaking his head experimentally. 'My head's a bit sore, but I'm okay now.'

'I'd rather he went home,' I say to Sam, rudely, as though Tim wasn't there.

'So would I,' says Jake, 'because then I could have the sofa. Tam's not taking my calls. I could drive, I suppose . . .'

'I don't think you should,' says Sam. 'You might get stopped.'

'I'd like to stay,' says Jake, suddenly looking very old. 'I don't want to go home by myself.'

'Have another drink,' says Sam.

The atmosphere in the kitchen is calmer than it has been in a couple of hours, and I should leave it. I should go upstairs and sort out some bedding and a pillow for Jake, and plump up the sofa. Instead I say, 'You know earlier, Tim? When you were so astonished that I took myself for a drink at the Connaught?'

'What?' says Tim. And then, 'Oh yeah. I remember.'

'And you said Sophie would never do a thing like that, and she agreed?'

'Yes,' says Tim. 'What about it? She wouldn't.'

'But why is it strange for me to do it and not at all strange for you to do an extreme version of the same thing right here at my house?'

'We've had this conversation already,' says Tim. 'It's a weird thing for a woman to do. I mean – if you wanted to go for a drink, why didn't you go with your husband?'

'Because he wasn't there. I was by myself in the middle of Oxford Street, doing the Christmas shopping.'

'I don't think it's that weird,' says Jake.

'Thanks,' I say, as though he has just given me a jewel.

'I'd better head back to the missus,' says Tim. 'Cheers, Sam, for a fun evening.'

'Any time,' says Sam. 'Drink on Boxing Day, maybe?'

'Sure, sure. Thanks, Clara,' Tim says, avoiding my eye. 'Well, bye then.' And off he goes.

'It *is* pretty weird,' says Sam, still on about my drink earlier. 'The timing of it, Clara. It's hectic, it's chaos, and you bugger off to the Connaught, all dressed up.'

'You don't like me being dressed up? I thought you were just saying that women somehow owe it to men to make an effort?'

'I'm saying nothing else,' says Sam, pouring himself another whisky.

'No, but you're implying. What are you implying, Sam? I mean, you know why I was dressed up. I told you this morning. I was meeting my editor. I'm hardly going to do it in sweatpants, am I?'

'You were wearing a lot of makeup,' Sam says.

'Well, there you go. I am the Whore of Babylon,' I say, rage rising inside me again, so much rage that it tamps down the guilt. 'I always wear makeup.'

'Not that much. And not lipstick.'

'Do you have any idea of your levels of hypocrisy?' I say. I can hear how shrill I sound, and I have time to register that shrill isn't a good look. Also that, right now, attack may be my best form of defense. 'Of your, your . . . outstanding, *award-winning* levels of hypocrisy? Your new friend Timbo can get shit-faced and he's just having fun, being a bloke, letting his hair down, and I can't go for one lone fucking drink *by myself* without you making it sound like a *betrayal*? I mean, what happened? Two minutes ago you were saying that I used to be fun, that I used to be *charming*, that I used to drink cocktails, like you were fucking sobbing over the corpse of What Used To Be. So then I go and drink a cocktail, charmingly, but that doesn't work for you either? What does work for you, Sam? What do you *want*?'

'Why didn't you call me?' Sam says.

'I think I'll just go and catch forty winks,' says Jake, who has spent this entire time slumped mournfully, sending texts to Tamsin.

'I'll get you some bedding,' I say.

'Linen closet, second floor. Towels, too. Help yourself. Sleep well, mate,' says Sam.

'Night, then,' says Jake. His leather trousers squeak poignantly as he shuffles away, his gait now that of an old man.

'Why didn't you call me?' Sam repeats. 'I could have joined you. I'd have been there within twenty minutes.'

'It didn't occur to me,' I say. 'It was a completely spur-of-the-moment thing. Spontaneous. It felt like a treat. I don't spend that much time by myself. It just felt like a fun thing to do.'

'Really,' says Sam. 'Well, there you go. And what happened when you got there, for your *treat*?'

'I told you what happened. I had a champagne cocktail and remembered I'd forgotten Tamsin's present.'

'Isn't that nice,' says Sam.

'It was, yes. What do you want me to say?'

'Less,' says Sam. 'I want you to say less.'

'Why?'

'Because I used to love it when you talked. But now you just talk at me. You used to be full of opinions, and now you're just full of judgments. This is good and this is bad and this is not allowed, dear me no – we couldn't have people sleeping on *sofas*, we can't have men getting *pissed*, we can't have men telling the truth about how they think and feel.'

'Sam,' I say, more plaintively than I'd ideally like. 'You're talking like you hate me.'

'I don't hate you,' he says. 'I don't want to talk about this anymore.'

'But I do.'

'That's too bad,' says Sam. 'Are you coming to bed?'

'No,' I say, quite stupidly, because I am suddenly extremely tired and Pat's in the spare room and Jake's on the sofa.

So then he goes, on his long legs and with his jaw all tight, and I sit there, in my kitchen, which is festooned with Christmas cards strung on cheerful red ribbon. I sit and think. And what I think is: this isn't just a row. I mean, it *is* a row, at one level, but it's a symptom. It's the lump before the diagnosis, the crack of bone before the thing is officially called a fracture. I get up and make a cup of tea; there's a painting of a snowman that Maisy did at school pinned up on the wall by the kettle. I'm so tired. And I don't know what to think. One should really always have arguments in the morning, or at least in the daylight: you can't entirely trust your thoughts at night, or at least I can't – they get distorted. Did the bone crack, or did we just bang our shins? How much of this stuff are you supposed to put up with? The lump needn't be fatal, after all, and bones heal. I don't know. I don't know anything, except that I'm not feeling especially festive. Also, I feel sorry for everyone (myself included). I can't stand the way everyone is so scared of being lonely: I don't want to be one of those people. Poor Hope, so badly behaved, who'd really save a lot of time and effort if she wrote PLEASE LOVE ME all across her forehead in indelible marker pen. Poor Tamsin, making so many compromises (she told me last week that when she has an orgasm, Jake says,

'Good girl.' Call me shallow, but that alone would be a deal-breaker). Poor Jake, and poor Jake's sex-vocab and poor Jake's children. Poor Sophie, who bought into the mad nuclear-family dream and doesn't know how to ask for her money back, and poor Tim, who's not a bad person, just a bit of a twat. Who else? Oh yes: poor Sam, being married to me. Because perhaps I really am a terrible cunt. Perhaps he's right. Not just about how I used to be fun and I'm not anymore, but about things generally. I mean, I don't love him as much as I used to, as I was thinking only this afternoon. That's not very nice, is it? I love him more than I love my really fantastic range, and considerably less than I love my annoying children. That's part of the problem: there's nothing to compare any of this with. I suppose if I loved my stove more, at least I'd know. If I *fancied* my stove more, that would be my clue, right there.

The one thing I know about love is that it means having somebody who's always on your side. When you're a couple, I mean. You exhale, and you think it's all okay, because the person you're with is on your side, and you're on theirs. You are, in this respect at least, as one. Your front is united. You support each other. You are complicit. Whether you behave well or badly, you know there is one person in the world who gets it, or trains themselves to get it, or pretends to get it, *because they're on your side.* They're on your side because they love you. And what tonight has taught me is that Sam is no longer on mine. You're not on a person's side if you call them out in public, or if you call them names, or if the tone of your voice suggests actual hatred.

I know how to make lots of things okay, but I don't know how to fix that, in him or in myself. I make another cup of tea. What I must try to be is the person I'm not, I decide wearily. I must be the person who is adult enough not to think, 'Fuck this for a game of soldiers.' I must be a good wife, like a wife in a book. I must work at things. I mustn't lie to my husband about what I did at the Connaught. In fact, I must avoid the Connaught and everything it stands for. It's already stopped feeling real; a few hours on, and it feels like a lovely daydream. None of this makes me feel especially better, and I have the whooshy, blurred feeling at the back of my head that you get when you lie to yourself, but it's late and I really need to get to bed. It's a shame I can't curl up on the kitchen table; having told Sam I wasn't coming up, I'm now going to have to creep in beside him.

I wrestle the bag out of the trash can, so it's there in the morning, in time for the last trash collection before Christmas. As I drag it outside, I notice it's snowing.

And as I come back inside, I see my phone is lit up. It's 12.36 a.m. on Christmas Eve and I have a text message. As I press the button to read it – it's from him, of course it is – I also notice, Miss Observant, that my hand is very faintly shaking.

PART TWO

3

25 December 2010, 7 a.m.

You wouldn't look at a live turkey and think, 'That bird's gagging for it.' Dead though, all plucked and huge-breasted and gaping between the legs – sorry to say 'gaping between the legs', but if you don't like it, imagine how I feel when it pops into my head at seven in the morning – there's an unsettling corporeal heft about turkeys, and also something faintly porno. I wonder if women all over the country are thinking the same thing, humping their giant bird out of the fridge and into the giant roasting tray, staring at its lifted-up legs and innards, into which they are shortly to insert their fists.

I'm fisting the turkey too. For God's sake: my life. I'm giving it a good stuffing with Mr. Lidgate the butcher's finest: apricot and cranberry in one half, walnut and bacon in the other. The wing tips shudder in response. It really doesn't help morale, or my rising feeling of nausea, that this bird, this monster, weighs very slightly less than Maisy did a couple of years ago. It's like roasting a child. Well, a child with giant goosebumps and bits of black quill left embedded at random in its flesh – bits of quill that you pay extra for, obviously. Bronze, innit.

I probably wouldn't be thinking any of this if it hadn't been for the text I received last night. From the man from the Connaught. Whom I met this time last year, and whom I have recently – because he lived abroad until three months ago – been seeing. 'Seeing': such a marvelous euphemism. Anyway, whom I have now been seeing for three months. And whom I 'saw' properly yesterday for the first time, *if you get my meaning.* It was the eve of the anniversary of our first meeting, sweetly.

And it was amazing. But the whole context is so weird, or maybe just so new, that I feel protective of myself, careful, half scared. I don't want to hold the man from the Connaught up to scrutiny. The man from the Connaught must just exist and be. If I sound cagey about him, it's because he makes me feel cagey even with myself. I don't want to fall in love with him. And besides, despite our intimacy, I have no idea at all about the man from the Connaught's intentions. Perhaps he doesn't have any.

Without the text, I tell myself, I would be hinged, stuffing the turkey like I do every year, not finding it remotely bosomy or gapey or porny. But the man from the Connaught's text has undone me. We normally communicate by phone or by e-mail; texts are rare beasts, and I don't think I fully understand the form in this context. Most of the night and all of this morning, I have been poring over single characters as though they held some eternal secret. He's put two kisses. Is that normal? Is two kisses just what he does? Is it in fact the definition of normal-for-him – does he send everyone who doesn't get 'best wishes' or 'yours' two kisses, and am I being sent the same number of kisses as, like, his nan? I reach for the phone again to check, smearing the keypad in sausage meat. *Happy Christmas, Clara. Xx*. Two kisses, one big, one small.

Yes, I know. I know that text doesn't look like much. But . . . actually. First, note the comma. I feel proud of his comma, and of being his comma's recipient. The man from the Connaught can punctuate, and that works very well for me, attractiveness-wise. Second, he sent me the text just before one this morning. He was thinking of me, and maybe he was even thinking of me while he was lying in bed. So. That is not entirely insignificant. Third, the kisses. Perhaps they denote an agony of longing. And what's with the first, big, kiss? Is that a kiss with tongues, or does the kiss automatically capitalize itself on his phone because it comes after a full stop? So you see my quandary: that text, that so-what, nothing-looking text, could actually mean, 'I am lying in bed thinking about you, in an agony of longing. These kisses mean I love you. I'm snogging with tongues. Actually, Clara, I want to marry you. Merry Christmas, my darling.'

Well, not the last bit, obviously. But the rest – well, it's possible, I think, smiling to myself at my own idiocy as I paint Nigella's maple-syrup-and-butter mix onto the bird's H-cupped bosom. Not necessarily probable, granted. But at least he texted. He texted! And even as I'm smiling at myself, there's a twinge somewhere in my abdomen, a little dart of hope. I think the penultimate sentence of the text probably doesn't denote an imminent proposal – let's get a grip here. And obviously I don't want him to marry me, because I'm married already. But still.

Daubs of butter, bacon on the breast, and – God, my back: I'm bent in two, like a crone – the bird goes into the oven. I turn my attention to the potatoes. We had a massive peeling session yesterday evening – me, the children, various rellies and friends who were hanging about – but I think the potatoes suffer from being peeled and left in water overnight, and frankly, if it were down to me, we'd chuck the turkey and feast on roast potatoes and bread sauce. So here they are, all four kilos of them, and here I am with my peeler in my hand and a cup of tea at my side, Radio 4 in the background, enjoying the last few moments of solitude I'll have all day.

I know exactly what's going to happen in approximately ten minutes. It is what always happens, and what will continue to happen until the End of Days (I push that thought right out of my head, because it makes me feel unpleasantly claustrophobic. I used to have it a lot, usually in various domestic contexts: I'd look at Sam sleeping, and think, 'Until the End of Days,' and sometimes I'd feel panicky and short of breath though

I know I should have felt comforted, secure, safe, bathed in the golden glow of eternal matrimony. But let's not go there again). Anyway, what will happen is that Pat will come downstairs and she won't have put her teeth in yet. Yes, I know – they're her teeth and if she wants to walk around with a broken-looking, caved-in face, it's her choice. And maybe the teeth are uncomfy; in fact I expect they are – how could they not be? Nevertheless, I will be temporarily irritated. I will also be irritated by the fact that, despite my having bought her four different dressing gowns over the years, she will choose to come downstairs in her sweet, old-lady, see-through nightdress. Why are sweet, old-lady nighties never sufficiently opaque? Buttoned up to the neck, cuffed to the wrist, virginally white, starched-seeming, practically Amish – but you can always see the bosoms. And the . . . I don't know what to call my mother-in-law's vagina. I don't understand it: my own nighties – less Amish, more flesh-exposing – are as densely woven as you like. I could stand in front of Klieg lights and nobody would see anything. Pat's nighties, not so. Good morning, Pat, and – hey! Long time no see! – good morning to you, Pat's tits and arse. Greetings, o loins.

And here she comes. 'You should have told me you were up,' she says, toothlessly. I can see her nipples. 'I'd have come down and helped.' She turns her back to get to the kettle, and yup – there is Pat's arse, glinting pearlescent through the fabric. And then she turns round again and . . . oh God. There it is, clearly visible and – help me – drawing my eye to it like a magnet.

I am suddenly filled with a sort of carpe diem vigor. If you can't carp the diem on Christmas Day, when can you? So after I've kissed Pat good morning and wished her a merry Christmas and stuck two pieces of bread in the toaster for her (I've cleverly remembered to buy her the plastic white bread she likes; she can't eat whole-wheat bread because she says the seedy bits remind her of 'wee moths'), I say, boldly, for the first time ever in the seven years I've known her, 'Pat. You know your nightie's completely see-through?'

'Is it now, darling?' says Pat, looking down at herself. 'Aye, so it is. Most of them are. D'you have any red jam? I don't like marmalade.'

'Here,' I say, fetching the jar. 'But, Pat?'

'Yes?' says Pat.

'Do you not feel . . . do you not think maybe a dressing gown?'

'You don't mind, do you?'

Tricky question. Admitting I mind suggests I am somehow affronted by Pat's parts, which – though true up to a point – isn't something I want to emphasize. I mean, what a downer for her, on Christmas morning, to feel her genitalia are somehow spoiling the vibe.

'Me?' I laugh, like this: ha ha ha. 'Me? Of course not. We're all the same, as I'm always telling Maisy.'

'Oh good,' says Pat, sitting down to breakfast, so that all I can see now are her practically bared breasts.

'But, you know . . . other people,' I say. 'The boys, and Sam, and . . .'

'Sam's seen it all before,' Pat says cheerfully of her sixty-something nudity. I have no idea of what goes on anymore. Perhaps they watch *Sex and the City* together starkers.

'I, er, right. But the boys, and people are going to start turning up in a bit, and I just think, I just wonder . . .'

'Ah, they're just my wee diddies,' Pat says. 'I'll go and get dressed in a minute. Now, what can I do to help?'

And that is the start of Christmas morning.

Everything happens at once, as it always seems to on Christmas morning. The children open their stockings after breakfast – I make them wait until then these days – and they all seem gratifyingly delighted with them; Jack and Charlie don't eye up Maisy's with any discernible dissatisfaction. And then there's a mini-lull, where it feels almost like an ordinary day, if we had ordinary days and lived in an idealized world. The house is calm, the children are in their rooms playing with their new things, everything is clean and shiny and there's a delicious smell. It is, frankly, blissfully domestic. Pat has put in her teeth and put on some underwear, as well as some clothes. There's champagne chilling on the balcony, what with the fridge still being crammed to capacity (I don't know why I buy stuff as though we were going to be under siege for days: the shops re-open tomorrow). King's College carols are streaming through the house via my computer; we even have a fire going in the sitting room. It's all extremely charming: a perfect scene, really. And I am delighted as I look at it. All that haring around, all that effort, and I think the result is worth it. Here we are: it's Christmas Day and the surface, at least, is gloriously lovely.

My former husband, Robert, is the first to arrive. He's been living in New York for the past three years, and Paris before that, which means the quality of his presents is really excellent. And I'm pleased to see him, too, obviously. Robert has gone, pretty much seamlessly, from being my husband to being my very good friend; we speak two or three times a week and hang out with the children when he's in London for work, which is every four weeks. It helped that I had already met Sam just before we separated: it cut the time I spent wailing and weeping. It also helped that I wasn't entirely inclined to weep and wail for long, once the shock of being dumped had passed. That's the main thing, really, about dumpage – the humiliation. Is that an awful thing to say? It's what I felt, at any rate. Twenty percent sad; eighty percent crushed with humiliation. Just really embarrassed, as though I'd farted exceptionally loudly, fusillade-style, at a very quiet wedding (an apt analogy, that – in all the time we were married, I was never aware of Robert having any bodily functions of the evacuative sort. He pooed in secret. *For eight years*).

Which isn't to say that being dumped doesn't suck, even when nothing very dramatic happens and you just peter out for no very good reason. You're like a stiletto when everyone's wearing wedges, all alone and unloved, gathering dust at the back of the wardrobe, not yet knowing – because you're too busy feeling miserable, and, er, also because you're a shoe and your brains aren't that huge – that your time will come again. I don't mean that my time with Robert will come again – Jesus, what a thought – but rather that you don't realize, when you're a shoe, that everything is cyclical. At some point you – shunned shoe, shoe of shame, shoe with the wrong heel and the unfashionably pointy toe, shoe with shoe-babies – will be in demand. You will be the shoe du jour. Sure, as Pat says, as eggs is eggs. But it's pointless telling a shoe that at the time of its despair.

'Hello, Clara,' says Robert. 'You look gorgeous. Merry Christmas.'

'My mummy always looks gorgeous,' says Maisy, who has appeared at my side, wearing a pair of felt antlers on her head and a dress with an appliquéd Christmas pudding on the front. 'It's because she has beautiful boobies. Daddy has *hairy* boobies, because he is a man. You're not my daddy, Uncle Robert. Come and see my presents now please.'

Robert sweeps her up and gives her a kiss. 'Boobies?' he says, raising an eyebrow at me. Robert's innate fastidiousness, which is legendary – he edits fashion magazines, and this has only made him worse – extends to language. 'Why not "knockers", while you're at it? Or "jugs", like the trusty print companion of my teenage years?'

'I didn't teach her "boobies",' I say. 'Obviously. She learned it at school. It could be a lot worse.'

'Come on, Uncle Robert,' says Maisy, already halfway back up the stairs.

'Are you okay?' says Robert, more solicitously than one might have expected.

'I'm delirious,' I say. 'Everything's fine.'

'Good,' he says, hanging up his coat. 'I'll just take these presents up and see my children. And I'll make you a drink. My mum's about half an hour away. Nice rack, by the way. As we say in the twenty-first century. Or *boobies*, if you must.' And, with a snigger, he runs up after Maisy. He's very annoying, my former husband, but he still makes me laugh. (I never, ever wonder – literally, not once – what things would be like if we'd stayed together. I don't think he does either. We were rather well matched, in that respect.)

Robert is followed by Kate, my mother, a vision in what appears to be – bold move, even by her standards – real fur. She is accompanied by my sisters, Evie and Flo, who are respectively thirty and thirty-two; Max, Kate's fourth husband, is en route from Devon, where he has spent the morning with his own grown-up children and grandchildren, and won't get here until teatime. I'm making it sound like my mother and sisters walk through the door in a normal, walking-through-the-door kind of way. What actually happens is, they sort of *explode* into the hall, thus:

'Who's got the truffle?' This is Kate. 'Hellodarlinghappy-Christmas. Flo! Did you get the truffle?'

'I have it in a little pot of rice, packed all sweetly,' says Flo.

'Like a little special egg, in a nest,' says Evie, who is wearing a silver lamé vintage dress of great beauty and dragging a vast stack of presents behind her on a red plastic sleigh.

'Yuck, eggs,' says Flo. 'Hen periods. Sickness. Don't say eggs, Eve.'

'Eggs,' says Evie, smiling an angelic smile.

'God, how I loathed periods,' says Kate, taking off her coat and handing it to me, her trusty major-domo. It *is* real fur. 'The bliss of menopause. You should write about it, Clara. I don't know why people moan about it – there is *literally* nothing nicer.'

'Everyone is saying periods,' says Evie. 'Periods, periods. Can they stop? It's kind of grossing me out.'

'Get in and shut the door, it's freezing,' I say, kissing them all. 'Happy Christmas!'

'Oh God – yes! HAPPY CHRISTMAS!' yell Evie and Flo.

'Happiest of Christmi,' says Evie, catching my eye – an old family joke dating back from childhood, when Evie thought it was spelled 'Christmus'.

'The truffle needs to go in the fridge right now,' says Kate. 'Clara! Right this second. The truffle. The fridge. They must meet and become one.'

'I read that menopause gives you vaginal dryness,' says Evie to Kate. 'That wouldn't be good.'

'No,' says Flo. 'That would be very challenging.'

'Except,' says Evie, 'there's always lube.'

'Vaginal dryness! Absolute nonsense,' says Kate. 'You should never believe anything you read. All journalists lie. They're paid to lie, basically.'

'Um,' I say. I've been working on magazines since I was twenty-one. 'Hello. I'm here.'

'Shameful profession,' says Kate. 'Ghastly. But never mind. The foul deed is done. Though I still don't understand what was wrong with medicine.'

'Kate. I'm forty-one years old. Bit late to retrain.'

'You're looking rather well on it, I must say,' Kate says. 'I was worried you'd be all sort of broken and hideous. Or that you'd have gotten fat again. It's so much harder to shift at your age. Have you had Botox?'

'No.'

'A man?' Kate is staring at me beadily; if she had antennae, they'd be quivering.

'Don't ask Clara if she's had a man,' says Flo, taking off her woolly hat and tousling her hair. 'We're still queuing in the hall and it's not appropriate *at all*. Though, Clara, have you?'

'A man!' This is Evie, practically shouting and hopping up and down. 'Is there a man? Oh, I knew it. Well, I *hoped* it. I prayed it.'

'Hello, Kate,' says Sam, coming down the stairs with a glass in his hand and looking rather stern. His eyes are very blue. 'Evie, Flo. Happy Christmas. What have you done with your children?'

'Oh pooey,' says Evie. 'Me and my shit timing. Sorry, Sam. Hello! Happy Christmas.'

'They're in the car,' says Flo. 'Hi, Sam. Merry Christmas.'

'And to you. Lovely to see you all,' says Sam. 'Are they going to stay there?'

'What?' says Flo, shedding her flat boots and slipping into massive four-inch heels: I never understand how Flo can actually walk, let alone run around after two little twins. '*Que*? Oh, no. Ed's bringing them inside in a minute. They fell asleep and we didn't want to wake them because they really need a nap.'

'Go upstairs,' I say. 'Take your presents. You're making a traffic jam. Sam, would you sort out drinks for everyone? And – hang on – there are some canapés somewhere, you can take them up too.'

'Probably in the fridge, where this truffle belongs,' says Kate, like a woman obsessed. 'Give me your arm, Sam. Lead on. Is your mother here? I long for her.'

'I'll bring them up,' says Flo. 'The snacks. Go ahead. I just want to talk to my sisters quickly.' We huddle into the kitchen.

'Sorry about saying "Is there a man?"' says Evie, looking contrite. 'Me and my giant beak.'

'It's okay,' I say.

'But is there?' says Flo. 'Clara, we must know. We can't sit here all day not knowing.'

'In agony,' says Evie. 'In ABSOLUTE AGGO, Clara.'

'Tell us,' says Flo. 'We beg it.'

I should perhaps point out that both of my sisters hold down responsible jobs, and that none of us talks like this except when we are with each other, and particularly when we are with each other and our mother. We just slip back into the jokes and cadences of childhood, the shorthand. It's comfortable, but I don't think that's the only reason we do it. It's also comforting. My sisters are as obsessed with Christmas as I am, and there's a reason for that: our childhood Christmases, our Christmi, when everything was fine, and before everything went wrong and Kate and Julian, the girls' father, split up in seismic fashion. The golden Christmases that we all try to recreate each year, along with the feeling that we are loved, safe, happy and that nothing bad will ever happen to us again. At this late stage, it would be fair to say that hope springs eternal in the Huttish breast.

'There isn't a man,' I say, grinning. 'No man. Manless.' I make a sad, upside-down face, but the grin won't entirely go away.

'I can tell from your face that thou lieth, Clara,' says Evie.

'I'm not lying, Eve.'

'You are totally lying,' says Flo. 'Your pants are on fire.'

'They are burning your bottom as you speak,' says Evie. 'Singeing your poor buttocks. "We burn," they cry.'

'Why are you so nosy?'

'Because we love you,' says Flo.

'I love you too. But I'm a grown-up – you don't need all the deets. And anyway, it's been going on a while and it's complicated. I met him a year ago. We spoke on the phone, and e-mailed. Very modern. He was working abroad at the time. But now he's back in London and we've been . . . seeing a bit of each other.'

'Clara!' says Flo. 'Oh my God. Please tell me the man isn't married.'

'Oh no, noooo,' says Evie, clutching herself around the waist. 'We always said that was the one thing we'd never, ever do.'

'Clara,' says Flo, her dark eyes on mine. 'Stop laughing. It's not at all funny. *You* told us. When we were little. *You* said, a person does what they have to do, but they never nick people's spouses, because it is sordid.'

'And you said,' says Evie, 'that it was a monstrous betrayal of one's own gender, also really bad karma.'

'It is,' I say. 'You reap what you sow. Christ, I sound like Pat.'

'It's still true, though. Hurry up and tell us so we can stop feeling sick,' says Evie. 'I want to go and say hello to Pat. And I want to squidge Maisy. And the boys. And everyone. They will all be squidged. And I want to know you're not shagging a married man.'

'Why's it complicated?' says Flo.

'You don't owe anything to Sam, and besides you two split up ages ago,' says Evie. '*Quel est le problème?*'

'We only split up eight months ago, Eev. Hardly ages. It's not entirely non-weird. First Christmas and all that.'

'You are obfuscating,' says Flo. 'Is the man married?'

'No.'

'Well, then,' says Evie, with a theatrical sigh of relief. '*Je répète: quel est le problème?*'

'There isn't a problem,' I say. 'I just fear the jinx if I tell you too much.'

'Why didn't you say in the first place?' says Flo. 'The jinx, we can understand.'

'God, yes,' says Evie. 'Totally mustn't jinx. We'll speak no more of it.'

'Also, I haven't told Sam yet,' I say. 'So. Hushed beaks. But mainly, it might not go anywhere, and thus I fear the jinx.'

'Gotcha,' says Flo. 'But can I just ask – why isn't he married? Is he, like, twenty-five?'

'Ew, toyboy,' says Evie. 'Bit suburban, Clara.'

'Bit "Hello, big boy, I am a lady of a certain age and I am wearing my lucky negligee." Ack,' says Flo.

'No, no. He has been married, but he isn't anymore,' I say.

'Hm,' says Evie. 'You've been having sex, obviously. I do believe it is the thing to which our mama alludes. You glow with sex, Clara. You are like a glowing beacon of the goodness of sex.'

'Eve!' says Flo, giggling. 'You're so mad.' She turns to me. 'Have you?'

'Not answering anymore. Respect the jinx,' I say, and we all go laughing up the stairs.

'Deep breath,' says Flo, taking my arm as we enter the sitting room.

4

25 December 2010, 11.30 a.m.

Our sitting room is big and square, and on an ordinary day you would find it airy and pleasantly spacious. Today, there's already nowhere left to sit, and the presents – the obscene tsunami of presents, which has been added to by every new guest – has by now pretty much engulfed what remains of the floor space: people are standing about like little person-islands, an ocean of packages at their feet.

Kate and Pat are sitting together on the sofa, champagne flutes in hand. Pat's flute contains brandy mixed with lemonade: she doesn't drink wine of any kind, claiming it's 'too strong' (she also claims that salad leaves are 'too scratchy', gesturing to her throat and wincing as she says it; I note this isn't a problem with jumbo bags of chips). She and Kate are screaming with laughter, God knows what at. You wouldn't think they had an enormous amount in common, but it's like this every year: BFFs, or at least best friends for Christmas. They're practically sitting on each other's laps by the end of the day. I think the love strikes because Kate makes no concessions of any kind when she's talking to Pat. So if she's just been cruising around the Aegean on Max's yacht (Kate prefers to say 'boat'), she assumes Pat is familiar both with island-hopping and with yacht-life generally. Pat likes this approach very much, and picks stuff up incredibly fast, including all the detail of Kate's social circles: 'Ah yes, that'll be the one that got divorced because in the end she couldn't make herself sleep with him,' she'll say. 'Even though he was so rich.'

'Exactly, Pat,' Kate will say. And then they'll both howl with laughter.

Robert and Sam are by the fireplace, engaged in earnest-seeming conversation; I briefly wonder, paranoiacally, whether they are talking about me and my disastrous failings as a spouse: 'And then she got fat.' 'She'd sorted that out by the time she met me. With me it was more, she just got boring.' 'Well, yes, she got boring with me too, obviously.' 'She started complaining.' 'Yep, yep, I hear you. She got the whining degree with me, but the doctorate with you.' 'I wish you'd warned me.' 'Well, you seemed very into her.' 'I was, then.'

Jack is perched on the arm of another sofa, his laptop balanced on his knee – I expect he's busy wishing every one of his 829 Facebook 'friends' a happy Christmas. Charlie is rifling through the presents like a locust, pointing out to a desperately overexcited Maisy which ones are hers, while Maisy dances around, begging her brothers and anyone else who cares to listen to let her open 'just one teeny-tiny present'.

'You have to wait till everyone's here, Maise,' Charlie says. 'It might be tomorrow.' He sees her face fall and adds kindly, 'Not really. If you're good it'll only be about five more minutes.'

'Your daddy is over there,' says Maisy. 'He is talking to my daddy.'

'I know,' Charlie says.

'Your daddy is Robert,' Maisy continues. 'And my daddy is Sam.'

'Yep,' says Charlie. 'Got it in one, clever-ass. What are you?'

'A clever-ass,' Maisy says.

People are still arriving: here comes Ed, Flo's husband, shepherding in their two-year-old twins, who waddle in giggling and make straight for the snacks. Flo kindly let Evie choose the twins' middle names, so they are called Grace Moomin (after the Moomins) and Ava Timothy (after Timmy, the dog in *The Famous Five*). Unlike Flo, Ed didn't appear over-impressed with these choices at the time. 'But what can you do,' as Evie said, 'if someone simply refuses to see the goodness? I wonder if I should have been more modern, maybe gone with something like Gruffalo or Iggle. Ah well, next time.'

'My aunties!' Maisy screams, hurling herself at my sisters, who shower her with kisses, one to each side of her. 'Like a sandwich,' Maisy says happily, 'and you're the bread and I'm the ham. No, the cheese. No, the cucumber. No, the *egg*.'

'I wish your mummy had let me choose *your* middle name, Maise,' says Evie. 'It would totally be Egg.'

And here come Tamsin and Jake (still together, and getting married next year) and Maisy's great crush, Tamsin's daughter Cassie, who at seven is a whole and significant year older and therefore an object of purest admiration. They are followed by Hope, traveling solo except for the laptop from which she has become inseparable: having worked her way through most of the dating sites with predictably unhappy – and occasionally downright grotesque – results, Hope has recently become obsessed with Facebook, which has opened up entire new worlds of disastrous flirting possibilities for her. ('It's different on Facebook,' she claims. 'You meet friends of friends, so you know they're going to be okay.' It doesn't seem to bother her that the online definition of 'friend' is 'someone you've never actually met in the flesh'.) She goes to perch next to Jack, recognizing a fellow social networker. Perhaps they'll sit there side by side, and send each other special Facebook Christmas gifts.

Everyone is eventually gathered – Robert's mother and stepfather have arrived, as have Sam's old friends Laura and Chris, who he's asked this year for moral support. They're currently standing in the middle of the room looking slightly overwhelmed and in need of support themselves, as well they might: there are an awful lot of us and it would be easy enough to feel swamped at the best of times. Which this isn't. It is a weird time, though today the weirdness is on the back burner, because it's Christmas. Sam moved out eight months ago, though he's living locally and is around most days, to see Maisy. She seems to be coping remarkably well with the new arrangements: the only evidence of any disquiet is her constant stating and restating of people's relationships to each other. Poor thing: in the context of our family, it's as though she'd asked for a six-piece, chunky wooden puzzle and been given a white Rubik's Cube.

'You can open a present now, Maisy,' I tell her. We walk – well, I walk, she hops – to the tree holding hands, trying not to step on people or gifts. While Maisy tears into wrapping paper festooned with jaunty reindeer, I start distributing presents to everybody else, so that they each have a little pile to open. Sam tops up glasses; Cassie passes around plates of canapés; Ed is in charge of garbage bags to stick the debris in, because if you're not careful the sea of presents transforms into a sea of wrapping paper that things get lost under. The noise is unbelievable: you'd think we were having a party for a hundred, though at a party for a hundred there would be fewer children's squeals and less beeping from their battery-powered new toys.

When everyone seems happily ensconced, kissing each other thank you, holding things up delightedly and pronouncing that they love their gift – 'I LOVE MY GIFT!' if you're one of my sisters; 'You're that good to me,' if you're Pat (tearful); 'Charming. Anyway, as I was saying . . .' if you're Kate – I go down to the kitchen to check on the roast potatoes, which disloyally, given how devotedly I love them, challenge me every Christmas, presumably because the giganto porn-turkey is absorbing all the heat; I need to swap them from the bottom to the top of the oven. Sam's down there too, unexpectedly (in the kitchen, I mean, not nestling among the spuds), feeling around the medicine drawer.

'I'm looking for headache pills,' he says. 'Do we . . . do you have any? Would they be in here?'

'They should be. It's a bit of a mess in there. You have a sore head?'

'Little bit,' he says. It strikes me – for the first time, oddly – that he looks a lot like Captain Von Trapp from *The Sound of Music*. Except younger, obviously. And real.

'It's very noisy upstairs, and hot too. Here, let me have a look. Could you just check on the potatoes?'

'Funny how quickly you become unused to things,' says Sam, grabbing the oven gloves. 'When you live on your own. I mean, this – it's just a ramped-up version of normal house noise, isn't it? It's not that bad. But it's given me a headache.'

'Here,' I say, putting two ibuprofen on the countertop, which is covered in stray crumbs from the bread for the bread sauce. 'It might not just be the noise, you know. That's giving you a headache, I mean. Do you like it?'

'The headache?'

'Living alone. The solitude.'

'Yes, I think so. I get a lot done. It's very peaceful. Calm. I miss Maisy. And the boys.'

'You can borrow the boys any time,' I say, heading for the fridge. 'Have them to stay. Adopt them, if you like.'

Obviously he wasn't going to say he missed me, the mother of the people he misses, and still – technically – his wife. I wouldn't have particularly liked him to say it, either: awkwardness. Except, clearly, I would, because now I'm narked by the omission.

'They're still a bit pale. The potatoes,' he says, giving them a shake.

'They'll be okay. The thing to remember is that they always are, in the end.'

'Like you,' says Sam, mirthlessly. He gulps down the headache pills.

'Sam. First, don't compare me to a potato, it's really exceptionally unflattering. And second, you have absolutely no idea whether I'm okay or not,' I say, trying not to sound exasperated. If there's one thing I really dislike, it's being told what I'm like by people who aren't me. I especially dislike the assumption that a person knows me better than I know myself.

'I observe that you are,' he says. 'You're very good at holding it together. Always were.'

Wrong thing to say. Just because I'm not doing ugly crying with nose stuff doesn't mean I have no feelings, the git. Second, it's so easy to tell someone what they're like – it exonerates you from having to do any thinking or empathizing: 'Oh, Clara, she's absolutely fine, because she's really good at holding it together. Me, on the other hand . . . Me, I'm sensitive.' I mean: fuck off. Three, there are *reasons* for me being good at holding it together – which I don't deny I am – and he knows what they are, so he shouldn't pretend that my 'holding it together' is simply what happens, a default setting, how I was born.

We're interrupted by the doorbell – it's Niamh, a friend of Sam's, who has popped in for a drink before her own family Christmas. She gusts in, followed by a wave of cold air, kisses us both hello and then disappears to the bathroom. When she's been in there for more than three minutes, Sam catches my eye and the atmosphere in the kitchen lightens considerably. He starts laughing before he says anything, shaking his head at me at the same time. 'You're so loopy, Clara,' he says. 'You're obsessed.'

'What?' I say innocently.

'And now I've caught that thing off you, and I find myself

thinking it too,' he says, still laughing. 'Even though it's completely deranged.'

'I just think it's so rude,' I say.

'She can't help it,' Sam says, now properly laughing out loud. 'People can't. It's just, you're so deeply weird that you notice. I can't believe you've contaminated me into thinking it too.'

'As I've told you nine million times before,' I say, 'people absolutely *can* help it. It's called sphincter control and we all have it, unless we're gravely ill or gastrically disabled.' I'm laughing too now, but I do think I'm right. Etiquette tip: don't go to people's houses for a drink, rush in, wave hello and immediately – or, frankly, at any point – go and take a long, leisurely dump. Just don't. You are an adult. Go before you leave home, and if you're suddenly overwhelmed with the desire to poo – well, hold it in. It won't kill you. It's really uncharming to come and crap all over somebody else's lavatory when you're only going to be there for an hour or two. It is the definition of bad manners. I'd understand if Niamh had traveled some huge, looless distance, but she only lives twenty minutes away. Why couldn't she poo before she left home?

Plus, another thing about pooing in other people's bathrooms is that everyone knows you've pooed. You might as well cancan back into the room, doing jazz hands and singing, 'Hey everyone, I done a crap.' And that's okay, in a way: I mean, we all *go*. But for me – and maybe I *am* loopy – I picture the person on the toilet, and when they come back for their pudding I think less of them and feel faintly disgusted.

The absolutely worst thing that can happen – the thing that makes you want to end the acquaintanceship right there, if you're me – is if someone you don't know especially well comes to your house, craps, and leaves a floater. That, my friends, is *the end* as far as I am concerned.

Sam and I had a row about this once. We were on a plane and lunch had just been served. Or what passed for lunch, at any rate. Anyway, the second it was over – literally, *the second* – an enormous queue started forming for the bathroom. I said, unwisely as it turns out, 'My God, these people are like animals. Food passes through their alimentary canals and they immediately have to defecate. They're like hamsters.' I pointed out that you didn't get the lav-stampede if you traveled business class, and Sam accused me of being a horrendous snob. I don't care. It's true. The cheaper the flight, the bigger the queue for the toilets after feeding time. 'You're unbelievable. You're basically accusing people like me of being in some way anally incontinent,' Sam had said, which made me laugh a lot – he wasn't laughing at all, which made it much funnier. He slightly spoiled his point by then joining the queue, throwing me pitch-black looks as I sat convulsed in my seat, making toothy little hamster faces at him.

We're both standing there, laughing like a pair of village idiots – too much, really, but I guess it's relief at the lightening of mood as well as the simple goodness of trusty poo laffs – when Niamh comes back into the room. 'That's better,' she says, fatally. Sam emits a strangulated sort of noise; I am aware that my face is weirdly contorted with the desire not to actually start barking with laughter, like a dog.

'Let's go up,' I say.

We *are* a bit much, I think to myself – not for the first time – as I cast my eye around the sitting room. Laura and Chris are still looking startled, Chris's mouth having just fallen slightly open at the sight of Pat, extravagantly bejeweled around the neck thanks to Kate's present. 'You really shouldn't have,' says Pat. 'It's too much. I don't know what to say.' Kate has given Pat a pearl necklace, the pearls huge and a beautiful, nacreous gray-pink. The gift is perfectly judged: the pearls shimmer beautifully against Pat's pale skin, and – this is very Kate: she loves luxe but hates ostentation – you'd only know they were the stonkingly expensive real thing if you were some kind of pearl expert.

'Don't go on, darling,' Kate says to Pat. 'But I'm delighted you like them. I chose them particularly carefully. You have that lovely coloring – I didn't want to get ordinary white ones, in case the whole effect was too revoltingly albino.'

'I love them,' says Pat happily.

'And I love this,' says Kate. 'I love the fact that you made it yourself. I'm enormously flattered and touched.'

'Oh, it's nothing,' says Pat. Her present to Kate is a hand-crocheted tissue-box holder, vividly turquoise and topped with an enormous orange starfish.

'It's divine,' says Kate, squeezing Pat's arm. 'It's the present to beat.' It is entirely possible that Kate means this.

I notice that Sam has positioned himself near 'his' friends – I always thought they were 'our' friends, but anyway – and is saving all his terms of endearment, his 'darlings' and 'babes' and so on – for his old mates Niamh and Laura. When I take him my gift – a shirt from his favorite tailor that I spent ages choosing – and present my cheek to be kissed, I also notice that he has some trouble with the question of physical contact with me. I stand there, waiting – not for Clara's especial kiss from her especial Sammy, but because kissing thank you is what everyone in the room is doing once every five minutes. But kiss comes there none.

'Thanks very much, Clara,' he says. 'It's lovely.' Then he just stands there, grimacing faintly, his face a rictus and his body rigid. It's galling, to be honest. It's particularly galling because Laura and Niamh are practically being snogged thank you for their presents (whisky and shaving stuff), and because he keeps patting and touching them: he's always been very physically demonstrative. Now I think about it, there hasn't been a kiss hello in all the times he's dropped round to see Maisy, or indeed a kiss goodbye. I am suddenly annoyed about this. Indignant. I am vexed. It's only my cheek. I'm not asking him to kiss my bottom.

'Sam,' I say. 'Aren't you going to give me a kiss? To say thank you for your really nice shirt?'

He stares at me. It's not a loving stare.

'You want me to kiss you?'

'Yeah. With tongues,' I say, which is probably a mistake, but which seems amusing at the time.

He stares at me some more. Now the stare is downright hostile.

'I'm not getting a loving Christmas vibe off you,' I say. 'I was joking about the tongues. No tongues. It would be inappropriate in the circumstances.'

Laura, Niamh and Chris are staring too now, as though I'd kindly provided a floor show.

There's a pause, and then he kisses my cheek, very quickly. It's as though he has been forced, pushed forward by evil invisible alien overlords with superhuman strength. The body language is Not Good, let's say. It's so bizarre, this whole situation. We can snigger like loons about guest-poos, but he can't give me a kiss, like a normal.

'There,' he says. 'Okay?'

I don't reply because I'm thinking about our old sex life, where 'old' means 'a year ago'. It's not that long a time, is it, twelve months? And yet in twelve months we've gone from total, ultra-intimate intimacy to the point where kissing my perfectly nice cheek is somehow repellent to him. I really don't understand it. I mean, I understand that when you break up with somebody, you immediately sever all intimate ties, though even that seems quite stupid to me. Because it's just pretend. It's adults thinking they're being adults by pretending that you click your fingers and boof! Everything's gone, just like that. Memory bank wiped, desire killed, fondness amputated. Let's be honest: there is no way on earth that in the normal course of a normal break-up you fancy someone one day and absolutely, 100 percent, don't fancy them the next – or ever again as long as you live. I can see the fancying dying overnight if a terrible thing has happened – domestic violence, say, or even someone behaving incredibly badly. Doom. Betrayal. But in an ordinary situation, where things just peter out and then you split up, I find the idea that everyone suddenly has to find everyone else utterly physically repugnant overnight very odd indeed. It's silly. Mind you, so is nostalgia-shagging. I'm not wishing Sam and I would nostalgia-shag. I can't think of many things I'd like less, actually. But I do wish he'd get a grip and find it possible to kiss my cheek without looking like his mouth has suddenly filled with sick. Apart from anything else, it hurts my feelings.

Over by the window, Tamsin has just opened Jake's present. She knows him well enough to quickly look round and check that there aren't any children nearby as she tears into the wrapping, but they've all wandered off as a posse and made a lair behind the big sofa. The present is, with almost tragic inevitability, 'sexy' underwear. But there's sexy and there's sexy, if you know what I mean. Tamsin catches my eye, and I can tell by the way she's biting the inside of her cheek that she's trying not to laugh. 'Thanks, Jakey,' she says. 'Very naughty. Cor.' She catches my eye again. 'I'm just going over there to show Clara,' she says. 'Show her my wonderful gift from my fiancé.'

'Help me, Clara,' she whispers to me. 'I mean, look. It's time-warp pants and a bra. Crotchless. Nippleless. Nylon mesh. I didn't know you could get stuff like this anymore. He must have gone to an actual sex shop. I didn't think there were any left. What's wrong with Ag Prov?'

I look up and smile at Jake approvingly. I am so craven that I even give him two jaunty thumbs up, like Paul McCartney. He winks back at me. Inside, I am nearly weeing with laughter.

'The thing about giving underwear is that it's basically a version of giving you a blender or a Hoover,' Tamsin says. She is very analytical, being a schoolteacher. 'It's a present from which he is going to derive all the benefit. If he'd given me a blender I'd have made him some soup; if he'd given me a Hoover we'd have a cleaner house. Giving me the underwear is basically giving himself a boner. I don't think that's fair, do you, Clara? I mean, it's all for the benefit of Mr. Penis.'

'What?'

'I'm saying, it's not really a present for me . . .'

'Yeah, I got that bit. But after that. Did you actually say the words "Mr Penis"?'

'Oh. Yeah. Haven't I told you about Mr. Penis before?'

'No, Tam.'

I'm thinking it's just as well I had three Caesareans. If my pelvic floor were even minutely compromised, I would actually be peeing with laughter all over the parquet.

'Are you sure?' says Tamsin. 'I thought I'd told you.'

'I don't think I'd have forgotten.'

'Must have been Tara. Well, you know about the ongoing vocab problem, right?' She stuffs the hideous underwear under a cushion, thinks better of it and stuffs it into her handbag instead. 'How he says awful bed things.'

'Mm,' I say. I am at this point unable to trust myself to speak.

'Remember? It started with the "good girl" come thing. Well, I couldn't have that. I mean, for God's sake. But actually, Clara, it's much harder than you'd think to get someone to not say bed stuff. I let him say it for ages because I couldn't think of a tactful way of telling him it made me want to be ill.'

'Mm.'

'Anyway, eventually I just came out and said it. It was driving me mad. I would feel myself getting to the point of, you know, and I would have to get the pillows and put them on my head.'

'Didn't he think it was strange?'

'No. He just thought I was so wildly into it that I had to clutch pillows and put them over my head so they covered both my ears.'

'Right.'

'Anyway. I told him I didn't like "good girl".'

'Good girl,' I say, in a deep voice. 'Well done, babe. Come for Daddy.'

'Not funny. Gross. Anyway. Then he started on the other stuff. And in many ways, it's worse. Not as bad as "Daddy", but . . .'

'I need another drink,' I say, refilling both our glasses from the champagne bottle on the coffee table.

'Thanks. The first thing was "Take Jake's cock."'

The laughter is so rapid, so violent, that I actually choke on my champagne, like in a sitcom.

'I know,' Tamsin says, patting me on the back. 'I know. And there's that awful internal rhyme. Also, who else's cock would I be "taking", you know? Plus of course the third-person thing. That's not good.'

'No. That's never good. Tam, can I ask you something? How do you keep a straight face? How do you not lose, you know, momentum?'

'The thing is, he's very good in bed. Plenty of practice and all that. But he will keep up this running commentary, and it's all seventies porno-speak. It does my head in.'

'Could you not just tell him that silence turns you on?'

'I don't think he can help himself. It's obviously just what he does. It's part of his technique. I have no complaints about the actual technique. He is skilled. It's just the words.'

'I don't want you to tell me any more of the words.'

'Please let me.'

'No. It's making me want to wee. Also, I think it's too much information. I have a very vivid imagination, Tam. You're forcing me to picture intimate moments between a man and a woman I know. Special moments. Secret moments. It's not right.'

'Well, you asked. You're the one who mentioned Mr. Penis.'

'Stop now.'

'He invented it as a substitute for "Jake's cock" and "my hard tool".'

'Tamsin!'

'What? He said I could hardly complain because it was just . . . factual. It's a penis, and penises are masculine, and therefore it's Mr. Penis.'

'I get a Mr. Man cartoon, except with a disturbing head.'

'Me too. At least with Miss Gina you don't get an immediate visual. Because of pronouncing it Geena. If it was 'gina, like in vagina, it would be awful. But I can live with Miss Gina, as it happens.'

'Do you ever think, Tamsin,' I ask, moving out of the way of Pat, who is carrying refills and cheese crackers to the residents of the sofa opposite, 'that it's all too much work? I know bad bed vocab isn't the end of the world, but I mean . . . all the compromises. All the things that make us laugh or cringe and that we have to put up with because otherwise we wouldn't be in a relationship? Don't you think it's tiring? And sort of unfair? And – well, hard work?'

'Yes. But I lived with the alternative for five years and I didn't like it.'

'But don't you think there must be a middle way? Like, a sort of Blairite Third Way? Where you can have a boyfriend or a husband or whatever, but the whole thing isn't quite so tiring and ridiculous and constant? Separate houses, maybe. Except not, because nobody could afford it. I don't know. But there must be some kind of solution.'

'Marriage!' says Tamsin, clinking her glass against mine. 'That's the basket I've got my eggs in.'

'Yeah, well, good luck with that one,' I say, clinking back. 'I'd offer expert advice, except, you know.'

'I know,' says Tamsin sympathetically. 'It's different though, with me and Jake.'

Unwilling to point out to the blushing bride-to-be that at least neither of my husbands had sex-vocab problems (she also once told me that Jake's face, at the point of orgasm, 'reminds me of someone having a stroke'), I go back to the other side of the room.

'You are my granny,' Maisy is saying to Kate, 'and you are my granny –' this is to Pat '– but you –' to Robert's mother '– are not my granny. You are the granny of my brothers but not of me.'

'That's right, Maisy,' says Eleanor, Robert's mother. 'But I am almost your granny, because I love you so much. Come and sit with me.' This Maisy happily does, clutching her favorite present, a second-hand portable games console, bought for her by both her brothers. I go off to find them.

'Come and talk to your loving mummy,' I say, embracing Charlie, who says 'Gerroff' but doesn't make any effort to move away.

'We love our presents, Mum,' says Jack. 'Thank you so much.'

'Thank your father and Sam too, please,' I say. 'They're joint presents, most of them.'

'Yeah, thanks Mum,' says Charlie. 'Cool-ass gifts.'

'You're very welcome. Happy Christmas. I wanted to say thank you for getting Maisy that DSi. She absolutely loves it. And I know they're not cheap. You must have saved up for ages. It was very, very nice of you to get it for her.'

'Yeah, well. We traded in some old games, so it wasn't that bad. She's quite cute, when she's not being a totally massive pain in the ass.'

'Do you think maybe you could stop saying "ass" every two seconds?'

'No. Soz.'

'Also, she won't bug us so much because she'll become totally addicted to playing it,' says Charlie. 'So it's win-win, we reckoned.'

'And she's had kind of a crap-ass time, you know, with her dad leaving,' adds Jack. 'We felt a bit sorry.'

I honestly spend quite a lot of my time wanting to put these boys in the trash, but I am suddenly so overcome with love for them that I just stand there staring, feeling quite choked.

'You're very nice boys,' I eventually manage to get out. 'I'm proud of you.'

'Whevs,' says Jack, looking embarrassed. 'Can you get out of my hair please, Mum?'

'We told her it would be okay,' says Charlie. 'We were okay when it happened to us.'

'I don't even remember it,' says Jack.

'It's not that big a deal,' says Charlie.

I don't know. That's always been my line: it's not that big a deal. It *has* to be my line, really, otherwise everyday life would be intolerable. And I think it's broadly true: sadness aside, it doesn't matter if relationships go wrong. What matters is how you deal with the aftermath in relation to children. This – the dealing, the absolute need for some sort of continuity – I am able to do. Sam sees as much of Maisy as he ever did: possibly, if you totted up the hours, he actually sees slightly more of her. The boys and Robert's relationship is more detached, out of geographical necessity, but they are fundamentally close: they certainly don't do that thing of being in any way confused about who their parents are, or who occupies parental roles. My worry now, though, is how they feel about losing their stepfather – the man who effectively helped bring them up. I don't want to put a downer on Christmas, but now seems as good a time as any to ask them. 'Are you still okay with it? With Sam no longer living here, I mean. I know we've talked about it before, but now it's a long time later, and I just wonder . . .'

'Oh God, mum chats,' says Charlie. 'On Christmas. That's so lame-ass.'

'We're fine,' says Jack.

'No, we're traumatized,' says Charlie.

'Charlie walks up to strange men in the street and says, "Will you be my daddy?" ' says Jack, laughing at his own joke.

'Jack wets the bed about it,' says Charlie, reluctantly laughing himself. 'He says "Sam, Saaaaam" in his sleep. "Come back, Sammmeeee." '

'We're fine,' Jack says again.

'We did it in PSHE,' says Charlie. 'In a module called the Blended Family.'

'Can you stop staring at us weirdly now, Mum?' says Jack. 'We were going to go and set up the new game on the Xbox before lunch. Mum?'

* * *

Christmas 1981. I am twelve years old. I live in Notting Hill with my mum and dad, whose names are Kate and Julian. Notting Hill isn't Notting Hill yet: it may sound hilarious from the vantage point of the twenty-first century, but it's considered rough and not quite *comme il faut*: a borderline slum, partly because of its large immigrant community. I have two little sisters, Flo, who is three, and Evie, who is just over a year old. It is Christmas Day.

Our house has a spectacular central staircase that spirals four storeys up, and our Christmas tree sits at the bottom of it in a pot wrapped in red crepe paper: it must be twenty-five feet high. Its delivery every year, on 17 December, is a momentous, thrilling occasion, as is the ceremonial decorating of it. Julian does the lights first – it takes him ages, because he is quite the perfectionist – and then my mum and I come along with our decorations. The result is heart-rendingly beautiful, even to a child with no sense of aesthetics. Our tree is majestic, Victorian, with its blaze of white lights and its hundreds of red baubles, and every year, once it's all ready, we turn off the main lights and sit looking at it for twenty minutes or so, beaming at each other. Elsewhere, there are big branches of spruce threaded through the banisters, going up all four floors. The whole house smells resinous, piney. All the presents are on the steps of the staircase, starting at the bottom and also spiraling out of sight. Kate is a genius at wrapping, and the sight of the presents – thick, glossy paper, velvet ribbon, a riot of colors – is viscerally pleasing, gasp-makingly lovely. In the living room there are thousands of Christmas lights tenting from the ceiling, like a sparkling canopy. Kate put every strand of them up herself two weeks ago. I got back from school one day to find Evie bolstered by a cushion on the sofa while Kate was on a ladder, getting tangled up in wires, a dozen multi-socket adaptors piled next to the sleeping baby. She wanted it to be beautiful for when Julian came home; my job was to watch Evie, occasionally detangle my mother, and be in charge of what wire went where. When Julian did get home, he exclaimed in pure delight, congratulating Kate on her cleverness and ingenuity. (This was back in the day where Christmas lights only lived on Christmas trees and got one outing a year.) Later that night we had supper together – me, Kate and Julian – eggs on toast, on trays balanced on our laps, in the twinkling Christmas light. I felt like I was inside a fairy tale: I wouldn't have been especially astonished if a unicorn had galloped past, shooting rainbows from its hooves.

Aged twelve, I don't remember ever living anywhere else, though Kate says, somewhat vaguely, that we did, and that we only moved here when I was five years old. But I have no recollection of any other home. Every inch of this house is as familiar to me as my own face: I know which floorboards squeak and which don't when you tread on them; I know that I like laying my cheek on the wall outside the third-floor bathroom, because it is an especially cool-feeling bit of wall on a warm day; I know there's a patch of damp behind the left-hand curtain (a William Morris print of green leaves on buff background) in the living room; I know that my favorite room is the kitchen, with its preponderance of pine, because it's so warm in there, and so cozy, and it always smells delicious. I know the best places to hide – it's a huge, rambling early Victorian house, full of odd nooks and crannies and doors that lead to closets big enough to make little lairs in. I know everything, and I love it all. I have friends at school who are starting to feel that their home is really their parents' home, and very little to do with them. I know that that's true of my house too, technically, but I don't feel that way. I love our house like I'd love a person. It is a part of me, and me of it.

I especially love it at this time of year, because Kate makes such a fuss of Christmas. The day starts early, because Flo is an early riser. Just after 6 a.m., Flo pads into my bed and we huddle for a while; I use her excitement about the day as an excuse to give full rein to my own. As soon as I hear Evie babbling to herself in her cot – the girls' room is next to mine – I pick her up, deftly change her nappy and carry her, warm and giggling, into Kate and Julian's enormous bed. We all clamber in. I am twelve years old but I feel no shyness or awkwardness about us all being hunkered in together (that will come, two years on, when I will also – finally – stop playing with dolls, and when I will choose to perch on the edge of the bed instead of getting in. I will sit and flick bits off my black nail polish, and then I will escape to my bedroom for a cigarette, and Kate and Julian will exchange a long look).

Kate excuses herself for a moment and comes back with a huge wooden tray, laden with cinnamon-scented buns and a stout teapot and mugs, as well as with Evie's bottle. 'Breakfast in bed!' she announces gaily. 'Merry Christmas, my darlings.' She kisses all of us. She looks so happy, and radiantly beautiful. She is barely thirty years old. She feeds Evie tiny pieces of bun after she's finished giving her the bottle, and laughs at the greediness with which the baby opens her little mouth for more, like a bird.

It is still dark outside. Julian glances at the steely sky and promises us all that it'll snow later. Flo says she would like to make 'an enormous snow bear', and he assures her that he'll help her after lunch. When we've eaten our cinnamon buns, we solemnly troop into the living room. The fireplace is decorated with yet more branches of spruce, the ceiling canopy is glinting merrily, and there are our stockings. Flo squeals with excitement, and so do I. I am a sweet girl, young for my age, bookish (I was an only child until I was nine, after all), quiet, family-minded, and if I know that squealing at stockings left by a pretend person isn't cool, I don't let it stop me.

The day progresses in the same vein: in my memory, it is bathed in a kind of golden light. All our Christmases – our

Christmi, as Evie was to christen them only a few years later – were. Kate's infinite generosity, her capacity for joy, love, celebration and the grand gesture all combined to make high days and holidays indelibly memorable, none more so than Christmas. And the feasts! My God, the feasts. Kate, not obviously a domestic creature in her later years, was a veritable Mrs. Beeton in those days – a cool one, in Biba and kohl-rimmed eyes. Cakes, perfectly iced, with elaborate snowscapes made of royal icing. Spiced cookies, permanently warm from the oven. Homemade stollen and panettone, before either had become commonplace. Goose, and turkey, and two kinds of gravy, and four different vegetables: she was amazing.

A little before lunch, I am chatting to some of our guests in the living room, pausing every now and then to lean back and examine my lovely stack of presents, including a longed-for Sony Walkman. Kate and Julian have headed off to the kitchen – we're moments away from sitting down to eat. I notice that Evie is absolutely covered in rusk – she really *loves* rusks – her little face practically orange with it, and I pick her up and head toward the guest bathroom to wipe it off her. The guest bathroom is just past the kitchen. I am walking very quietly, padding like a cat, because I am wearing my new knee-high stripy socks with toes, a gift from Father Christmas, and no shoes. Evie is sucking her thumb and staring at me with big eyes. There's even rusk in her eyebrows. As we pass the kitchen, I hear Julian saying, 'This report's going to get lost. I'm putting it in the dresser, Kate.'

'Thank you, darling. I meant to tidy it away.'

'She's done brilliantly at all the languages again, it says here. Isn't it interesting? Nature versus nurture and all that. I always thought there wasn't anything of her father in her at all.'

'Apart from her ear,' Kate says, which is when I realize they're talking about me. The bit near the top of my left ear is pointy. Not like an elf or anything, but it's there, and distinctive, if you look for it.

'Yes, apart from that. Though you're not bad at languages yourself, I suppose.'

'I'm better than you,' Kate says. I can hear the laughter in her voice, and the silence as she gives him a kiss. 'Which isn't saying much. Bonn-jewer mon-sewer,' she says. 'Boo-ay-nas deee-as, sen-nore.'

I carry Evie into the bathroom and wipe her face with damp toilet paper, and a few minutes later we all come back downstairs for lunch. And it is at lunch, somewhere between the smoked salmon and the second helping of roast potatoes, that I realize that Julian isn't my dad.

It all makes sense afterward, of course. One of the things that has occasionally puzzled me over the years was my presence at Julian and Kate's wedding, where I was the bridesmaid. I'd just turned six. I had a silver dress with puffed sleeves and lily-of-the-valley in my hair. Their wedding is perhaps the abiding memory of my early childhood. People get married – or not – after they've had children all the time nowadays, but in the mid seventies, even among Kate's haut-bohemian circle of friends, you got married and then you had kids, the model was still broadly nuclear: marriage then kids, in that order. I remember my friends at primary school being amazed by the concept of being a bridesmaid at your own parents' wedding. Nevertheless, I took it in my stride. And I'd asked Kate about it, some years later. She'd said, perfectly reasonably, 'We had you, and then we got married. Julian was working abroad at the time, you see. When you were born. And then he came back, and then we tied the knot. Do you see?' And I did.

The discovery that Julian wasn't my dad also cleared up another puzzling thing, that of the enormous – nine years –

age gap between me and Flo, my closest sibling. I must have also mentioned this to Kate, or maybe she preempted me, but I remember her saying that I was 'so wonderful' that there was simply 'no rush', which was a brilliant, and brilliantly jealousy-busting, thing to say to a child. I took everything I was told for granted: why wouldn't I?

Nevertheless, it was pretty shocking, at the time. I'd say devastating, but that wouldn't be quite right: the devastation came later. I told Julian and Kate that I'd overheard them later on Christmas Day, when everybody had gone home and Kate was lying on the sofa in Julian's arms. They were incredibly in love, Kate and Julian: you noticed it all the time, even when you didn't yet know what grown-up love meant, or what it looked like. They set the bar quite high, I see in retrospect.

I didn't know how to phrase it, and – more curiously – I didn't know how to feel. I was sad, obviously, and shocked, and angry with them for lying to me, though not as angry then as I would become over the next decade. I wanted them to reassure me, I suppose, to flick a switch and undo the conversation I'd heard.

'Was my father, whosoever he may be, good at languages, then?' is how I started. I remember the ridiculous 'whosoever' because I'd read it in a book that week, and I felt pleased to be able to slip it into a sentence. It felt dramatic, appropriately filmic.

Kate paled, but didn't dissemble for a moment. I suppose it must have been a relief for her, after twelve years, at some level.

'He was studying them when I met him,' she said, reaching out for my hand. 'Postgraduate. He was very good at them, yes.'

'Where?'

'At university. Oh, Clara. Come here. Sit down. I'm going to make you a hot drink and then we'll sit properly and I'll tell you all about it.'

'Clara,' Julian said when Kate was out of the room. 'This must be weird, I know. I can imagine. But you know all this stuff – who is or isn't your father, genetics, nature?'

I nodded.

'None of it matters. Kate thinks it and I think it. What matters is love.'

'I thought you were my dad,' I said.

'In every measurable respect,' Julian said, 'I am. I took you to your first day at nursery. And to your first day at school. Do you remember? Your little red uniform. I taught you to swim. I told you off when you were naughty and I cuddled you when you were good. I read you bedtime stories. Your favorite was *The Little Mermaid*. Have you forgotten?'

I shook my head.

'I don't make those sorts of distinctions,' Julian said, sighing and taking in my expression. 'I know that's a very complicated and unhelpful thing for a child to hear, especially a child who feels a sense of, of betrayal, which I suppose you must. But remember, Clara. One day you'll understand. And yes, maybe it was wrong to lie to you . . .'

'Maybe?' I said. '*Maybe?*' If I could have snuck another 'whosoever' in there, I would have.

'. . . but we had our reasons, and they came from a good place. You were tiny, Clara, when I first met you. You were younger than Flo is now.'

'I remember you,' I said. 'At least I think I do. Maybe that's made up too.'

'Kate and I were together for a couple of years before we bought this house,' he says. 'You and I first met when you were two and a bit. I loved you then, and I love you even more now.'

Kate came back into the room and handed me a mug of hot

chocolate. She was wearing a cashmere kaftan, very soft and brown, nicer than it sounds, and long amber earrings.

'I'm going to tell you everything,' she said. 'And you can ask me anything you like. I'm sorry you found out by overhearing: that must have been horrid for you. But nothing else in the story is horrid, darling. It's a story about love.'

And she told me. There wasn't much to tell. Kate was a student. She had a relationship with another student, called Felix. She became pregnant. She decided, on the spur of the moment, that she would keep the baby. She was pretty, clever, comfortably off due to her background: 'It would have been an awful indulgence not to see you as a blessing.' Her parents were furious, 'though less so once they met you'. Her father was not as cross as her mother, and he bought her a little flat. Kept afloat by a generous allowance, she and I lived in the flat 'as happy as two clams, darling. You were adorable.' Felix was long gone, by this point.

'Were you in love with him?' I remember asking, hoping at least for some romance.

'No, Clara. I was briefly infatuated with him, because I was young and giddy and he was very handsome. And,' she smiles, 'good at languages.'

'Did he love me?'

'He . . . He wasn't terribly good with babies. Or terribly into them. You have to remember, Clara – I was six years older than you are now, and he was only three or four years older than me. We were babies, really. All of us. You, me, him. Well, you were the *actual* baby. But, you know. Not much in it.'

'What happened to him?'

'He went back to California, where he'd come from. And then he moved to Mexico. He behaved impeccably. He sent money every month, but we didn't need it, so I asked him to stop. And he used to send Christmas cards and birthday presents, except we . . . we pretended they were from us. From me and Julian.'

'God, Mum,' I said. 'When were you going to tell me?'

'I didn't see the point,' Kate said, looking defeated. 'Julian really loves you. He's always loved you. I found you the best possible father I could. I found you a father who loved you. I thought . . . Clara, darling, I thought it was an improvement.'

'I suppose,' I graciously conceded. 'I have to go to bed now, to think about it. The thing that's really bothering me is that Flo and Evie aren't really my sisters.'

'Never say that!' Julian shouted. I remember it like it was yesterday: he actually bellowed, and Julian never really raised his voice. 'They are *absolutely* your sisters. You are absolutely loved and we are absolutely a family. And we always will be.'

I lay in bed that night wondering whether he was right, or whether he was lying to me again. Both, was the answer to that one. Christmas 1981: memorable in all respects.

* * *

All of this popping into my head, and Maisy's current fixation with everybody's genetic lineage, reminds me that I haven't heard from Felix for some time. We spoke on the phone a couple of weeks after the Christmas bomb detonated, round about January 1982 ('Julian's a good man,' Felix had told me. 'He loves you. Don't forget that, Clara') and a handful of times since: I called him up to tell him I'd had children, for example. But we haven't spoken for years now, partly because he moved to some even remoter bit of the Mexican desert. I'd get the annual Christmas card but really, there is no relationship. We have never met. I'm not naive enough to think we'd fall into each other's arms, and besides Felix has never expressed any interest in it. And, to be fair, neither have I, not seriously.

Now, aged forty-one, I wonder whether this is quite as it

should be. I thought about it long and hard when Kate and Julian got divorced, which happened when I was twenty-one, half a lifetime ago. That was a bad time. Not only was there the seismic shock of it – none of us had seen it coming: I suppose by then we were all too wrapped up in ourselves – but, after the event, the realization that my nearly real father had, just like that, gone from being almost the real thing to . . . to nothing much. A man my mother used to be married to. 'My former stepfather' is how I took to referring to him: it was like self-harming every time the words came out of my mouth. I can't express the sense of bereavement I felt without sounding like a mad person, so I shan't try, but it was awful, particularly when Julian remarried and inherited a fresh batch of stepchildren. Lovely, each and every one. Nothing to complain about there. But . . .

Anyway, I briefly considered trying to establish some kind of relationship with Felix, my biological father, at around that time. I toyed with the idea, even as I knew it was doomed. Julian was right: he taught me to swim – and the rest: everything else that 'taught me to swim' is shorthand for. I told myself that I should be happy for that, and not go desperately searching for something, or somebody, that could never be as good as the reality of my childhood – which was that I was raised by two people who loved me. So, no Felix.

But today, for some reason, I wonder what happened to him, and make a note to ask Kate later today. Maisy doesn't have a grandfather, as such – Sam's father died years ago and, after all these years, it would be absurd for her to call Julian 'grandpa'. We should maybe all go and see him, I think. Felix. Mexico: family trip. Just to say hello. Not to fall into each other's arms. But just so the children get a sense of where they've come from. Maybe.

Meanwhile, it's time for lunch.

*

Sam normally does a placement for where we sit at Christmas lunch, but he hasn't this year, what with not living here any-more and possibly finding me repulsive to the point of mouth-sick, and I'm so busy giving the bastard potatoes a final blast while trying to make un-revolting gravy – I find gravy-making particularly challenging, for some reason – that I just wave my hand vaguely at the tables and tell everybody to sit where they like. This is possibly a mistake.

In addition, in the general chaos of trying to hump lunch out of the oven and onto the tables (two huge trestles, hired from the community center for the occasion – and the kit-chen's not big, so there's much squeezing myself past people and bumping into things with my bottom), I have (the horror) forgotten all about the truffle. Kate and my sisters are vegetar-ians, and though I did once attempt to fob them off with chestnut soup and nut loaf, Kate pointed out that nut loaf was for hippies and soup was 'for the homeless'. 'Even lobster bisque?' I'd said, startled. 'Lobster bisque would be for the homeless of Chelsea,' she replied, 'or for rich invalids. We are neither. We have teeth. And homes. Feed us accordingly, Clara.'

So, the truffle, or more accurately, The Truffle. White truf-fles, as you probably know, cost more than gold, pound for pound. The Truffle, therefore, costs the same as the whole of Christmas lunch for twenty people put together, Bronze tur-key, organic veg and pudding from Fortnum's included. We started sourcing The Truffle in October. It's about an inch and a half long. It's also completely slipped my mind.

'The Truffle!' Kate cries, as I finally sit down. My hair is damp and clinging unattractively to the side of my head, and I can feel my flushed face and burning cheeks, as though I'd given myself a quick blast in the oven along with the parsnips.

'We forgot all about it!' says Flo. 'Oh crap.'

'Oh God,' I say.

'I'll do it, Clara, if you move out of the way,' says Kate.

But I can't move out of the way – I am absolutely wedged in due to the number of people and the two tables and the narrowness of the room.

'It's okay,' I say, getting up again. 'I'm closest.'

At least I haven't forgotten to buy the linguine – not spaghetti: spaghetti is not allowed near The Truffle, being unforgivably tubular – or the Parmesan or the heavy cream onto which The Truffle will be shaved. But there aren't any clean pans left, so I start washing up the one I parboiled the potatoes in earlier. The Truffle is getting on my nerves.

'We need a toothbrush,' says Kate.

'What?'

'To clean The Truffle!' she says. 'I'm not eating a dirty truffle that a strange pig has snuffled all over with its *snout*.'

'In a bosky glade,' says Evie. 'In autumn. Quite a poetic pig, as pigs go. I don't think it matters terribly. Can't we just give it a wipe?'

'Toothbrush!' says Kate, much as a surgeon might say, 'Scalpel!'

'Oh God,' I say again, not on purpose – it just comes out. And then, 'Ow, fuck,' because I've just burned the top of my forearm trying to extricate the tray of extra stuffing from the top shelf of the oven.

'It's okay,' says Flo. 'I've got it. I'll go and get one from upstairs.'

'Florence!' Kate says. 'For God's sake. We need a clean toothbrush, a new toothbrush. We don't need the toothbrush that's been in Clara's mouth.'

'It's my mouth, not my arse,' I say. I am feeling hotter and hotter, plus I'm starving, plus I feel a bit dizzy from all the champagne, plus my burn is starting to throb. Everyone else is tucking into their lunch with gusto. I can feel my hair frizzing and sweat beginning to trickle down the back of my neck.

Also, there's turkey fat on my really nice new lace dress – this is the first time I've worn it – and I don't think it'll come out.

'Good grief,' says Kate, shaking her head with sadness and pity. 'You are so unbelievably coarse, Clara.'

'I've burned my arm. I don't have a brand-new toothbrush,' I say. 'And the shops are shut, otherwise obviously I'd crawl there on my hands and knees through the snow. So. Why don't we use Maisy's? You can't object to Maisy's mouth, surely?'

'My new princess toothbrush?' says Maisy. 'What are you going to do with it?'

'Scrub the dirt off The Truffle,' says Kate. 'I'm no happier about it than you are, Maisy.'

'Pigs find truffles. Will it have pig on it?' says Maisy. 'Afterward.'

'Yeah,' says Jack. 'It'll be covered in pig's bogeys.'

'But I don't want –'

'That's enough,' I say, more loudly than I mean to.

'I'm getting the toothbrush right now,' says Flo. 'From upstairs. Excuse me, everybody.'

'And I'm holding the linguine in my own fair hands,' says Evie, getting up and grabbing the packet from the countertop. 'I will be poised by the pan. I will monitor its cooking. Sit down, Clara. Eat your lunch.'

'I can't,' I say. 'If I sit down you're not going to have any room to get to the stove.'

Now Kate gets up. 'You are all creating complications,' she says. 'I will do it.'

'You sit down too, Kate,' says Evie. 'Everybody's standing up and it's making me feel claustrophobic and if they keep doing it I might have a panic attack, actually. I am now officially the only person in charge of The Truffle.'

'Oh God,' says Sam, who's two people away from me. He's getting on my nerves as well. At least he's eating his lunch, instead of being persecuted by burns and frizz and The Truffle's complex needs.

'What?' I say. 'What, do you mean, oh God? Is your lunch not to your satisfaction?'

'No, it's delicious,' he has the grace to say. 'It's just, all this *fuss*.'

'Fuss?' says Kate. 'Fuss? Poor Clara's been working like a donkey. Like two donkeys, *one of whom is absent*. She's donkeyed about all day while you've sat there smooching your friends thank you for their frankly banal and unimaginative gifts. There would have been a great deal less *fuss* if you'd given her a hand.'

'Steady on,' says Chris, giver of unimaginative gifts.

'Kate,' I say. 'Now's not the . . .'

'It is, actually,' says Kate. 'Now is absolutely the time. It is time for a toast to you, even though your language is intolerably gross.' She taps a glass with the edge of a knife. 'Shush,' she says. 'Sam's going to make a toast.' Her face is deadpan but her eyes are sparkling with mischief.

'Mum,' I say. I only say 'mum' in extremis, partly because Kate prefers 'mummy', and I'm forty-one. 'There's no need for him to . . .'

'Quiet, Clara. If you don't pipe down, no one will hear the toast.'

Flo reappears with Maisy's toothbrush just as the room falls silent. All eyes are on Sam. Sam's eyes are on me, and there is desperation in them. Shall I help him out?

'Hurry up, Sam,' says Kate. 'Spit it out. People's food will get cold.'

No, I don't think I will. As he has made more than clear, the time for complicity is over.

'Ooh, isn't this nice,' says Pat, putting down her fork and leaning back in her chair contentedly. 'A toast! Lovely.'

'I'd be happy to say a few words,' says Jake.

'Sweet of you, but no,' says Kate firmly.

'Ahem,' says Sam, clearing his throat.

'Stand up,' says Flo. 'It's more traditional.'

'Put your paper crown on,' says Evie. 'It's more regal.'

'And so chic,' says Robert. 'On an adult male.'

Sam glares at Robert and throws both my sisters black looks but pushes his chair back and rises.

'Well,' he says. 'Here we all are. Again. For Christmas. Merry Christmas, by the way.'

'Merry Christmas,' everyone choruses. Cassie blows a lone tooter – paaarp, it goes, quite poignantly.

'And a happy New Year,' says Maisy. 'And I hope the Easter Bunny visits you, chocolate face, ding-dong.'

'Dong!' says Ava the baby, ensconced on Flo's lap.

'Kate would like me to thank Clara for this . . . delicious lunch, and what Kate has decreed must of course come to pass.'

'Hear, hear,' says Kate loudly.

'And it *is* a delicious lunch,' Sam continues. 'So . . . thank you for that, Clara. For making it. And having us all round. And being so . . . giving of yourself.'

'Do you mean that to sound like it sounds?' guffaws Jake. 'Because it sounds like . . .'

'Shush, Jake,' says Tamsin.

'Possibly,' says Sam. 'Anyway. It's a great virtue you have, Clara, the ability to gather everyone together and make them feel welcome and included no matter what the circumstances might be. Even when the circumstances aren't straightforward. And we're all very grateful to you. For your, your warmth.'

'Yes,' says Robert. 'We are. And we love to give loving speeches about it.'

'Piss off, Robert,' I say.

'No, really,' says Sam, meeting my eye. 'You make Christmas

lovely every year. And I know how much hard work it is. So, from all of us, and from me – thank you. To Clara,' he says, raising his glass. 'And Christmas.'

'Clara,' says everybody. 'Christmas.'

'The water's boiling,' says Evie. 'For the pasta. I'm beside myself with excitement. The Truffle is ahoy, Kate. The Truffle cometh.'

It's extraordinary to me how quickly the food disappears. I think this every year, and yet it still takes me by surprise. All that work, all that effort – not that I resent any of it, but it's a lot of man-hours – and whoosh, gone in five minutes. Well, not quite – we sit at the table for ages afterward, but the actual eating is terrifyingly swift, as though my friends and relatives were starving hyenas.

I notice that Hope has been taking photographs of the food, leaning over the plate of roast potatoes and zooming in on the Brussels sprouts. Now she stands up on her chair to get an aerial shot of what remains of the turkey.

'Hope, what are you doing?' I eventually ask.

'I'm live-blogging lunch,' Hope says.

'I didn't know you had a blog,' says Tamsin.

'It's new. I started it a couple of weeks ago.'

'What happens on it?' I ask. 'You should have let us all know. Is it a work thing?'

'Can we get down until pudding please?' asks Cassie. 'Me and Maisy want to go and play upstairs.'

'Take the babies,' says Flo. 'Boys, can you keep a vague eye on the babies?'

'Suppose,' says Jack. 'But only for a bit and only if they don't crap.'

'Fair enough,' says Flo. 'Call me if you need to. And don't let them eat small stuff.'

'Yo, babies. Let's go, nappy-asses,' says Charlie.

'I love blogs,' I say. 'I'll bookmark it. So, what, is it a work thing? Some sort of branding exercise?'

'No, it's just for fun,' says Hope. 'It's a sort of online diary in which I share my hopes and dreams. It's got quite a few hits, actually. And comments. I've linked it to my Facebook page, you see, and to Twitter.'

'Cool,' I say. 'What's it called?'

'*More Than a Woman*,' says Hope. 'Because that's what I am. Like it says on my blog: "Woman. Entrepreneur. Tycoon. Maverick. Friend. Sister. Lover. Survivor".'

'Bee Gee,' says Robert.

'Ah. Right,' I say, a bit feebly. 'Um, survivor of what?'

'Tummy ache?' says Robert. 'Horrid sniffly cold?'

'Life,' says Hope with simple dignity.

'Explain it to me, darling,' says Kate. 'I don't understand. You post photos of our turkey carcass onto a website?'

'That's what I'm about to do in a minute, yes.'

'I see,' says Kate. 'How insane. Why?'

'Why?'

'Yes. What is the purpose?'

'Well,' says Hope. 'I suppose it just gives my fans a little insight into my everyday life.'

'Your fans?' says Kate. 'But darling, who are they? Have you become a pop star since I last saw you?'

'Not really fans,' says Hope. 'I mean, my Facebook friends and my Twitter followers. Do you know about Facebook, Kate?'

'I'm not a hundred and three,' says Kate. 'My grandsons showed me years ago, although if I remember correctly – IIRC in your parlance, Hope – that was MySpace. I can see why they like it: it looks rather jolly, if you're a teenager. Tell me, Hope – what about you? What do you use it for, mostly?'

'Kate got out of the naughty side of bed this morning,' Flo says to me quietly. 'Inside, I am crying with fear.'

'Primarily?' says Hope, connecting a cable from her camera to her laptop and uploading the images of our lunchtime vegetables.

'Mm,' says Kate. 'Primarily.'

'For . . . contacts,' says Hope.

'I knew it,' says Kate. 'You use it for sex.'

'Kate!' I shout. 'Stop it.'

'Don't be such an old prude, Clara,' says Kate. 'There's nothing wrong with using it for sex. Good for you, Hope.'

'I, er, thank you,' says Hope.

'One can perfectly well imagine doing it oneself,' says Kate. 'In different circumstances. Everyone's on Facebook these days.'

'Can one?' says Evie. '*I* can't.'

'Are you on drugs, Kate?' says Flo.

'Drugs! Not since that nightclub someone took me and Julian to in the mid-eighties. In Manhattan. Now, what was it called? Area, I think. Absolutely packed with dwarves, for some reason. Rather attractive ones.'

'Gosh,' says Flo.

'What's that you're talking about there?' says Pat, who's been a million miles away at the other end of the table.

'Hope,' says Kate, 'is finding new boyfriends on the internet. For sex. Which seems as good a way as any, don't you think, Pat?'

'Oh aye, sure,' says Pat. 'Uh-huh.'

'Unless they're murderers,' says Tamsin. 'Or twenty-three-stone truckers pretending to be hotties. Or married. Or, you know, just complete and utter psychos from hell.'

'I like a nice wee fat man,' says Pat. 'A nice wee chubby man.'

'But they're the people I meet in real life,' says Hope. 'Nutters and psychos and married men, though few *really* fat ones.'

'Oh, that's a shame,' says Pat. 'It's nice to have something to hold on to, with a man.'

'So it's not like I have much to lose,' says Hope.

'Jesus Christ, women,' says Sam to nobody in particular. 'Jake, come upstairs with me? We can take our drinks and keep an eye on the children.'

'The bar is set low for you, Hope,' says Kate.

'You could say that,' says Hope. 'I – well, you know, Kate. We've had this conversation before. There simply aren't any good men left.'

'That's because they're hiding from you,' says Robert with a pleasant smile. 'Whimpering with terror.'

'Meanie,' says Hope, tapping him playfully on the arm. She might as well say, 'La, sir, forsooth!' and be carrying a fan. She honestly can't help herself: Robert's a man, after all.

'They're not hiding from Clara,' says Robert. He is relentless, more so with a drink in him. 'Judging by the little indicators one is so familiar with as her former spouse.'

'That's precisely what I was saying earlier,' says Kate, shooting me a triumphant look.

'Clara?' says Robert. 'Anything you want to share with the group?'

'No thank you,' I say primly. 'And keep your voice down.'

'What do you mean?' says Hope. 'What, you're seeing somebody?'

I heave quite a large sigh. In recent months, my relationship with Hope has been dramatically buoyed by her idea that we're both 'in the same boat', an idea I find unappealing in the extreme but go along with because it boosts her morale.

'No,' I say. 'Ignore them, Hope. They're just wittering on to make conversation.'

'I know my own child,' Kate says.

'I know my own wife,' says Robert. 'Former.'

'Fancy that,' says Pat. 'You're a dark horse, Clara, so you are.'

'I can't believe you would be seeing somebody and you wouldn't tell me,' says Hope, looking genuinely wounded and also quite angry.

'It's a low blow,' says Robert. 'I quite agree.' I know what I should have given him for Christmas: an enormous stick, all the better to stir the pot with.

'I can't understand it,' says Hope.

'What do you mean, you can't understand it?' This is me. 'Understand what?'

'Well,' says Hope. 'To be honest. To be blunt.'

'Yes?' I say.

'Never mind.'

'No, go on.'

'Yes, do,' says Robert, smiling wolfishly. 'Clara's dying to hear.' He actually starts laughing to himself before Hope's even opened her mouth.

'Well,' Hope says. 'And don't take this the wrong way.'

'You know,' says Flo, 'in my experience, anything you feel the need to prefix with "don't take this the wrong way" is better left unsaid.'

'Totes,' says Evie. 'Can I see your blog, Hope? Will you show it to me? Like, right now? I die to read *More Than a Woman*.'

'In a minute,' says Hope.

'You were saying?' I say.

'Well,' says Hope. 'I don't really understand how you – you, Clara – can meet someone and I can't.'

'You're always meeting people, Hope,' I say. 'You do nothing but.'

'Yeah, but that's not what I mean. I mean . . . well, look at you.'

'Me?' I say, startled. 'What about me?'

'Oh God, I didn't mean it like that. Nothing's *wrong* with

you. You're quite attractive. It's just . . . I do Pilates three times a week. And I see Guy, obviously.' Guy is Hope's personal trainer; he arrives every morning at 6 a.m.

'Right.'

'Feel these,' she says, proffering her upper arms. 'Just feel.'

'Yes,' I say. 'Impressive.'

'Thanks. And you've seen my abs. And I never have my roots showing, unlike you.'

'Okay.'

'And I don't have marionette lines.'

'What are marionette lines?'

'Those,' she says, pointing at the tiny lines between my mouth and nose. 'You should really get them filled in. I do. And maybe a tiny bit of Botox.'

'Mm.'

'And I weigh eight and a half stone.'

'I know. You've told me before.'

'Also, I've seen you in the changing room. Three kids: I'd have had a tummy tuck.'

'Hypothetically.'

'Sorry?'

'Hypothetically. *If* you'd ever had children, you *might* have had a tummy tuck. I guess we'll never know.' This isn't a kind thing to say, but I'm not really digging the demolition of my appearance.

'Clara!' says Hope. 'Why are you being mean to me? It's not my fault I haven't had children yet.'

'Modern women are so bizarre,' says Kate. 'In my day, if you wanted a child, you just got up the duff. Worked if you wanted a husband, too, come to think of it. Why don't you just get up the duff, Hope? Just get pregnant. I realize it's not ideal, but frankly at this latest of late stages . . . It's not like you couldn't afford to raise a child on your own.'

'I want to get married,' says Hope.

'Don't look at me,' says Robert. 'Christ.'

'Why am I not married, Robert?' Hope asks plaintively, laying a hand on his arm. 'Seriously. What do you think, as a man?'

'You try too hard,' says Robert. 'It's ball-witheringly off-putting. Simple as. Is there any cheese, Clara? I fancy cheese. Stilton. It's Christmas. You must have some Stilton somewhere.'

Hope looks absolutely crestfallen, so I pat her, even though I need a tummy tuck and filler for my lines.

'Fridge, I think,' I tell Robert. I turn to Hope: 'Everything that Robert says is purest nonsense,' I tell her. 'Don't listen to him.'

'Not nonsense,' says Robert from inside the fridge. 'Unvarnished truth. Horse's mouth. Ah good, here it is.'

'It *is* nonsense,' I tell Hope. 'He divorced me because I didn't try hard enough . . .'

'Yes, that's partly true,' says Robert. 'Where are the crackers?'

'. . . and now he's telling you that you try too hard. You can't win.'

'All I want,' says Hope, 'is for a nice man to love me. I don't even care what he looks like that much anymore. I used to have this great long list – he had to be tall, he had to be clever, he had to own property and have a decent income and be successful and maybe a bit glamorous – and I've scrubbed every single requirement out. All I want is for him to be nice and love me and want to have children.'

'Oh God, Hope,' says Evie. 'It's so tragic.'

'I know,' says Hope. 'It's a wonder I haven't thrown myself under a train. Anyway: where is he? I go to the shops and I see dozens, hundreds, *thousands* of couples. Ugly people, fat people, stupid people. Women with moustaches and men with breasts. They've all got partners. And I'm good-looking – I'm a goddess by comparison, to be honest – and I spend hundreds a month on maintenance. Plus I have amazing tits. And hair extensions you can't even detect. And my own business. And a palatial house. Do *I* have a boyfriend?'

'You do not,' says Flo. 'It *is* really sad.'

'I know. And now your sister has a man, and to be honest it just pisses me off.'

'I don't "have a man".'

'Well, something's up. I'm saying this in a nice way, Clara, but if there were any justice in the world I would have a man and you wouldn't. You've had some already *and* you've got kids.'

'What, I'd just sit here every night, doing the crossword and sewing my vagina up with artisanal yarn?'

'Clara!' says Kate. 'That is the most horrendous visual.'

'Well, honestly,' I say. 'I'm tired of it. Of women buying into all this, this *crap* in the completely *mad* belief that it'll get them *a man*. It isn't true. None of it is true. You've been sold a pup, Hope . . .'

'You've been sold a pup, Hup,' says Flo, who loves rhymes.

'You've been sold a pip, Hip,' says Evie.

'The difference between you and me is – and I'd worked this one out by the time I was twenty-one – you don't have to do anything. Well, you have to do *some* stuff, otherwise . . .'

'The full bush,' says Flo. 'You can't have the full bush.'

'Some people like a full bush,' says Evie. 'Just saying.'

'And the 'tache. Gotta bleach the 'tache,' says Flo.

'Yes, okay, you may have to deal with the full bush. And probably only Diego Rivera liked the 'tache–monobrow combo.'

'I think South Americans in general are partial to facial hair,' says Kate. 'Or at least indifferent to it.'

'And you have to wash, and brush your teeth and have baths

and go and get waxed every now and then. And not be morbidly obese or have stains down your clothes, and maybe not burp your appreciation repeatedly when someone buys you dinner. And that's kind of it. The other stuff is so many cherries on the already quite appetizing lady-cake. You know, Hope? We're nice. There's nothing wrong with us. We don't have to go on as though we need to starve ourselves or have extensive plastic surgery and a personality transplant . . .'

'Wouldn't hurt,' says Robert.

'. . . and an interior-decorated mansion just to "get a man". It's just such balls.'

'Word,' says Flo. 'Also you forgot our teeth.'

'What? Oh. Yes, quite. It's bad enough that none of us can drink red wine because we all bleach our teeth.'

'I don't,' says Kate.

'I just wash mine in Steradent,' says Pat. 'Is there any cake?'

'Over there,' I say, pointing to the dresser. 'I made it with Maisy.'

'It's all very easy for you to say,' says Hope.

'There is no man on earth who's going to love you more because your highlights cost £300,' I say. But this entire conversation is pointless: I know Hope simply doesn't believe me.

'Is she still going on about wanting babies?' asks Jake, coming back into the room. 'Sam sent me down to get the whisky.'

'Are the children okay, Jake?' asks Flo.

'What? Oh yes, perfectly happy. Yours are watching a thing about some pigs that live in a human house.'

'Peppa,' says Flo. 'I fancy Daddy Pig.'

'Everyone fancies Daddy Pig,' says Evie. 'Obviously. Where's Ed?'

'Upstairs with us,' says Jake. 'You okay, Tamsin?'

'Enjoying you being the babysitters,' says Tamsin, smiling at him.

'The whisky's on the side, there,' I tell Jake. 'The Scotch. If you want the Irish, it's in the cupboard.'

'Thanks, Clara. I'd better go back up. Sperm donors,' he says to Hope as he's halfway out of the room. 'You can have some of mine, if you want. The Jakester's seed is mighty.' He does a rather upsetting little thrust to illustrate. 'You coming up, Robert?'

'Yeah, I think so,' says Robert. 'I'm scared of Hope.'

'I think your fiancé just offered me his semen,' says Hope, giving Tamsin a wild-eyed look.

'Your poor life,' says Evie sympathetically. 'It just gets worse.'

As everyone sits in the kitchen with wine and coffee – the general consensus is that we're still too stuffed for pudding – I take Kate aside and lead her upstairs to my bedroom, which is a blessed oasis of calm compared to the bazaar-like chaos of the rest of the house. The boys have retreated to their top-floor lair, and the smaller children are still being watched over by the men, an anthropologically unusual occurrence that I feel ought to be taken advantage of.

My bedroom is large enough to have a sofa in it. Kate perches on its worn velvet arm while I sit on the bed, the soft embrace of which immediately makes me feel exhausted. It fleetingly occurs to me that I could not have this conversation and instead go for a quick, refreshing catnap – I am suddenly unbelievably tired – and so I inch forward a bit, in order to be not so comfortable and more likely to stay awake.

'I wanted to ask you something, Kate. It's a weird kind of question.'

'Shoot,' says Kate. 'Though you do look awfully tired, Clara. Are you sure you wouldn't rather be lying down?'

'I *am* weirdly tired, actually. I was just thinking that.'

'Well, you've barely stopped. I know you think I don't notice anything, but actually I am unusually observant. I'd have made an excellent sniper, I always think. You must be exhausted. You really are a goose for not taking advantage of Conception and Pilar, you know. I say it every year.'

This is a reference to Kate's housekeepers, who – although their names suggest an almost permanent state of genuflection – don't apparently 'do' Christmas. She's always offering to lend them to me at this time of year, to help with clearing up and so on, but as we have established, when it comes to 25 December I have my own strange compulsion to do everything myself.

'I just don't want, you know, *staff* milling about. It's not . . . it's just not very me.'

'Think of them less as staff and more as your very own Christmas elves,' says Kate. 'Sent by the mothership in your hour of need.'

'Mm. But then what? You know – we'd get them presents and they'd feel obliged to get us all presents, which would bankrupt them, and then we'd sit them down to lunch and there's no room and the whole thing would feel a bit uncomfortable.'

'Why?'

'Well, remember when you asked them to Sam's and my wedding? It was nice of you, but I had a bit of a problem working out the placements.'

'They were next to that grand friend of yours from school, if I remember. The heiress.' Kate starts to laugh, catches my eye and then laughs more loudly.

'She's a very committed feminist socialist. I just wanted to see what would happen when she met people who were actual Filipina maids. I mean, it's beyond parody.'

'What did happen?'

'Well, disappointingly she was slightly insulted to be seated next to them, I could tell by her face. I think she'd have preferred a hot man.'

'Not very democratic of her,' says Kate. 'And rather sexist.'

'Yes. She asked them whether they were paid the minimum wage –'

'The nerve!' says Kate. 'I never liked her, even when you were at school. *Mimsy* sort of girl. They're paid it many times over, because I am not a monster.'

'And then – well, she just sort of ignored them.'

'Rather a waste of them. They're very jolly. Of course they're also extraordinarily right-wing, it always takes people aback.'

We are both laughing now.

'Oh, this is silly, sitting like this,' Kate says. 'Let's get into bed for a little while. It looks so cozy. Come on, shove up. I feel rather tired too. My ancient bones are weary.'

'You're fifty-nine, Kate.'

'I know. It's unspeakable. And don't tell anyone. I've started saying I'm sixty-five, though actually I'm thinking I might bump it up to seventy.'

'Why?'

'Because they literally gasp in disbelief at my extraordinary state of well-preservedness. People really are stupid to lie in the other direction. When I meet a woman who lies about being younger than she is, I think, "Poor thing, forty-five and so unutterably ropey."'

She's already kicking off her shoes and easing herself out of her wrap. Twenty seconds later we are in my bed, propped up on a slew of fat, squishy pillows.

'You gave me these a couple of Christmases ago, remember?'

'Siberian goose down,' Kate nods. 'Nothing to beat it. I know you thought it was a dull present, but – life-changing, don't you think?'

'Oh, God yes. The only trouble is, it makes all other pillows give you neck-ache.'

'The princess and the pea. How spoiled we all are,' says Kate. 'When I think of how you and I used to live.'

'Hardly in a shoe gnawing on trash, Kate.'

'No, but in a studio flat with very few mod cons.' She sighs. 'We used to share a bed you know, rather like this but with desperately inferior pillows. And sheets and blankets rather than a duvet. I rather miss sheets and blankets. We were blissfully happy.'

'That's kind of what I wanted to ask you about, actually.'

'Bedding?'

'No, my father.'

'Julian? Good Lord. Well, I assume he's fine, darling. As you know, we aren't on what you'd call best-friend speakers. Ask the girls, they're going to see him tomorrow.'

'No, I mean my father-father. I mean Felix.'

'Felix?' Kate almost splutters. 'Good grief. What brought that on?'

'I don't know, really.' I note I'm twirling my hair, like I used to do as a child. 'I was thinking how Maisy doesn't have any grandpas, and you've noticed how obsessed she is with who goes where?'

'Yes.'

'And I thought – a bit earlier, when we were all upstairs – that maybe I should meet him.'

'Felix?' says Kate, looking astonished.

'Yes. Felix.'

'But . . . but darling, *why*?' asks Kate.

'I don't really know the answer to that, either. To lay something to rest, I suppose. To see where I came from. To show my children.'

'You know where you came from,' Kate snaps. 'You came from me.'

'I know, I know. But do you not see? I feel like it would give me – and maybe the children – a sense of . . . of something that might eventually be important.'

'It hasn't been important for forty-one years,' Kate says.

'I know. But still.'

'Don't romanticize this, Clara. Don't be sentimental. You're not going to fall into each other's arms in slow motion. The world isn't suddenly going to rearrange itself. Scales will not fall from eyes. All will not be explained.'

'I know that too. But still. I quite fancy the idea. I'm not explaining it very well. But I'd like to do it. I think. I mean, he *is* my father. Genes have got to count for something, right?'

'I see,' says Kate.

'So, can you help? I haven't heard from him in years. Where is he, for instance?'

'Do you have a cigarette?' says Kate. 'I used to love smoking in bed.'

'There was half a packet in the drawer,' I say, rootling through the bedside table. 'Here we are. Might be a bit stale. And . . . here we go, matches. No ashtray. You can use that empty mug.'

'How sordid,' says Kate. 'Marvelous.'

We sit in silence for a while. There are knots of anxiety in my stomach, which is odd because I didn't think I cared that much. About any of this. Anymore.

'Well,' Kate eventually says. 'It's funny you should ask about Felix.'

'Really? Why?'

'Because it so happens that I saw him ten days ago.'

'What?' I say, sitting bolt upright, like a meerkat. 'Felix? My father?'

'Yes,' says Kate, inhaling. 'We kept vaguely in touch, you know.'

'I didn't, actually.'

'No. Anyway.'

'What do you mean, you kept vaguely in touch?'

'I mean I've seen him, what, two or three times over the past decade. If that.'

'I see.'

'I wonder if you do.'

'I see that you didn't choose to tell me that you were seeing him. I might have liked to clap eyes on him. Or . . . or him on me.'

Kate sighs. 'I'm sorry for all my failures,' she says. 'I've always tried to protect you.'

'How do you mean? Protect me from what? You're making him sound like a psychopath. Or, or a paedophile or something. What? I really don't see what's remotely funny.'

'He is neither. Anyway. Do you want me to continue?'

'I suppose so,' I say, feeling about fourteen years old and quite mutinous.

Kate pauses again and smokes for a bit. It's very irritating, particularly as she makes it look so elegant. Most people smoke like navvies (not unattractive in itself, in the right context), but Kate smokes like a film star from the 1940s, and now I want one.

'For heaven's sake, darling. Smoke if you want to, only don't sit there with that ghastly longing expression.'

'I gave up years ago.'

'Don't be *worthy*. So dull. I smoked throughout my pregnancies. Everyone did. Drank rivers of wine. Ate blue cheese and liver, so nutritious. And we all produced these absolutely gigantic, bonny children, not the shrimpy little wraiths I see nowadays.'

'I know, but you can do that thing of smoking five a day. Anyway. Carry on.'

'Where was I?'

'Protecting me.'

'Oh yes. What I mean, Clara, is that I have always tried to protect you from Felix's *absolute* lack of interest.'

This would be painful to hear if what she was saying wasn't demonstrably true, and hadn't been demonstrably true for over four decades. Nevertheless, the words are not pleasing to my ears or heart.

I don't say anything for a while.

'Are we playing Pinter Play?' Kate says. Pinter Play is a game Kate invented for long car journeys when I was a child. The aim is to say as little as possible while still just about making sense.

'Where did you see him? I thought he lived in the middle of a desert.'

'He does. In a cactus, practically. Like a character from those books you used to love. Richard Scarry. Do you remember? There was a worm that had an apple house.'

'Lowly Worm. Maisy loves those books too. Anyway. You were saying?'

'Where was I?'

'You saw Felix in the desert.'

'Ah yes. No, I saw him in Harley Street. Well, Marylebone High Street, to be precise. He'd come from Harley Street and I'd come from Regent's Park.'

'*Harley Street?*'

'Yes,' says Kate. She pauses again for a while. 'Where his physician is.'

'He's lived in Mexico for nearly forty years, but his doctor's in *Harley Street*?'

'I know, isn't it odd? Some Professor Thingy. Touching faith in the superiority of English medicine. Or English addresses. I don't suppose he nips over every time he has the flu. But he, but, ah . . .' She falls silent again.

'Kate, this is unbearable. I hate playing Pinter Play.'

'All right,' Kate says with a sigh. 'He asked to meet me. I met him. He wanted to eat cheese, so . . .'

'What do you mean, cheese?'

'Darling, don't shoot the messenger. He loves cheese, Felix. He is absolutely mad about cheese.'

'Great. That'll give me something to remember him by: "My father. He loved cheese. Your grandfather? He loved cheese." Maybe I could get a tattoo. A heart with a dagger going through it and "Mum" in curly writing, and on the other arm a block of Emmenthal.'

'Don't be silly, Clara. The point is, there is no cheese in America,' Kate continues. 'It's the worst place on earth for cheese lovers. His desert *is* literally a desert when it comes to cheese. All you can get is that ghastly sliced plastic stuff that tastes of worse than nothing.'

'Mum, please. Fast forward past the cheese.'

'So I met him in that cheese place, you know, La Fromagerie. They have a big communal table. We sat down and ate cheese. He almost swooned with joy.'

'This is surreal, Kate. It's doing my head in.'

'It's rather a revolting word, isn't it, "cheese"? But I am reporting events as they unfolded. As I was saying, we ate cheese. He ate industrial quantities of it, actually – rather gross, though one forgives because of the cheese hiatus. The cheese exile.'

'Kate!'

'Fine, fine. I'm getting to it. He looked pretty peaky. He told me he was unwell. On his last legs, Clara, to be perfectly straightforward with you. The final stages of some ghastly cancer that nobody knows what to do with. He was saying goodbye.'

'Oh my God,' I say.

'It was rather touching. Do you mind if I have another cigarette?'

'Help yourself. So, what, he's going to die?'

'Yes, darling, I'm afraid he is. Imminently.'

'Where is he? I'll have to change the plan . . .' I'm thinking aloud now. 'See him at his bedside. Take him some grapes. Some *cheese*. But not take Maisy, too distressing. I wonder if the boys . . . It's sooner than I wanted. Oh God. Where is he? Private or NHS?'

'He's back in Mexico.'

'Great. Fan-fucking-tastic.'

'Darling, there was nothing anybody could do. He wanted to die at home. Perfectly reasonable of him.'

'I suppose.'

'Though of course if one were him one would die at Claridges, with a trolley of cheese at one's side. I did offer, but he just laughed rather wildly.'

There is another pause, the longest one yet.

'Are you angry, Clara?'

'Yes, I think so.'

'Are you angry with me?'

'Yes.'

'I understand,' she says, taking my hand. She has worn the same shade of nail polish – Chanel Rouge Bengal – for as long as I can remember.

'I . . . I wanted to fix it, and it can't be fixed,' I say. 'It's too late.' The tears come out of the blue and plonk onto my lap.

'I know,' says Kate.

Eventually she says, 'May I say something?'

'Be my guest.'

'It isn't anything I haven't said before,' she says, 'But I want you to listen carefully. Clara. It's important. Are you listening?'

'I'm all ears. I'm made of ears.'

'Now isn't the time to be sarcastic.'

'No. Okay. I'm listening.'

'Do you want to blow your nose?'

'What?'

'I think you should blow your nose. It's off-putting.' She climbs out of bed, goes into my bathroom and comes back with a roll of toilet paper. 'Here. Blow.'

'Kate! I'm not five years old.'

'Nevertheless.'

I blow my nose.

'I put a family together,' Kate says, turning so that she is looking me straight in the eye. 'And I made it the best family I could. I found you the best father – someone I genuinely believed to be the best father in the world. He and I have had our differences in recent years, but I still believe that to be the case. I stand by my choice. And it was a choice, Clara. There would never have been any question of me marrying Julian if I hadn't thought he'd make you a perfect father. And I think he did. And we loved you, and we loved your sisters, and we all loved each other.'

'I know all of that.'

'I know you *know*, darling, but I don't know if you *feel* it. I suppose it was inevitable that at some point, at some point after you found out about Felix, there would be a part of you that wondered if you wouldn't be happier elsewhere.'

'Kate. I never thought that.'

'Maybe not happier, but – better understood. There must have been a seed of doubt, I quite see that. It kills me that I planted it. There was a time, when you were a teenager, when I thought it would grow into some monstrous mutant plant. What I want to say to you, Clara, and it's important, is this: in our case, water is thicker than blood. I can only say it subjectively, because our family is all I know. But I know I'm right.

What matters is love. What remains is love. It doesn't matter if the love comes from *genes* or elsewhere. And you're making a mistake if you assume that the former is better or stronger than the latter.'

'I don't assume anything,' I say sadly. 'I just wanted to meet him once.'

'But what do you think would have happened? Some bolt of recognition? Some sense that the universe had finally fallen into place? We don't live in a soap opera, Clara. It's not *EastEnders*. What forms us isn't some ancient heap of *genes*. It's the way we're brought up, what we're taught, everything we experience. And Felix hasn't offered a single contribution to any of that. Not one.'

'Here,' I say, handing her the toilet paper. 'Blow.'

'I just can't bear that you can't see it,' Kate says.

We sit there in silence for a bit after that. I understand what Kate is saying – of course I do. And I realize perfectly well that it *is* absurd to suddenly decide you want to do something like go and meet your father for the first time several decades too late. Perhaps it was a stupid idea – Kate certainly seems to think so. But what I liked was the possibility of it being a possibility. Now that the possibility has been removed – for all I know Felix fell off his perch last week – there is, of course, nothing I want to do more than to meet him. I suppose I could always hop on a plane tomorrow . . . but no. The deathbed reunion isn't what I ever had in mind. I don't want to slide my hand downward to close his dead, staring eyes – I was thinking more of going for a coffee. She's right: it's not *EastEnders*. But still. It's bothersome, all of this.

'Did you feel like you were carrying out some bold experiment at the time, Kate? You know, like those tabloid headlines about how men are going to become obsolete? Did you think Felix was just sort of surplus to requirement?'

'Darling, he *was* surplus. He didn't particularly want to have anything to do with either of us – certainly not at the time, and not subsequently either. It made me indignant on both our behalves, and then I thought, "Well, more fool him." But if you mean, was I conducting some exercise in matriarchy, then the answer is no. I married Julian. Children need fathers.'

'Except me.'

'No, not except you. You aren't *listening*. Yours was utterly hopeless, so I got you another one. I thought Julian and I would stay together, Clara. He was never meant to occupy a temporary position.'

This is the difficulty with stepfathers, I think to myself. They come with their own detonators built-in, and as a child you have absolutely no idea if – or when – the detonator's going to detonate. So you put all your eggs in that particular basket – well, your one egg. Your Egg of Self. One egg, one basket, like one man, one vote. You put your egg in the basket called 'my new daddy', and you think, 'Well, there's my Egg of Self, I don't know why I made such a fuss about putting it there: it's so happy in the basket. Everything's fine. The egg and the basket are a pretty good match.' Sometimes this goes on forever, in which case everybody is extremely fortunate. But sometimes something comes along and BOOM. Your egg is smashed, tipped out of its cozy basket through no fault of your own. 'Where's my new daddy now?' you think, lying on the ground, which frankly isn't a very nice thing for any child to think.

This is true of ordinary, mummy–daddy relationships too, of course. Nobody likes a break-up. But there's an extra level of trust involved, with new daddies. A leap of faith. You think, okay – maybe *you're* the one. The last one didn't work out, but maybe you will. I'll give it a go. Again. And then, boom. Again. This is why, although Kate's current husband Max and I get on perfectly well – I think she's probably met her match – I'm pleased to finally be old enough not to mind the idea of anything going wrong between them. I'd mind for Kate, but not for me. His predecessor, Maurice, barely featured on my radar, though to be fair I don't think he much featured on Kate's, either.

And then of course you have to gather up the bits of broken shell and patch your egg together again. That's a drag too, especially when you look around for the basket and find it's moved on. The basket is elsewhere. There are other eggs in it.

'It's enough to make you want to join a nunnery,' I say out loud. 'And never procreate.'

'A nunnery! Can you imagine? The idea that sexual frustration can be subsumed into growing vegetables. As though saying novenas was foreplay and nurturing *potatoes* equivalent to going to bed with someone. Perfectly mad. Those poor women.'

'It's not ideal. But maybe it's better than all this mess.'

'Clara, you've gone loopy. What mess? There is no mess. Here we all are, perfectly happy. Your children are happy. You're happy. You're just having a strange moment, like when poor Granny had an infarct, do you remember?'

'I'm not having a mini-stroke, Kate.'

'You're having an emotional mini-stroke, I think. And do you know, it's entirely possible that it isn't about Felix at all.'

'Share your Freudian analysis.'

'Christmas is always very emotional, one, and two, you feel some guilt about the Sam situation in relation to your children. Fathers, stepfathers, absences, break-ups – you're conflating your past and their future, and not seeing that there's no comparison. Not really. Times have changed. We've all evolved. And darling, I'm bored of this conversation. I've said my bit. I hope you digest it in time. And now I think we should probably go back to your guests. All of this emoting is rather vulgar after a while.' She squeezes my hand, and we get out of bed.

Ack, stress. And now Hope is drunker than she might be. It's hardly front-page news, but I wish she wasn't. I often wonder whether I, too, would have become a borderline alcoholic if I'd been single – as in uncommitted, not necessarily as in sex-deprived – for a very long time. It doesn't seem terribly probable, but then I've noticed that it's on the up, the drink-until-you're-sick single-woman-in-middle-age thing. More and more of my friends are doing it – women in their forties and beyond, who go out at night and can't quite remember how they got home. And it's not a good look, no matter how you approach it. I love drinking, and I love being drunk, but now that the hangover from even the mildest drinking session lasts forty-eight hours, I'm meticulous about choosing where and when to do it: it needs to be really worth it. I pick my occasion and then go for it. There's nothing worse than going out, drinking because you're bored, going home and then finding yourself ill for two days, with only a dull evening to show for it.

These days, though, I have girlfriends – two or three – who drink methodically, joylessly, most nights and some lunchtimes, just because it's there and that's what you do. You meet them for coffee at 5 p.m. and they suggest a glass of wine; you have the glass of wine and they suggest a bottle. And then another. It's not fun, wahoo-why-not drinking; it has nothing celebratory or illicit about it. Nobody laughs. And so you say no, and you go home as they order more drink, and you think, 'What are you going to do now, all by yourself, sitting there pissed?' And you worry. Having said that, I'm annoyed with myself for a) noticing that they do it, and b) disapproving. It is, after all, Christmas Day. And if you can't drink on Christmas

Day . . . Also, I have the horrible feeling that there's something sexist in my disapproval, some sort of deep-seated, prehistoric objection to the fact that middle-aged women getting that pissed is somehow *unladylike*. I'm as bad as Tim last year, flipping out over my own Connaught expedition. I am a monster of hypocrisy. So that's a bit grim.

But it doesn't detract from the fact that Hope is tottering about the kitchen and that, horribly, the adjective that springs to mind is 'frail'. She seems somehow doddery, brittle-boned, *old*. She's not crashing around the furniture or anything, but she's all blurred-seeming, her gestures hesitant, her arms too thin. I hate to think of her doing it elsewhere, in bars and clubs and other places where the majority of the clientele is at least fifteen years younger than her. The problem is – and there's a gap in the market, I always think – that society assumes that women our age are at home with our kids and husbands. But what if you don't have either? And what if you do, and you just want somewhere nice to go and have a drink? There's no bar or club that caters properly to the middle-aged, so if Hope and I want to go for a drink and don't fancy the pub, we end up surrounded by twentysomethings. It's perfectly jolly, and more aesthetically pleasing than sitting at home staring bleakly at each other from across our matching recliners with footrests that flip up, but I'm not surprised it puts a downer on Hope's morale and confidence. I wonder whether there ever comes a point where being the oldest woman in the room is actually fun. Maybe if you're the widow of a Mafia don.

'Hope, darling. Would you like me to make you some coffee?' I ask.

'I'm just finishing off this wine,' says Hope, topping up her glass. 'Seems a shame to waste it.'

'What are you doing down here anyway? Everyone else has gone upstairs.'

'Yes. I'm going up in a minute. I just updated my blog, and now I'm updating Facebook.'

'Do you think . . . what are you saying? Can I have a look?'

'Sure,' says Hope. 'I'm just having a chat with Phil.'

'Who's Phil?'

Hope angles her laptop toward me. She is having a conversation with a very good-looking man who is topless in his profile picture. Maybe it was a hot day.

'Do you know him?'

'Phil? Yeah. Well, you know. He's a Facebook friend. We chat a lot. Actually, Clara, I will have some coffee. No – it's okay. I'll make it.'

Hope busies herself with finding clean mugs and washing out the cafetière, and I get a chance to examine the Facebook page she's on, which is her own homepage. She's been busy: whereas most people have posted a lone 'merry Christmas' or variants thereon – weariness with in-laws, exclamations of delight at certain presents, pictures of said presents and of cats wearing tinsel ('19 people like this') – Hope's timeline is full to bursting with her own comments and replies to other people's. You can tell pretty much exactly when the fourth glass kicked in. Phil wishes her a happy Christmas; Hope replies, 'Are you going to come over and say that to my face?' 'Is that an offer?' says Phil. 'It's a firm one,' says Hope. 'Firm, LOL,' says Phil, who is clearly possessed of a marvelous sense of humor as well as a fine pair of pecs. 'Naughty,' Hope had just replied, before I interrupted her. 'Get a room, you two!' someone called Elsa has added ('12 people like this').

Elsewhere in the timeline, among the YouTube clips and the imaginary gifts ('Alan has sent you a kitten'), Hope has – and this seems to me to be a fairly intractable problem with Facebook generally – given vent to an unappealing mixture of neediness, vanity and fishing for compliments. 'Why am I spending Christmas at my mate's and not my boyf's?' she asked her friends earlier, illustrating her point with a little upside-down smiley. She answered herself: 'Because I don't have one.' Two sad smileys this time. Which is okay, up to a point. But then: 'Here's a pic of me last summer. Am I ugly or something?!' 'No!' cry her Facebook friends. 'You're gorgeous!' 'You're beautiful!' 'I love what you've done to your hair!' 'Perfect 10,' and so on. Hope – thumbs up – 'likes' these comments, which is good as there are two dozen of them. 'I wasn't fishing, btw!!' she's written with what strikes me as really breathtaking disingenuousness. I mean, if you wouldn't dream of saying this stuff out loud, why write it down?

I scroll back through the timeline and find more of the same – along with a photograph of our Christmas tree, two of Hope's pile of presents and one of Christmas dinner with a link to her blog – and I suddenly feel quite depressed. It's so poignant, somehow. I absolutely see that it has the potential to go right, this whole stalk-your-next-shag business – but it does also seem to have the potential to go horribly wrong. I sigh internally. The problem with Facebook is that it makes me like my friends less.

'Hope? Don't you sometimes think that this is all a bit, I don't know, a bit . . .' I can't think of a word that isn't grossly unflattering, so I just make an 'ick' face.

'You were on it, I seem to remember,' says Hope, downing half a pint of black coffee in one gulp.

'I still am somewhere, I think. I didn't like it though – it seemed like a way for people I've spent years avoiding to track me down and then show me pictures of their babies. And I had to "like" the babies, otherwise it would have been mean, and after a certain point I just thought, "This is stupid. I don't give a shit about these babies or their parents." Also, do you remember that child who died in really monstrous circumstances last year, and you could become a "fan" of it? That kind of did for me.'

'Yeah, well. Half a billion people can't be wrong. Half a *billion*, Clara.'

'That's a lot of potential new friends. Or shagees.'

'That's partly the point,' says Hope. 'Most people nowadays meet online.'

This is true enough. 'What about dating sites, though? Wouldn't they be a better bet? I mean, at least with dating sites everybody's clear about what they're after.'

'Too prescriptive. The only men who are interested in somebody my age are in their sixties. There was one quite good one called ToyboysRUs, but after a while, you know . . .'

'Bit depressing.'

'Yeah. And I don't have trouble getting the shags. I just have trouble holding on to them afterward.'

'I know. I wonder why. What do you *say* to them, Hope? Do you yell, "I want your babies" the moment they look at you?'

'No, of course not.'

'Do you say, "I love you" on the first, er, date?'

'No. Well. Perhaps once or twice, by accident.'

'Maybe stop doing that.'

'I know, though actually it's not that bad. I'd be delighted if someone said they loved me.'

'You wouldn't. You'd think, "Stop talking, weirdo."'

'I don't think I would. I think I'd say, "Thanks very much, I love you too." Anyway. I don't need your advice. I just need to meet the right person.'

She looks at me, less blurred now but still not what you'd call sober, and her expression is not warm. This happens sometimes, with vampire friends – not a category I'd necessarily place Hope in, though given her earlier outburst, things are perhaps headed that way. The needier friends can mutate into vampires overnight, I've found. You know vampire friends, right? The ones who claim to love you but always leave you feeling slightly deflated. They say they're desperate to see you and then moan about every single aspect of their lives for three hours, in minute detail, until it's time to go home. You set off to meet them feeling perfectly cheerful and happy, and you come back feeling like crap, for no reason that you can quite put your finger on, and it happens every single time you see them. Vampire friends never ask you anything about yourself, and if you do manage to shoehorn something into the conversation (so-called: it is really a monologue) – something like, 'I'm worried about my father's Alzheimer's' or 'My granny was run over by a bus today' – the vampire friend says 'Oh, bummer' and then uses your remark as a springboard to tell you about the state of their own short-term memory or how they still miss proper double-deckers. If you told them you had breast cancer they'd start talking about their bra collection, and if you had an axe through your head they'd tell you about the time they had a papercut. And then – and this is the really remarkable thing about them – after a while, they start resenting you. You sit there, for months or years or decades, listening to this stuff and wishing with all your might that you were somewhere else, but you stay put in the name of friendship. (Vampire friends don't – surprise! – have many friends, which gives them another thing to moan about.) No good. Either because they can sniff out pity or because you appear to have no problems – none that you've ever been allowed to articulate in their presence, at any rate – they suddenly, randomly decide that you need taking down a peg or two. So the vampire friend starts telling you that X doesn't like you, or that Y thinks your work is rubbish, or that Z thinks you could do with losing a few pounds. I wonder whether that was the direction Hope was headed in earlier, with her incredulity at the idea of my 'having a man'. I hope not.

Regardless of vampires, I think as I load the dishwasher – Hope's wandered off upstairs now, still clutching her laptop – this whole question of 'having a man' really does render women my age insane. I understand biological imperatives, and that nobody likes the idea of being lonely, of course I do. What I'm less clear about is how going on and on, to the point of obsession, every moment of every day is going to attract people rather than send them running away screaming.

It's six o'clock now, and dark outside. Inside, the light is yellow and comforting, somebody's chucked another log on the fire, and we all look like characters in a feel-good movie. Some people are lying on the sofas, watching the obligatory screening of *Kind Hearts and Coronets*. Sam has Maisy on his lap – he is absentmindedly stroking her hair – and Maisy – beep beep – has her new games console on hers. Jake is having a snooze, Pat and Kate have reprised their chat-howl-with-laughter-chat thing on a couple of adjoining armchairs. Charlie and Jack have reappeared because they're finally ready for pudding – more than ready: 'starving', they claim.

'Oh, but can we wash these children first,' asks Flo. 'Would you mind? We need to hose them all down and then come down and have pudding. Otherwise it's going to get too late – for mine, at any rate.'

'Did you forget to feed them, Flo? I thought they had tea at half past five.'

'They do normally, but look at them – they're so stuffed they can barely walk, the pair of puddings. They've been helping themselves to leftover canapés all afternoon. They're not really children, they're mini-pigs.'

'I love mini-things,' says Evie. 'I like everything mini. I wish

I was mini and lived in a mini-house and ate mini-food at a mini-table.'

'How small?' says Flo. 'You'd have to get the size exactly right, otherwise it might be creepy. Like, Borrowers-mini?'

'Thumb-sized,' says Evie immediately. 'I've given it a lot of thought. Hand-sized would be odd and toe-sized would be dangerous.'

'I agree,' says Flo.

'Right,' I say, trying to round up the children. 'Who wants a bath?'

'Ach, they don't need a bath,' says Pat from her armchair. 'They're on their holidays.'

We have this debate every time Pat comes to stay with us, which is usually outside term time. If Pat had her way, no child would be washed from July to September. This, she says – being humiliatingly filthy and stinking to high heaven, basically – would constitute the most tremendous treat for them.

'The thing is, Pat, kids *like* baths these days. Baths are fun. Hot water, splashing, bubbles, toys – what's not to like?'

But she's unpersuadable. In Pat's world, baths equal sitting in two inches of tepid water and being scrubbed with a Brillo pad, and all holidaying children should neither bathe *nor wash their teeth*. When I questioned the wisdom of the latter approach a couple of years ago – the idea of not brushing your teeth is completely disgusting to me – Pat said to just 'freshen their mouths with something nice and clean, like a wee kiddies' fruit yogurt', which is akin to sprinkling their gums with sugar and which is indeed what she does when she babysits. Pat feels sorry for Maisy's daily bathing ordeal, to say nothing of the four minutes of tooth-brushing she must endure at the hands of her mother.

'Is it Child Soup?' Maisy asks. 'Please can it be Child Soup? With the twins in it?'

'Absolutely,' I say. 'We'll make Child Soup. Giving each one of you a separate bath's going to take too long.'

Flo and I start to wrangle the children, who squeal with excitement and run, or in the twins' cases waddle (going 'Soooooup! Sooooooup!'), up the stairs.

'Would you look at that,' says Pat. 'You're that funny, in London. Kiddies in baths!'

'Do you want me to do it?' says Sam. 'Or at least give you a hand?'

'Oh you *angel*,' Flo says before I've had a chance to reply. 'Would you? Then I could actually spend some time with my poor ole husband, Edward the Neglected.'

'Shall I help too?' asks Tamsin. 'Though I don't know that Cassie wants to be a part of Child Soup. What do you think, Cass?'

'I'm too grown-up for it,' says Cassie matter-of-factly, 'but I'd still like to.'

'Yaaay,' Maisy yells dementedly. For her, a bath with Cassie would be equivalent to Madonna perching companionably on the lav, chatting away while I shampooed my hair.

'Do you want me to come up?' says Tamsin.

'No, it's okay, Mum,' says Cassie. 'I know Sam and Clara. He is not a bad man.'

'No, of course I'm not,' Sam says, looking surprised.

'I know,' says Cassie, who is a solemn, big-eyed child. 'That's what I said. There's no stranger danger with you, because I know you.'

'Though of course, statistically, a child is more likely to be assaulted by someone she *does* know,' says Evie.

'Evie!'

'Sorry, Sam. I'm not at all suggesting that you're a child-botherer. You know, like an awful peed. God, the things that come out of my mouth. No self-editing, you see. Sorry. Up you go, Cassie. Sam is *a good man*. He will not harm you.'

'You're making it worse,' I say. 'Stop talking.'

'My body is private,' says Cassie. 'It's my body and it's private. No one can touch it without my permission.'

'Jesus,' says Sam.

'School,' mouths Tamsin with a helpless shrug.

'My body isn't private,' says Maisy sadly. 'Everybody is always touching me.' I am really, really glad that we know everyone in the room.

'Darling, of course it is,' I say. 'Everyone's body is private.'

'But my brothers squidge me and tickle me and put me upside down all the time and say, "Who's the boss of you, who's the boss of you?" And you bite my bottom.'

'They are no respecters of privacy,' says Evie. 'Your mummy was the same with me and Auntie Flo.'

Delighted by the idea that I may have held her aunties by the ankles, Maisy takes my hand and we make our way to the bathroom. Cassie solemnly puts her hand in Sam's, giving him a long, wary look as she does so. The twins are halfway up the stairs.

'I don't feel comfortable, Clara,' Sam whispers as we get the twins out of their nappies and the little girls dance around, shedding their clothes. 'Cassie's looking at me strangely.'

'You are a *good* man,' I say, grabbing the bottom wipes out of the twins' changing bag. 'You will not harm her.'

'Don't, it's creepy,' Sam says. 'Oh God, Grace has done a poo.'

'You can deal with a poo, can't you? Or do you want to swap?'

'Here,' says Sam. 'Swap.'

'But you did Maisy's poos. Well, some of them.'

'Yeah, but she's my daughter.'

'So, what – you think I mind other people's poos less than you?'

'No – well, yes. It's your niece's poo, for a start.'

'Your niece by marriage, too.'

'I know. But . . . I just don't really like the poo. And you're a woman.'

'That's a despicably sexist thing to say. Women are not genetically predisposed to like poo more than men. Honestly, Sam.'

But he's just standing there, staring at the poo and looking repulsed.

'Hold Ava then,' I say, wishing the now-naked toddler would pee on his arm.

It's funny, isn't it, about poo. I can't claim I ever *loved* any of my children's poos, but you just get on with it, partly because it's family poo and partly because there's no choice. Poo belonging to others, though: not so keen. For a moment I feel like leaning over the banisters and shouting down to Flo that there's a poo that's come from a bottom I didn't give birth to, and could she come and deal with it. Instead I get on with it myself and remember the other really unattractive thing about toddler poos, or indeed baby poos: the horrid shock of realizing that they're sometimes adult-sized.

'I'm naked now,' says Cassie.

'Won't be a minute,' I say.

'Sam! Clara!' she shouts, causing both to turn and look at her.

'What, darling?'

'This,' says Cassie, pointing at her vagina with both index fingers, 'is the most private area of all.'

'Oh my God,' says Sam. 'I'm going to have to leave you to it.'

'And this,' she continues relentlessly, turning round, 'is very, very private too. The bottom.'

'So, the fronty,' says Maisy, looking interested. 'The fronty and the bottom, Daddy. THE PRIVATE AREAS.'

'Yep,' says Sam, averting his eyes. 'I know, Maise. No need to shout.'

I have an inappropriate but overwhelming urge to howl with laughter.

'The thing is, Cassie,' I say instead, 'that everyone has a fronty and a back bottom. They're private, but not that interesting. Is the thing. So . . .'

'That's not true,' says Maisy. 'Daddy doesn't have a fronty. And neither does Charlie. And neither does Jack.'

'Sam has a peeeenis,' says Cassie, who hasn't smiled once since we came upstairs and is giving Sam her stare again. I have to admit, it's quite disconcerting.

'Sam has a penis,' says Grace the toddler.

'Is a penis a willy?' asks Maisy.

'Yes,' says Cassie. 'But it's silly to say fronty and willy. It's what babies do.'

'Oh,' says Maisy, crestfallen.

'The proper names are penis and vagina,' says Cassie.

'Bagina,' says Ava, who has a slight cold, or has maybe just misheard.

'Moving on,' I say briskly. 'It's bathtime. Child Soup. In you get.'

'I think I should maybe go downstairs,' says Sam, 'and get Tam to come up.'

'Nonsense,' I hiss, like matron at school. 'This is ridiculous. Cassie can't help it – she's just repeating something she's been taught. And since as far as I'm aware you have no sinister designs on her person . . .'

'Clara!'

'Well, *really*. It's completely absurd. I didn't know anything about people having sinister designs on children until I was about eighteen. It was bad enough finding out at that age – gave me nightmares. Imagine what it's like knowing that kind of stuff when you're still in Year 1. I knew not to get into cars with strangers and it served me perfectly well. I never needed anyone to tell me that my vagina was very private when I was still practically a baby. I didn't even know what a vagina *was*.' I point downward with my two fingers, like Cassie did. 'It's a question of context, I suppose. But since our context in this house is only dysfunctional in the emotional sense, I think we're probably okay.'

'I don't think it's something you should joke about,' says Sam. 'Seriously, Clara. Stop doing that with your fingers.'

'Well, *I* don't think little children should be terrified of adults raping them. I don't think it should be the norm. I think it's fucked up. Most people are nice – that's what we should teach them. Anyway. Moving on.'

The girls are in the bath at this point, the twins wedged in between Cassie and Maisy, who are at either end. I throw in a load of fish-shaped bath toys. I sit a few feet away, on the toilet seat, and Sam leans against the entrance to the bathroom.

'So,' he says. 'Nice Christmas Day.'

'Thank you for your charming speech.'

'Don't be sarky, Clara.'

'No, I mean it. It was nice.'

'Hard to know what to say. I mean, given the situation.'

'There is no situation, Sam. You were here and then you left me and here we are. It's not a situation. It's just normal life.'

'I guess,' he says.

'By the way,' I say. 'I've been meaning to ask all day. Do you find me physically repulsive?'

'What?'

'You flinched when I kissed you. It hurt my feelings.'

'I did not.'

'Yes, you did. You went all stiff, and I don't mean in your pants.'

'You need to adjust your vocabulary, Clara. You can't say that kind of stuff to me anymore.'

'Why not? Do you think it's a come-on? Because ding-dong, you're wrong. It's just how I talk. As you know. Anyway, you're not answering my question.'

The girls are shrieking with laughter in the bath. They have decorated the twins' sweet little round heads with bubbles. Ava is laughing so hard that she has got hiccups.

'Come on, Sam. It's simple enough.'

'No, of course not. Of course I don't find you physically repulsive.'

'Oh good,' I say, meaning it.

'I don't find you anything,' Sam says. 'Not repulsive – nice dress, by the way – and not . . . attractive either. I think of you as the mother of my child. Which is what you are.'

'Seriously?'

'Well, yes. Unless you wore padding for nine months and stole her from a pram.'

'You don't see me in any other way at all?'

'No. What do you want me to say?'

'I just think it's so weird. I was thinking about it this morning. You know – we live together all that time, and we sleep together, and then overnight I'm "the mother of your child" and nothing else. Like your eyes have fallen out of your head and rolled away down a drain hole, or something.'

'It's what people do to hold on to their sanity, Clara.'

'Hm. I'm not sure. I think it's what men do because they only know two types of women: the ones they'd like to shag and the others, who become invisible.'

'Right. You've got your feminist dungarees on. Always a look I liked.'

'Yes. I know.'

'Hm. Shall we wash these children, then? I think you'd better do it. Fuck knows how Jake deals with all this.'

'I don't think Jake has much to do with childcare. Do you

remember, when he and Tam first got together he dressed Cassie one day and Tam said he put her in a vest, pants and a cardigan?'

'And then took her to tea at Fortnum's for bonding. Yeah, I remember.'

'Do you think they'll last?'

This used to be one of our favorite games. Sam invented it. At first I thought it was rather a mean, negative game, but after a while I joined in enthusiastically. He was obsessed with the game: the happier the couple we spent time with, the more likely he was to ask, 'Do you think they'll last?' Oddly for someone who is basically good-natured, he was pessimistic about most people's chances, usually because of the female half of the couple. I wonder if anybody played it about us.

'Tam and Jake?' he now says. 'Yes.'

'But why?'

'Because they need each other desperately. They're both horrified by the idea of being alone. Remember Tam's love life before?'

'Yeah. Not great.'

'And Jake goes on about being a stud, but he's old. He's scared of being by himself. Like I say, they need each other. And they love each other too, I think. Proper love.'

He's said a perfectly simple thing, but I can't stop thinking about it as I scrub the four children. For some weird reason, this has never really occurred to me before, but it's when you stop needing each other that it all goes wrong. It's when one or both of you become surplus to requirement. It must go some way to explaining why so many couples split up once one of them 'makes it'. Everybody starts off needing each other, and then they get used to each other, and then gradually they need each other less, and then one or both of them thinks, 'I'd have more fun on my own, or with somebody else.' Or maybe someone thinks, 'I don't need them, why do they still need me? It's creepy, clinging to me like that.' And the relationship crawls away to die, along with the need.

It's at this point that my phone – a new one I got given this morning by my sisters; it only finished charging half an hour ago – beeps in my dress pocket. I'm in the middle of extracting the twins from the bathtub and wrapping them in towels to take them through to my bedroom. I can feel the phone vibrate against my thigh as it beeps. 'Please let it be him,' I say to myself in my head. 'Please.' I put fresh nappies, vests and pyjamas on the toddlers – which takes a while because they're so wriggly – and hand them to Sam to take back downstairs to their parents. Then I go back into the bathroom, which is by now quite swamp-like, and dry Maisy and Cassie before sending them upstairs to Maisy's bedroom to find a couple of nighties. I take out the bath plug, gather up all the plastic fish, wait for the water to drain away, and rinse out the tub. I pick up the load of wet towels and put them back on the rail near the radiator. All the time I am thinking, 'Please let it be him.' The phone beeps again, to remind me that I haven't read my text. I get a mop from the closet on the landing and quickly swish it over the worst of the puddles. I turn off the bathroom light and go back into my bedroom, to sit on my bed.

'The girls said you were bathing the children,' the text says. It's from Julian, my former stepfather. 'So doing this the modern way to wish you all a very happy Christmas. Love to all, J x.'

He could have called back later. He could have left a voice mail. He could have rung earlier, to be honest, if he wanted to talk to me.

It's when you stop needing each other that it all goes wrong.

We turn the lights out for the Christmas pudding. Everyone is gathered around the kitchen tables. I've asked Sam to light the pudding, because that's what we've always done. He comes through holding it aloft, burning on a white plate, to awed gasps from the smaller children. The blue flames flicker in the darkness, lighting up the faces of my babies, my friends, my family. Here we all are. Will we all be here next year, and will it be the same? Will we all still be together? I say a quick prayer in my head – 'to health, to love, thank you God, amen' – and blow out the flame.

PART THREE

5

24 December 2011, 5.57 a.m.

Terrible, terrible mistake. Fatal error. Monstrously bad call. We're at the airport. *The airport.* On Christmas Eve. Whose brain-bleedingly moronic idea was this, then? Oh, that's right. Mine. My idea. It came from me, who loathes flying and whose only motto in life is 'We spend Christmas at home.' Cherry on the cake: it's just coming up for 6 a.m. We got up before 3 a.m. You can imagine the levels of good humor. Jack and Charlie are slumped over a trolley, their faces gray, moaning about wanting breakfast and having a half-hearted argument about thin versus fat fries. Maisy is in my arms, which is breaking my back. Her legs are dangling down by my knees: we must look absurd. She's far too big (and long) to be carried, but she was so overexcited about our trip that what with falling asleep late and getting up inhumanly early, she's only had a couple of hours' sleep. She's got the mood to match. I don't know where her father is – he's supposed to be meeting us here, in the hideous, unforgiving neon lighting by Counter B6 (like a vitamin), but there's no sign of him. I push our two trolleys forward and somehow manage to bang myself on the shins. What I would really like to do at this stage is lie down on the floor and have a snooze, and maybe a little cry.

It all seemed like such a good idea. I was at the hairdresser's last month leafing through the kinds of magazines I never buy anymore. It was late November and it had, by that point, been raining solidly for nine days: proper, award-winningly miserable English weather, without even one crisp, cold-but-sunny morning to atone. In the right mood, I can totally work with torrential rain and it being dark at half past three: I embrace fires and endless cups of tea and blankets on the sofa and making cakes, and I quite like it. But it was still term time, our car was at the garage waiting for a part that seemed to elude capture, and walking Maisy to and from school in the deluge before going to buy food in the deluge before going about my normal business in the deluge began to get me down. The boys were like sun-starved plants longing for photosynthesis, setting off for their own schools in inadequate rainwear – they really needed to be wearing wetsuits and rubber balaclavas – and coming home looking like drowned rats every afternoon. We all got colds, so the soundtrack to all of this was sneezing and honking and coughing, with the odd up-at-2-a.m.-to-administer-acetaminophen-and-cough-medicine-to-Maisy thing thrown in. Our house was awash with tissues, which I kept forgetting to remove from pockets before doing the laundry, with the result that everyone's clothes had a light and unshiftable sprinkling of white fluff on them.

We were weary, it is fair to say. The mood was bleak. My own mood wasn't helped by the knowledge that Kate kept trying to show me various bits of paperwork that had been sent through to her following the death, nine months ago, of my biological father, Felix. I didn't ever want to run across a field and into his arms, but it's a bit odd suddenly losing the possibility of access to half your DNA – to say nothing of suddenly being half orphaned. I kept batting her off, with her documents and her forms that needed signing: if I thought about it too hard it slightly melted my brain.

Jack started it: we were having breakfast one morning, watching the miserable torrents of rain outside – it was so bad that I was contemplating letting them off school on compassionate grounds, just so their poor bones could get a chance to dry out – when he said, 'You know what would be really nice?

To go somewhere a bit warm for Christmas. Not, like, somewhere flash – just somewhere it isn't raining. Do you think we could, Mum? Please.'

I said I understood the impulse, but that Christmas was sacrosanct. 'We always have it at home,' I said.

'Yeah,' said Charlie, 'but that's mostly for us, isn't it? The thing is, Mum, we get it. The whole trad Christmas thing. It's really nice. We'll always remember it. We can do it again next year. But, just once. Somewhere warm.'

'Please Mum,' said Jack again.

'Christmas *in the sunshine*? In T-shirts?' said Maisy, just before she sneezed. 'That would be so, so cool.'

I said I was very sorry and repeated my mantra, that Christmas happened at home, like it always happened and like it would keep happening until the end of time. Then Maisy and I swam to school.

Anyway. So there I was in the hairdresser's a week later, having my roots done. The weather hadn't improved. There was a glossy travel magazine in my lap. And there it was: Marrakesh. Specifically, an article about a lovely-looking, newly done-up big old villa, a riad in the medina – the old town – with a little courtyard pool and orange trees in big terra-cotta pots. I love Morocco. Sam and I went there on our honeymoon, as it happens. I fell into a kind of daydream for a while, and then I sat up straight and read the article. The house sounded divine and was alluringly photogenic. The flights only took three and a half hours. But then, most incredibly of all, the price for a week's rental was not nearly as astronomical as the pictures of the house suggested: if you split it by the number of people it could accommodate, it was actually affordable. I photographed the letting agency's number with my phone and when I got home an hour or so later, I called them, on impulse. I had a feeling. And my feeling was right: the house was available from Christmas Eve, for seven nights: they'd had a cancellation that very morning. I barely even thought about it: I booked it. It felt like fate. And then I rang round my relatives and quickly booked a bunch of the cheapest flights I could find, which, despite the dates, were very cheap indeed – I don't suppose that many people go and spend Christmas in a Muslim country. And then I stared into space for ten minutes, gasping at my own audacity. I'd broken all my Christmas rules in the space of fifteen minutes.

And so here we are. It's going to be great – of course it is. I am the boss of Christmas and I decree that it shall be so. But first we have to get there. I wonder if it's too early to take my sedative. I *really* hate flying – not so much the bobbing along in the sky bit as the acute claustrophobia, the massed, helpless humanity hurtling about sealed inside a metal tube.

Everyone seems to arrive at the same time. There's Sam, looking bleary-eyed, accompanied by Pat, who is wearing a comedy-enormous sombrero and practically trotting with excitement on her size-four feet: the general effect is 'jaunty donkey'. 'This is great,' she says, kissing me and Maisy and waving to the boys, who are still leaning comatose on their own trolley, bickering weakly. 'Is this not great? This is great. Morocco! Africa!'

'I like your hat, Pat. Yes, it's going to be great,' I say, giving her a hug. 'Good Lord, is all this luggage yours?'

'Yes,' says Pat. 'I'm not keen on that foreign food, so I just brought along a few bits and pieces from home. Couple of wee pies. And toilet paper. Plenty of that. They have those toilets where you squat down and *pigs are waiting underneath to eat your business*.'

'I've tried telling her,' laughs Sam. 'She won't listen. And she's brought an unbelievable number of presents,' he adds, kissing my cheek and taking Maisy off me. 'Hello, my lovely girl,' he says to her.

'Hi,' I say. This is possibly the most ancient joke in the world, but it makes me laugh like a simpleton every time. I also like saying 'Thanks' when the three of us are in a room and Sam says 'I love you' to Maisy.

Sam rolls his eyes. 'The old ones are the best. Hi, Clara. I see you're not doing too badly on the luggage front either.'

'A mere five suitcases,' I say. 'Nearly one for each day of the week. Mostly presents and, um, Christmas stuff.'

'I'm surprised you didn't pack a tree and baubles. I can't believe you organized this,' Sam says. 'I'd have bet money on you never, ever spending Christmas anywhere other than at home.'

'I know,' I say. 'I don't know what came over me. But I'm so pleased everyone else liked the idea. And that they could all come.'

'Where's Robert?'

'Meeting us there. He managed to get a direct flight.'

'Yoohoo!' yells somebody. 'YOOHOO, Clara, Sam, Maisy, Pat, Jack and Charlie!' The other people in the queue turn round to stare at my sister Evie, who is channeling a kind of Talitha Getty vibe with loosely pinned-up hair, a silk kaftan, enormous hoop earrings and half a ton of kohl in each eye. She is wearing an enormous parka on top and a pair of green woolen mittens on her hands. 'Pat! Your hat! The beauty!'

'Just a wee sombrero,' Pat says shyly but looking very pleased. 'For my holidays, like.'

'I'm absolutely mad about it,' says Evie. 'Hello, everybody. Merry Christmas Eve. Hello, people in the queue staring at me. Merry Christmas Eve to you too, guys.'

Flo, Ed and the twins are next. The twins are dressed as princesses under their bulky coats; Ava is wearing a crown and Grace is waving a scepter around with some force. Maisy perks up at the sight of them and all three clamber onto one of my trolleys, installing themselves among the suitcases.

'My children are hell,' Flo says. 'They literally haven't slept. They wouldn't have breakfast. They insisted on coming in costume. They're like crazed beasts. I wish we could put them in a suitcase. I'd cut holes in it first so they could breathe, like when you carry guinea pigs home from the pet shop. Otherwise they'd suffocate, which would be awful. Also, we brought too much luggage. It's mostly gifts. We're going to have to pay a massive surplus charge.'

'I think we all are,' I say. 'And take some deep breaths. Where's Kate?'

The queue for the check-in provides me with my answer, now turning almost as one in the direction of the Departures entrance. Ah yes, here's Mummy. She is wearing her floor-length fur coat (it was Granny's, I found out last year – not that this appeases anyone), enormous dark glasses and has tied her hair up in an Hermès scarf. She literally cuts a swathe – people actually move out of the way – as she approaches Counter B6. Kate's trolley is piled high with two reasonably normal suitcases and – good grief – two trunks, each one gigantic, as though she were a missionary moving to the Congo. Max, her husband, is a reverent five feet behind, smiling to himself, which is pretty much what he does: smile to himself and make business deals on his BlackBerry.

'Hello, Clara!' Kate starts shouting from about forty feet away. 'Are you going to the gym? What on earth are you wearing? *Leisurewear*, I do believe. Mine eyes. Comfort is not all. Pat – your hat! Beyond divine. Oh dear, look at this monstrous queue.' She's now about thirty feet away but feels no apparent need to lower her voice. 'I absolutely *loathe* airports, do you? Ought to be poetic – romance of air travel and all that – but, no. Rather reminds me of the thing someone said about Dunkirk, or do I mean the Somme? "My dear, the people! The noise!" That's how I feel. Hello, Sam. Clara says you've stopped being peculiar to her – marvelous news. Hello, grandchildren. Boys! Alertness! Posture! If I can manage it, being as I am an antique, anyone can.' True to her word if not to her passport, Kate is now officially sixty-five, five years older than her real age, for vanity purposes.

'Yo, Nan,' says Charlie, because he knows it annoys her.

'Kate, short for Katharine,' bellows Kate. 'Not Nan, short for Banana.'

'Wotcha, Kate,' says Jack.

The people in the queue stare at Kate. She waves benignly back at them, like the ruler of a small principality surveying her dear serfs.

'I'm approaching!' she shouts. 'Coming through. *En départ pour le Maroc*. Make way.' I sometimes wonder whether Kate has a secret cocaine habit. How else to explain being this full-on at six in the morning?

'Everyone's staring at us,' observes Maisy, not inaccurately. I barely notice anymore. Every time we're together in a public place, we basically become the floor show. You get used to it after a while.

'I know, darling,' I say. 'We're making rather a lot of noise, I think.'

'Like a circus,' Maisy says, 'and we're the seals.'

'Yes, a bit like that. No, darling, don't honk. It doesn't help. Look, here comes Cassie.'

Jake and Tamsin – now married – are headed toward us, with their own inevitably gigantic pile of luggage. Jake is wearing a cowboy hat at a rakish angle; it's made out of some kind of hide. Though I'm still occasionally startled by Jake's sartorial choices, and though I wouldn't fancy any of his sex-chat (brrr), I have revised my opinion of him. Tamsin has never been happier, and he's turned out to be an unexpectedly wonderful stepfather to Cassie, who took her time thawing but who now appears delighted with the first father she's ever had, really. When he made a speech at their wedding, Jake devoted ten minutes to saying what a great little girl Cassie was, and how much he loved her, and how he might have cocked up with his own children but wasn't planning on making that mistake again. There wasn't a dry eye in the house. Cassie smiles nearly all the time now. All three of them do. Maybe that's the trick: marry grandpas. Also, he is the stepdad who can't run away, because he's too old. Bonus.

Half an hour later, having finally checked in – and had to traipse round to the Freaks With Macro Luggage counter to pay our excess-baggage charges, which come to roughly the same amount as the actual flights – we're all ensconced at a fish and chip restaurant, a poor choice given the ungodly hour but the only place that could accommodate us. ('No room at the inn,' Kate said, turning away from the vaguely brasserie-ish place we'd initially made a beeline for.) My children all eschew breakfast in favor of jumbo portions of haddock and fries – it's not yet seven in the morning – and seem enormously perked up by being thus nourished. Jack and Charlie resume their bickering, and Maisy does her favorite thing of wandering about the restaurant in search of the roughest family she can find. Having located them – the dad is drinking pints, the mum's on what looks like shots (it's always seemed odd that airports serve alcohol so early in the morning: surely it just makes the cabin crew's job harder?) and the rest of the brood are busy seeing how many four-letter words they can cram into a sentence – she stands by their table, gazing upon them in absolute admiration. Her eyes are literally shining with love. Maisy also does this on beaches: she finds the roughest tattoos – prison-style, ideally – the most litter, the greatest embarrassment of empty beer cans, the music that's blaring the most anti-socially from the loudest radio, and then she goes and stands there, longing to be asked to join the party (which, often, she is). It's been the bane of many a summer, because eventually I have to go and get her back, which involves toning down my accent and putting on what the boys like to call my 'taxi voice', whereby my usual 60:40 mix of 'middle class' and 'London' transforms into 20:80 or, in extremis, 10:90. The children make fun of me, not least because I do it brilliantly – even though they had learned to do it for themselves by their tenth birthdays. It's funny, I don't know of any other capital city where the natives are masters of accent fluctuation, or where accent fluctuation is a daily necessity. I'm so adept at it that I can no longer do it in the other direction – up the middle class and mute the London – which is probably for the best.

Just as we're about to board I get a text from Hope – she's flying out to Ibiza from the same terminal and we'd hoped to hook up for a coffee, but it is not to be. She sounds extremely cheerful, though. She's going with Phil, the half-naked man she 'met' on Facebook last year and whom she has been happily dating since the spring. Just goes to show how much I know. I do worry, though, about my friends and compromises. I also worry about my own ability to ever contemplate them.

The flight is as hideous as you would imagine – horrible plane, horrible squashed seats, horrible food, horrible enormous queue for the bathroom the second the horrible food has been consumed – though I am desensitized via the judicious swallowing of a sedative, which makes me so woozy that I don't even have the energy to talk: I just zone out in my seat, trying to control my urge to dribble. And then, just like that, we're disembarking at Marrakesh airport, where it's a balmy 19 degrees and still only late morning. I am astonished by air travel. *Astonished*. I know it's the twenty-first century and even babies are used to long-haul flights, but I genuinely marvel every time at the fact you were in place A not so long ago and now you're in place B, in a whole other country – continent, in our case. It strikes me as one of those things that is actually a proper miracle – albeit one that can be explained – and that we all take it for granted: if I had my way, the entire passenger list would whoop and punch the air and maybe faint in thrilled amazement every time they landed. Air travel blows my mind. Actually, any kind of travel that isn't walking blows my mind: I cheer at getting in a car in London and ending up in Cornwall six hours (though occasionally more like nine) later, too. And trains! Trains are my favorite, particularly sleepers. The boys find this extraordinarily funny every time I mention it – which I do every time I travel – but I know that I am right and that they, and everybody else, are simply horribly blasé. Happily, today Pat shares my shock and awe.

'That's grand,' she says, 'being here so quickly,' and I smile at her and say I quite agree.

'Mum's flipping out about planes again,' says Jack to his brother with a snigger.

'Because in her day they only had mammoths,' says Charlie, 'and it took ages to get anywhere and it was really itchy sitting on them.'

'And they were so poor they couldn't afford a dinosaur,' says Jack. 'She used to stare all sadly out of her cave and wish they had even a small diplodocus, like the other families. But no.'

'She could only sit and dream of pterodactyls,' says Charlie. 'Poor Mum. Hard life. But it made her stronger.'

'Did you, Mummy?' asks Maisy.

'No. Your brothers are being silly.'

'Nice to be here though, Mama,' says Jack. 'Thanks for bringing us. Blue sky!'

And indeed there is. After we've cleared customs and waited an age at the luggage carousel – our assorted trunks and suitcases look like they need a plane of their own – we saunter out into the glorious day and into two eight-seaters sent by the letting agency. The children sit at the back, their noses pressed up against the glass, as we make our way into Marrakesh, through the new town ('Camels! Mum! Camels! Horses! A sheep!') and from there into the warrens of the old city. It's at this point that the excitement really kicks in.

'It's a wee assault on the senses,' says Pat, who has been studying the guidebook. 'So it is. Everything's that different.'

'Look at the colors,' says Kate. 'So beautiful. People in the West really have no idea.'

'They're all brown,' says Pat.

'I mean the buildings and the clothes,' says Kate.

'Aye,' says Pat. 'They're colorful.'

We twist and turn through the crowds before coming to a slow crawl down a little lane, boys on scooters on either side of us – one holding a chicken under his arm – the sides of the road crammed with people, and eventually arrive in front of a pair of massive old wooden doors. An elderly man in an embroidered white djellaba is standing outside, waiting to welcome us in. 'Home,' I say. 'For the next week. Merry Christmas. Out we get.'

The house is, if anything, lovelier even than it was in the pages of *Condé Nast Traveller*. The little pool shimmers green in the tiled central courtyard, the edges of which are lined with low-level seating and round, ornate brass coffee tables. There are colored glass lanterns everywhere, and metal ones all around the pool. The man in the djellaba is called Moustafa; his wife Fatima is standing in the courtyard with fresh dates and almond milk for us all. I notice Pat is staring at the couple intently; they smile back at her.

'Thankee,' she says loudly, accepting her glass of almond milk and sniffing it suspiciously. She does this with any unfamiliar foodstuffs and it drives me mad: it's so canine. 'Thankee kindly.'

'Why are you talking like that, Mum?' asks Sam.

'Abroad,' says Pat authoritatively. 'It's all right, this nut milk, even though you can't milk a nut. Doesn't make sense. Still, nice and sweet.'

'They have tiny udders,' says Evie. 'All nuts do.' She puts her glass down. 'Urgh, I was trying to make a joke and now I've made myself feel sick. This house is glorious and I wish I lived in it. Well found, Clara. Oh, I really wish I'd asked Jim now.'

'You look very at home,' I tell her. 'Perfect outfit. And you should have done.' Jim is Evie's relatively new boyfriend; she was anxious about subjecting him to the fullness of our family Christmases, probably with good reason, so he's stayed in London.

'One of the advantages of not having children is that I can wear really fabulous clothes,' says Evie. 'You know, without anyone peeing on them. Do you think Hope's going to get up the duff, by the way? Now she's found that man?'

'Phil. I don't know. I suppose if she got on with it there's still just about time for her to bang one out.'

'I never understood it, you know,' says Evie. 'That total compulsion to breed. I don't have it at all. Never did. Don't expect I ever will.'

'Well, you never know. You've got a while to make up your mind'

'But I do know, that's just it. I love the neffs and nieces to death, you know I do, but they do give one a *startling insight* into what parenting is really like.'

'I love that you don't particularly want children. It's so refreshing,' I say.

'I think so too. I love myself for it,' Evie says with a delighted smile. 'There's only one boredom, except it's a biggie.'

'What? Does Jim want them?'

'It's never been mentioned, so I'm guessing not. He has two

already. No, the boredom is other people's fixation with kids,' says Evie. 'We should get this luggage upstairs, come on.'

'*Non, mesdames!*' cries Moustafa as soon as we approach our cases. 'I will do. My friends will do. Please.'

'How nice,' says Evie. 'Very kind of you, Moustafa. *Vous êtes très gentil.*' She grins her megawatt smile at him and he beams back at her.

'Let's just find our rooms, then,' says Evie. 'Come on, Clara. What was I saying? Oh yes – the bummer. The bummerus giganticus.'

'Other people's children?'

'Not so much the actual children,' says Evie. 'I like the children. Well, I like most of them. And Jim's are sweet, as you know. But the endless *going on about them*. Why do people do that? You don't and Flo doesn't. But if I go out with my girlfriends and they've had children, they can literally spend the whole evening telling me about potty training or choosing a nursery.'

'I know,' I say. 'I've never really understood it.'

'I mean,' Evie continues as we climb up the stairs, 'I can see that those things would preoccupy one. But I'm pretty much the only one left who doesn't have kids, so why pick on me? Why not tell the other people who are interested, and talk to me about shoes or politics or the weather or books? You know?'

'Yes,' I say. 'I remember it well. I *do* have children and I used to hate those conversations as well. Ten minutes, fine. Entire evening: you start longing for death. See also schools, school places, church attendance, moaning about the teachers, moaning about the governors, moaning about the lack of facilities in inner London state schools – there's no end to it just because you leave babyhood. Actually no, that's not true – no one much discusses teenagers, which is pretty weird because they're the ones shagging and smoking weed.'

'It's so off-putting,' says Evie, pushing open the door of one of the bedrooms. 'Oh my God, look at this. I have died and gone to heaven. I want it. How shall we do it – shall we draw straws?'

'They're all nice, I gather,' I say. 'Have this one.'

'Oh, blissful joy. I suppose it's to do with how women define themselves,' Evie continues, flinging herself onto the enormous bed as I open the elaborately carved shutters. 'I don't really get that, either. I must be the purest imbecile. You're you, and then you go and get knocked up, and then you're not you anymore, you're this other person who has literally mutated overnight, like in Kafka except not into a cockroach. Do you want to do flat bouncing?'

'Okay.' I lie on the bed next to Evie and we bounce on our backs, a traditional family pursuit when supine. The aim is to gain enough momentum to rise off the bed by several inches while still horizontal.

'I love flat bouncing. Anyway. Sorry to go on, very boring even to myself.'

'No, it's interesting. Tell you what I hate: when women play along with the idea that pregnancy and children make you giddy and thick. Oh, silly me – I used to have a degree but now my brain has turned to *absolute mush*, ha ha ha ha ha.'

'Ha ha ha,' says Evie, still bouncing. 'I do really cute eccentric things and I'm super-forgetful, *because I had a baby.* Why, I'm practically retarded. Yay feminism!'

'Can I play?' says Flo, coming into the room. 'Our bedroom's amazing, by the way. It's got a little room off it for the twins. Who are sleeping, thank the baby Jesus.'

'Feel free,' says Evie. 'Join us. We're flat bouncing.'

'I can see,' says Flo. 'Shove up. What *I* hate most is the bitching. There's this big fat lie that you're all sisterly and in it together because you've all had babies, and it lasts about two minutes. After that it's back-to-back competitiveness. Ooh, she's stopped breastfeeding. Ooh, he's already on solids and if you ask me it's a bit early. Ooh, I don't think she was watching him very carefully at the park because she took a call on her mobile. Ooh, *she's gone back to work*. The ghastliness.'

'Thank God we're us,' says Evie.

'Ah, there you all are,' says Kate, swishing in. 'The fruits of my loins. How nice to be here with you in this simple North African home.'

'It's not that simple, Kate,' I say.

'Oh yes,' says Kate, waving her hand airily. 'It's a typical Moroccan house. They may be poor, but *my God* they have style.'

'I don't think –'

'Kate, stop pronouncing it like that,' says Flo. 'It's "pore", not "poo-er".'

'Don't abuse me,' says Kate. 'I speak how I speak.'

'The poo-er are always with us,' says Flo.

'Don't be tiresome, Flo. Anyway, what are you doing? Max is having a nap, Sam and Pat have taken Maisy and Cassie for a dip, Ed's drinking mint tea downstairs, and I imagine Jake and Tamsin are in bed going at it hammer and tongs. Shall we go for a little stroll?'

'Let me check with Ed,' says Flo. 'In case the babies wake up.'

'Glorious news on that front. I was talking to Fatima about menus and she said she'd be delighted to babysit any number of children at any time.'

'A simple homestead, with typical staff,' I say.

'Exactly,' says Kate.

'Would they mind not knowing her?' I ask Flo.

'I shouldn't think so. They love strangers,' says Flo. 'Another one of my maternal failings. Show them a stranger and my children hurtle toward them, squealing with joy. So it's got to be worth a try. Provided she's kind. Is she kind, Kate? She seemed nice.'

'I thought she had kind eyes,' says Evie. 'You can always tell. Sometimes mean people have kind faces, which is so wrong and upsetting, but you can always tell by the ole eyes.'

'She is absolutely lovely,' says Kate. 'We had a long chat. I would trust her *implicitly*.'

'Excellent,' says Flo, bouncing off the bed. 'I'll go and tell Ed.'

'I need to decorate,' I say. 'Though I suppose I could do it when we get back.'

'How do you mean, decorate?'

'Well, I brought a few things from home. For, er, continuity.'

'Rather mad of you,' says Kate, 'though I suppose not a bad idea. It's marvelous to be here, but I can't honestly say Marrakesh *exudes* Christmas spirit. I brought a few things too, actually.'

'So did I,' says Evie. 'What shall we do, then? Shall we walk? I rather fancied the look of those horse-drawn carriages, except they were back in the new town. Do you remember, Clara, when you started me on Georgette Heyer? I used to want to go everywhere by phaeton.'

'I was made for sedan chairs,' sighs Kate. 'I was born in the wrong century.'

'I think we should walk,' I say. 'Get a bit lost and see what happens. We're bang in the middle of everything – we don't actually need any transport.'

'I want to take Pat with us,' says Flo.

'Flo! She's not a sort of *creature* you can carry about like a pet,' says Kate.

'I totally would, though, wouldn't you? If she was chihuahua sized and I could stick her in my handbag,' says Flo. 'I would ensure she never left my side.'

'I would feed her tiny treats,' says Evie. 'Wee snacks. She would be blissfully happy and well cared for.'

'I'd brush her fur,' says Flo.

'I'd put ribbons on her ears,' says Evie.

'You are absurd, girls,' says Kate. 'Quite ludicrous. But fine – let's ask her if she wants to come along. I'll go. We'll leave in ten minutes, to give Clara time to change out of her grotesque costume.'

'It was for the plane,' I say. 'Leggings have a lot of give. They help me curl up into the fetal position while I scream on the inside. I'll put on a dress.'

'Mind your bosoms,' says Kate. 'The exposure thereof.'

'I thought the dark blue, with the décolleté to the navel,' I say. 'And no underwear. No?'

'Teach us, Mother. Teach us the ways of the local peoples,' says Flo.

'The poo-er locals. I thought the boob tube,' says Evie. 'Or maybe just a bikini top.'

'Just pants,' says Flo. 'Let's all go in our pants. And maybe go and hang outside a mosque. You have raised us well, Kate.'

'You're exasperating,' says Kate. 'All of you. I was just reminding you to be culturally sensitive. I could go out without a stitch on and nobody would bat an eyelid, but you all have the wrong sorts of faces. You promise much. I wonder why. None of you got that from me.'

'What do you mean, "promise much"?' I ask, suppressing a laugh.

'She means we're hot,' says Evie.

'She means we're vulgar,' says Flo.

'She means we look come-hitherish,' says Evie. 'Not at all the vibe I was going for, which is much more *noli me tangere* glacial ice-queen.'

'I mean nothing of the sort. I mean you look knowing. Rather *wild*.'

'Grr,' says Flo, making tiger shapes with her hands. 'Roar. I'm a-swishin' my tai-yul, mamma.'

'Too silly,' says Kate. 'I'm going downstairs to find Pat now.'

Fifteen minutes later we finally head out into the heaving street. Kate almost immediately suggests that our first port of call should be 'a burka shop', which given the amount of attention we are getting – perhaps my sisters and I are leering wildly and knowingly without being aware of doing it – doesn't seem a bad idea.

'Go and ask that lady where the nearest one is, Clara,' Kate says, gesturing to a grandmotherly-looking woman.

'I don't know, Kate. It might be, you know, a tiny bit culturally dubious to stick ourselves inside burkas just because we don't particularly enjoy being looked at.'

'That is the *entire point* of burkas, you goose,' says Kate, rolling her eyes. 'That is why they were *invented*. To prevent ogling.'

'I adore being looked at,' says Evie.

'Yes, but I don't know that one can just turn up and appropriate a religious custom in that way . . .'

'Nonsense,' says Kate. 'Don't lecture me about local customs. I am exceptionally well traveled. Everyone will be thrilled. Not that many women wear them here. We'll be among the special few.'

'I still think –'

'Oh, for heaven's sake. Now you've taken so long that the old woman has gone.'

'The only reason people are staring is because of our clothes and because there are so many of us. It would help if we weren't walking five abreast,' I say.

'And because of our come-hither faces,' says Evie. 'That promise much.'

'And because of Pat's sombrero,' says Flo. 'To be frank.'

'Aye. It's getting a fair bit of attention,' says Pat, who is not tall and who looks like the cartoon drawings of Mexicans we used to do at school: a huge hat and two tiny legs. 'Oops!' she says, as she brushes the hat right into a man's face. 'Forgiving,' she says to him.

'Pat,' says Kate. 'Why have you been speaking in that odd way ever since we arrived?'

'It's easier for them to understand,' says Pat matter-of-factly.

'Ah. Right. Quite a lot of them speak English, you know. As well as French. And Arabic.'

'I *am* speaking English,' says Pat. 'That's the point.'

'I want to learn it,' says Evie. 'How do you do it, Pat? How would you say, "I'd like a mint tea, please"?'

'Greeny tea, choppy,' says Pat, without thinking twice.

'It's basically speaking in tongues. The power is flowing through you, Pat, you marvel,' says Flo. 'How would you say, "I would like a remedy for my bunion"?'

'Sore toot-toot. Fixy!' says Pat instantly.

'Open to hideous misinterpretation, that one,' Kate murmurs.

'How would you say, "Do you have it in the pink?"' asks Evie.

'Rosy have prithee?' says Pat. It's like automatic writing: she doesn't even have to think about it.

'Perhaps I'll do the speaking,' says Kate. 'Ah, now look. This seems interesting.' We have arrived at what seems to be an enormous furniture barn; its doors are open. Elaborate, multicolored glass lanterns like the ones in our house dangle enticingly from the ceiling; the tables are piled high with china, pottery, tea glasses, brass teapots, beaded quilts, cushion covers and so on and on: it's ye olde traditional tourists' Aladdin's cave.

'Let's go in,' says Flo. 'It looks fabulous.' Which indeed it is: beautiful things as far as the eye can see.

'It's that exotic here,' says Pat, looking around. 'Back home, we'd call it a pile of old junk. Don't they sell anything new?'

'Excellent point, Pat, to which the answer is no,' says Kate. 'It's to do with class, tiresomely enough. We like old junk, partly because we think it shows we have *souls* and partly because we don't think owning broken, rickety things makes us look like they're all we can afford. You'd probably prefer something shiny and new from a department store.'

'I would,' says Pat. 'Though I like a nice rug.'

'Rugs over there,' says the sales assistant, pointing to another room. 'And may I offer you all some mint tea while you look around?'

'He speaks English,' Pat says. The man is standing three inches away from her. 'He speaks English! Would you listen to that? Oh my days.' She looks the man straight in the eye, holds two erect thumbs aloft and says, louder than is necessary, 'Speaky bueno!'

The man from the shop smiles a tight little smile and gestures again toward the rug room, then claps his hands and asks a young boy to bring us tea.

'I'd like one with cats on,' Pat tells the man. 'They had one in the Argos catalogue. Do you have anything with wee cats on? Taily-miaow?' Still unconvinced by his demonstrably fluent English, she mimes being a cat, which involves an unbearably coy expression and doing weird paw-things with her hands, much like Flo's tiger act earlier, but creepier. I love Pat, but I am beginning to find her Abroad-mode challenging.

'It's so disturbing when elderly people do little-kid things,' says Evie. 'I hate to look upon it.'

'I can't believe you said, "It's to do with class,"' I tell Kate while Pat takes a seat and the men busy themselves unrolling carpets.

'What?' says Kate. 'Of course it's to do with class. Absurd not to say so when it's perfectly true. My relationship with Pat is based on honesty.'

'I know, Kate. But we're not supposed to allude to the fact that we are relentlessly bourgeois. We're supposed to be more sort of . . . elastic.'

'Ludicrous,' says Kate. 'Can't stand any of that nonsense. We're perfectly elastic but I don't have class shame, and neither does Pat. I don't see what the issue is. She is more proletarian than us. Simple fact of life.'

'Yah,' says Flo. 'Let's buy some old junk.'

The shop owner and his two assistants have by now laid a good two dozen rugs out for our delectation. We sit on some low banquettes while he explains the provenance of each, the differences in weave and pattern, the origins of the dyes that have been used – and, of course, the prices, which being in dirhams mean very little to any of us. The tea arrives; Pat automatically raises the glass to her nose before sniffing it deeply.

'Pat!' I say more sharply than I'd meant to. 'It's mint tea. It's mint leaves and water and sugar. It's delicious. Please don't sniff it.'

'Smells all right,' Pat says. She speaks before unwrinkling her nose, so that her facial expression is that of an especially dim and toothy hamster.

'Well, they're hardly going to serve you a glass of warm piss,' I say, which causes Pat to laugh heartily.

I'm not laughing at all. It's funny how you reach your natural threshold with stuff. Pat's dog-like sniffing of nice things she is given to eat or drink (often by me) has annoyed me for years, but today, for some reason – perhaps the fact that I've only had a couple of hours' sleep – the annoyance has mutated into purest exasperation. What does she think she is, some medieval food taster, checking the King's food for poison? It's just so rude: the implication is that people – kind people, who've gone to the trouble of making you a meal or a drink – have sneakily shoved in something disgusting, like ground insoles or powdered guano. Or that they are so inept at cooking that you need to smell their food to make sure it's not going to make you vomit onto the ground. I mean, you know – *really*. Of all the rudenesses. I make a mental note to brace myself against the orgy of plate-sniffing that's in store tomorrow, when we're served our atypical Christmas dinner – the plate brought, with great suspicion, up to the twitching nostril, or maybe the head bending down to the table, so that the nose is level with the plate. And then: sniiiiiiiiiiiff. Aargh.

'No cats, though,' says Pat mournfully, dismissing a selection of rugs with a sad wave of the hand.

'Did you want an actual cat's face?' asks Evie.

'Aye, or a face and a body,' says Pat.

'And a tail,' says Flo.

'You don't like these patterned ones?' says Kate. 'None of them? What about the plain ones? The colors are lovely.'

'No,' says Pat.

'Madame dislikes all of these?' asks the shop owner. 'I have many more.'

'They're not to my taste,' says Pat loftily. 'I collect cats, see. Oh, sorry, son. I mean, collecto puss. These ones, baddy. Caca rug.'

'Oh God,' whispers Flo. 'Please help me, Clara.'

'I can't,' I say helplessly. I am biting the inside of my cheeks. The poor man.

'*Caca* means poo in French, Pat,' says Evie, her voice

carefully modulated. 'And in English too, actually, I think. So, it's kind of quite a rude thing to say.'

'Oh!' says Pat. 'I didn't mean anything by it. No shitey,' she says to the man, who is now looking pretty irked, and who can blame him? 'Ruggies bueno, ruggies nice. But –' and here she mimes tragedy, pulling the sort of face one might make if one's firstborn had just been slaughtered ' – no pussy, see?'

'Pussy?' says the man.

'Aye. Taily-miaow,' Pat repeats, for emphasis.

'That's enough,' says Kate, whose eyes, I notice, have a strange sheen about them, almost as though she were about to cry with laughter. She turns to the man. *'Madame n'aime que les tapis avec des motifs de chats. Elle n'a aucun goût. Je suis désolée.'*

'Ça ne fait rien, Madame, ça ne fait rien,' says the man, perking up a bit (thank God).

'Moi, par contre, j'aimerais voir ce que vous avez de Berbère,' says Kate. 'Girls – why don't you take Pat for a coffee? There was a place just further down, on this street. I'll catch you up. Call me if you go anywhere else.'

'Sorry for saying caca, Kate,' Pat says humbly. That annoys me too, the suggestion of forelock-tugging in her voice and the fact she is addressing her apology to Kate, not to the man from the shop, whose rugs she has just compared to feces. Feces, for God's sake.

'I'll catch you all up,' Kate repeats, quite loudly. 'Please go. Now, ideally.'

We bundle Pat and Pat's sombrero out of the shop and walk down to the café Kate has mentioned. We're only fifteen minutes or so away from home, and it occurs to me that we could do with Sam being here. We could feed Maisy a snack and generally try to behave like normal people. I call him on the mobile and they arrive a short while later. Maisy immediately starts to demolish a plate of pastries.

'Robert's just arrived. He's having a shower and then he's joining us here,' says Sam. 'Did you have a nice time, Ma?'

'Oh, aye,' says Pat, sipping her Coke through a straw, so that her mouth looks like a tiny beak. 'Nice enough. Just a wee junk shop, you know. Well, a big one.'

We took Pat to Greece one summer. The house was beautiful. The pool was turquoise and you could walk from the garden to the most stunning beach, down a path that smelled of wild herbs. Pat began to look bored and sulky after three days: the trip, apparently, did not compare favorably with the time her old-age-pensioners' group went to Calais for a weekend. Not enough shops, no booze cruises, 'nothing to look at'. I wouldn't mind – each to his own – but why come in the first place, knowing the kinds of places I book? You know? Why come and sit there and make a face like I'd taken her to Darfur?

'The stuff in the shop we went to wasn't really Pat's cup of tea,' I tell Sam.

'No,' says Sam. 'I don't suppose it was.'

'I just wanted a wee cat rug,' says Pat plaintively. 'But never mind. Never mind me. You just go on and enjoy yourselves, son.'

'There's a herbalist four doors down,' says Evie. 'Let's go to it when Robert gets here. I love Moroccan herbalists, they have jars full of saffron and rose petals and special solutions of delicious oils.'

'We can go after this,' I say.

'I'll stay here with the wee 'un,' says Pat. How, *how* could I have forgotten how irritating she is in traveling mode?

We sit for a while, drinking coffee – Coke in Pat's case – and turning our faces to the sunshine like flowers.

'Maisy's that good at eating,' Pat observes. 'Foreign stuff, I mean.'

'They're just pastries filled with almond paste. You like marzipan, Pat – try one,' I say, pushing the plate toward her.

'No, you're all right,' Pat says. 'Don't fancy the look of them.'

'Try one, Ma,' says Sam. 'They're nice. You'll like them.'

'Don't make me *do* things,' Pat says to Sam, her good humor deserting her. There's a mutinous look on her face and her voice sounds both defensive and aggressive. 'I'm not *like* you lot.'

This is unimpeachable fact. As I may have mentioned, Pat is exceptionally keen on Hallmark-type greeting cards and on the sentiments contained within them, which she treats as though they were piercingly insightful, quasi-Buddhist aperçus into the human condition. This reliance – or perhaps dependence – on ready-made sentimentality comes at the expense of other human emotions, especially the ones requiring thought. There is no digging in Pat's world, no self-examination, no questioning – only greeting cards and the hysterical, over-the-top behaviors learned from soap operas. So if somebody makes Pat unhappy, she never thinks, 'But *why* are you like that, *why* do you do / say things that make me / you sad / happy, what can *I* do to help you / myself?' Instead, there are the comfortable, omnipresent platitudes, applicable both to herself and to her family: 'A mother's work is never done', 'Going abroad gives you diarrhea', 'Foreigners exist to rip you off', and a whole separate slew involving 'family', 'kiddies', 'love'. Every emotion comes with a pastel-colored teddy attached. To her, the words are enough: they don't require any action or examination – they merely need to exist and be said out loud. Pat lives in the kind of universe where, if you fell out with your mother twenty years ago over a stupid thing that neither of you can quite remember, you say 'I'll never forgive her' like a mantra until she dies, at which point you hurl yourself into the grave at the funeral, ululating like a maniac, and spend the next twenty years telling your kids about their marvelous gran, *who you made sure they never met.*

Anyway. Pat's ideal card would be one with a cover that read: 'We're That Different Now, Son, You and I.' (*We're that different now, son, you and I/ It wasn't always so/ But you had to make your way in life/ And so I let you go. PS: Now I just sit here crying, but don't mind me.*) Sam knows this, and sees the absurdity – which doesn't detract one iota from the fact that Pat is his mother, whom he loves and feels defensive about, and loyal toward. It's an awkward situation to navigate – but then, I tell myself, his navigation of it is no longer my business. It's another weird thing about separation: what was our joint problem is now his alone; what we took care of together – what was made a hundred times easier by our complicity – is now Sam's sole affair. The difficulty is, it's not easy to absent yourself completely from situations that have been ongoing for nearly a decade, even though the rules dictate that you must.

Poor old Pat. My own family would probably be the recipients of the *You Are Very Strange, But I Quite Like You* card, or maybe *To Me, You Are Like Characters in a Film*. Pat likes, and perhaps even loves, us, but she doesn't believe we're quite real; she thinks the whole thing – our whole lives – are a diverting entertainment, a bit like watching telly. I don't for one moment imagine that she believes we are capable of actual, real, painful, complicated feelings or emotions, and I don't think she believes Sam is, either: by making a comfortable life for himself, he has jettisoned his right to her sympathy. Pat's other children live in the world she recognizes, a bus ride away from her own home. They eat plastic bread and oven fries and cans of peas, they work shifts, they go to the pub. They are known creatures. Not so Sam, with his homemade pesto and his quilted toilet paper. And very much not so me, with my everything.

When her son and I separated – after a child, two stepsons and seven long years – Pat's sole words to him were, 'Are you all right, son?' and to me, 'Aye, it's a shame.' That was it. No 'Are you coping?', no 'Do you need a hand?', no 'Talk to me about it, I'm your mother.' God knows Kate has her faults, but at least she moved in for a week – nightmare: she literally shoved a toothbrush in my mouth every night and said things like, 'There's no need to be repulsive just because you're mildly depressed' – and sent food parcels for a month afterward ('C – There are other pleasures in life and food is one of them. Enjoy the duck confit, but please don't get fat again. Carbs are the enemy! Love, K'). My sisters rallied. Sam was alone. He has friends, obviously. But none of his family made themselves available.

I think of it and look at him feeding Maisy the froth from his coffee in the North African sunshine. He is watching his mother – Pat is sitting silently; she's finished sipping her Coke and has pursed her lips in a hen's bottom way – with that mixture of pity, irritation and absolute love, and I feel sorry for him. Zero assistance from his family: *pas une saucisse*, as Kate would say. He's the one who 'made it' and got away, ergo in the eyes of his brothers and of his mother, he is impermeable, always dealing, a Coper, successful, absolutely undesirous of help or any offer of support. It must have been horrible for him. On the other hand, swings and roundabouts: that's exactly what he thought about me. Nevertheless.

'It must have been horrible for you,' I say, patting his arm. 'When we split up. It was horrible for me too, but at least I have these mad people wishing me well.'

I am expecting Sam to make a joke of this, or to respond with some light, throwaway remark, or to tell me to stop pawing him. Instead he says, 'Thank you, Clara. That means a lot, you saying that,' and smiles a genuinely warm smile.

Robert appears just as Maisy finishes hoovering up her pastries. He has Jack and Charlie in tow. 'It's fantastic here, Mum,' says Jack. 'Can we move to Morocco?'

'I'm starving,' says Charlie.

Kate appears too, having purchased four rugs, two bedspreads and one crateful of hand-painted tableware, all of which are being shipped to London; she's also bought us six colored tea glasses each as an early Christmas present. 'You're that good to everyone, Kate,' Pat says, perking up. We order another round of drinks and cakes, after which Evie, Robert and I wander down to the pharmacy, or rather the traditional herbalist's, which looks extremely promising. The cool, stone-floored hallway is lined with jars of roots and petals, and the window display is dazzling – huge glass bottles filled with every kind of pigment known to man, lapis-lazuli blue next to fuchsia next to pea green next to ochre. But as ever in Marrakesh, pottering about browsing is not an option: the pharmacist finds us immediately, offers mint tea and leads us upstairs, to a room where, he promises, the really 'special' stuff is. The special stuff includes top-grade argan oil, which we buy by the half-liter at Evie's insistence – 'It's brilliant on everything,' she says, 'skin, hair, salad' – and a jar of some creepy-looking root which the pharmacist pulls out with great reverence. 'Viagra!' he says triumphantly, grinning at Robert.

'Goodness,' says Robert.

'For virility,' the pharmacist elaborates. 'Herbal.'

'I see,' says Robert. 'What do you do with it? Chew on it?'

'Make tea,' says the man. 'Infusion.' He turns to me. 'No sleep for you anymore, madame! No ladysleep for long time!'

'We're not togeth–' I start saying, but it's too late. The pharmacist is on a roll.

'Busy life make tired,' he says. 'Everyone. In your country, in my country. Whole world. Man work hard.'

'Why don't you give him your femmo lecture about how women work hard too?' says Robert. 'Now seems a good time.'

'Oh, be quiet,' I say.

'Man work hard,' the pharmacist repeats. 'He want so bad,

you know. He *want* to make good time in bed. Party time. But sometimes . . .' He looks down at his white-overalled crotch and makes a sad face. 'Little guy no wanna play,' he says, shaking his head.

'God, Americans have a lot to answer for,' says Evie. 'There should be a crimes-against-language tribunal set up in The Hague. I'm going back downstairs to look at the tisanes. I'm embarrassed in advance by how this dialogue is going to end. Get me some saffron, would you?'

'My little guy's okay, thanks,' says Robert.

'All man say this,' laughs the pharmacist. 'From the shame.'

'From the shame, Robert,' I repeat. 'D'you have peen shame, darling? About your little guy?'

'You're the most annoying person I have ever met, Clara,' Robert says conversationally, and very much not for the first time.

'Snap,' I say.

'I'm okay, really – thanks,' Robert says to the pharmacist.

'Apart from the peen shame you carry every day,' I say, making a helpful face. 'Poor Robert. All flooby and –'

'Stop it,' says Robert.

'You buy, huh?' says the pharmacist. 'You buy anyway. You buy many root. For friend, for family. Mans happy, happy ladies. Everybody happy! Many hours, hard.' He makes a fist. 'Hard. With these root.'

'I suppose I could get some for Jake,' Robert mutters. 'Give it to Tamsin for his stocking.'

'My husband would like a dozen,' I tell the pharmacist firmly. 'Twelve. For his own personal use. I sleep too well,' I add, making an unhappy face. 'Every night. His little guy . . . we have problems.'

'Haa!' the pharmacist shouts in delight, clapping his hands. 'I will help you! Take twenty, I give nice price, family price.'

'Two,' says Robert. 'I'll take two.'

'Six,' says the pharmacist. 'Happy Mrs.'

'Yes, watch out, my love,' Robert says. 'It's your lucky night. Now,' he adds, smiling at the pharmacist. 'My wife.' He gestures to me. 'She has very bad hemorrhoids. You know hemorrhoids? On the bottom. Well – *in* the bottom, horrendously enough. Piles. Protruding from . . .'

'Rob. Stop. It's not funny.'

'. . . from the anus,' says Robert. 'Yep. She is in terrible pain. Ow! Bottom-ache! Like that. All the time. And she's too shy – um, *trop timide* – to ask. But I love her, you see. So very, very much. So I am asking for her. *Is there a remedy?*'

Robert should have been an actor: he really does look like the definition of a concerned spouse refusing to let his wife's happiness be destroyed by her bottom problem. Every inch of his being is focused on the task at hand, the task being my humiliation. With the volume muted, you'd think I had a terrible sickness and lived in a refugee camp and he was begging a medic for antiretrovirals.

'And perhaps something for constipation, if you have it,' he adds. 'It seems to exacerbate the problem.' He looks at me and shakes his head sadly. 'Doesn't it, my poor darling?'

'I don't have piles. Hemorrhoids,' I say to the pharmacist. 'Or constipation. Monsieur is making a hilarious joke.'

'Many people from Europe have,' says the pharmacist with a shrug. 'I can fix. One herb for make small, one cream for itchy. I find.'

'*I don't have . . .*' I start to say, but it's too late: he's already rootling through his cabinets looking for suitable remedies.

'Robert!' I hiss. I am actually blushing. 'It's a totally inappropriate joke. It's a Muslim country. You can't go around talking to people – to strange men – about my bottom.'

'Oh dear,' says Robert. 'But I just did.' He bursts out

laughing. 'I win,' he says. I don't know why he and I can only communicate in the manner of really babyish ten-year-olds – sometimes I worry that it's because we don't have anything real left to say to each other – but it passes the time. Say what you like about Robert, but he does lighten my mood, even if it is at the expense of my dignity.

By the time we get home, the house is a flurry of activity. Moustafa is up a ladder, trailing multicolored paper lanterns all across the courtyard. Two young men have appeared from nowhere and are sweeping, polishing the brass tables and placing dozens of nightlights on every available surface. Foot-high candles have been put inside the lanterns surrounding the pool.

'What's this?' I ask. 'Are we having a party?'

'It's tonight!' says Flo. She is stringing silver baubles on meters of silver ribbon. 'Some of them got shattered in my suitcase, so annoying. But I thought we'd have these crisscrossing the landings. And then maybe hang some from the glass lanterns, too.'

'What's tonight?' I ask.

'Christmas! Well, it's tomorrow, obviously. But they follow the French model of doing most of the eating on Christmas Eve. Sniff the air, if you don't believe me.'

'Fatima is cooking us an absolute *feast*,' says Kate.

'Oh, but God – tonight?'

'Yes,' says Kate. 'Don't worry about it – there are hours to go.'

'Right,' I say. 'Okay. It's not what I'd have done but . . .'

'That's the point,' says Kate. 'Of not being at home.'

'Yes, I suppose so. I'll just go and get my decorations.'

'I brought one or two things too,' says Kate. 'Could you get them while you're up there? Maybe get them first, actually. They're in the older trunk, the battered brown one.'

'Yup. Where are the children?'

'Cassie and Maisy are helping Fatima,' says Kate, who seems to be holding everyone's social diary in her head. 'Or maybe hindering, who knows. But she offered and they seemed awfully keen. The boys stayed out with Sam. They've gone to the main square, the Djeema-el-Fna. They took Pat with them – I don't know that it was an entirely wise decision. Shamans and snake-charmers, you know. Tooth-pullers and dancing boys in drag. She'll either love it or be sobbing for home.'

'She'll like being with Sam and the boys,' I say. 'Little break from us.'

'She's in a funny mood, isn't she?' says Evie. 'Like she half wants to have fun and half wants to hate everything, and she can't make up her mind which it's going to be.'

'It's difficult for her. She is very much out of water. She cheered up a bit after you'd gone,' says Kate. 'Ate quite an exotic cookie. And I have the most wonderful present for her, which'll perk her up even more.'

'You're very organized, Kate, keeping tabs on everything.'

'I have my uses,' says Kate. 'Now – Max has gone down to La Mammounia to meet his old friend Richard for a coffee. He won't be long. And I've told everyone else to be here and changed for six o'clock.'

'Better get on with the decorating, then.'

I go upstairs to Kate's bedroom and make a beeline for the oldest and most battered trunk. I'm about to go downstairs again and ask her for the key, but then I notice that it's already unlocked. It takes me a moment to realize what's inside the trunk, and when I do I let out an actual gasp. There, nestled between layers and layers of white tissue paper, are our old Christmas decorations – the ones from home, from childhood, from Notting Hill all those decades ago. Boxes and boxes of them: red baubles – *our* red baubles, from the Christmi: I'd know them anywhere. I didn't think they still existed: I'd assumed they got lost or thrown away when Kate and Julian split up and sold the house.

I sit down by the trunk, holding a box of baubles on my lap like a loony, staring at them tenderly as if they were a basket of kittens. Kate has never, in two decades, mentioned that these decorations were still in her possession. She stopped hosting Christmas after the break-up with Julian, which is why I started doing it at my house in the first place: I couldn't bear to see the flame go out, so I became its keeper. I can't believe she had the baubles all the time.

I want to cry.

I want to cry even more when I start unloading the boxes – the boxes I know by heart; I can even tell you that the one I'm holding now got trodden on by me in 1984 – that's what the crumbling, yellowed Scotch tape on the corner is about – which was the year Julian's mother gave his biological children £10 book tokens and a £5 one to me, and Kate, electric with anger, took me aside and pushed a twenty-pound note (vast and unimaginable riches) into my hand. Here's the angel I made at primary school, with its pipe-cleaner halo; here are Flo and Evie's cack-handed deer decorations from nursery; here's the only tinsel we were allowed ('vulgar'), six feet of it, red, re-inforced with wire and bent into a heart. Kate's even brought our Christmas lights along.

I go into the hall and lean over the courtyard. My mother is talking to Moustafa in extremely rapid French; I can't make out what they're saying.

'Kate!' I shout down. 'I don't know what to say. That's like giving us the most amazing present.'

'I thought it was time,' says Kate, smiling up at me. I beam back at her, one of those mad smiles when you're aware of showing all your teeth.

'Evie, Flo. Come up and see. I need a hand.'

'Oh my God,' says Evie, peering into the trunk. 'They're the ones from home.'

'No!' says Flo. 'Let me see. God, so they are. Look, Eev, our deer.'

'And look, my Christmas robin,' I say, holding it up.

'And our baubles. There must be hundreds of them. And our thread. From that old lady who had a haberdashery on Portobello and used to give us sweets, remember?' Each bauble has a piece of thread going through the metal loop bit.

'I used to do them with pink thread, when I was obsessed with My Little Pony,' says Flo. 'Look, here they are. Oh, God.'

'Christmas Hamster!' shouts Evie. 'It's Christmas Hamster!' She pulls out a misshapen knitted lump with tiny ears. 'Oh, the sweet thing, he's lost an eye. I'll make him another one right this minute. I missed you, Christmas Hamster,' she says to it. 'I thought you were *dead*.'

'I had no idea these were still around,' says Flo.

'I know,' I say. 'It makes me want to cry.'

'Me too. Did you know?' asks Flo.

'No, I thought they'd got lost years ago, along . . .'

'Along with everything else,' says Evie. 'So did I. I thought they'd be lying smashed in a skip somewhere. But Christmas Hamster has risen again, and we rejoiceth.'

'He rises at Easter. He is born tonight,' says Flo.

'Man, I need an infusion, I got bad Jesus confusion,' sings Evie. 'I just made that up. I feel weird. It's the baubs.'

'There's an unChristmassy danger of us all sitting here sobbing into Kate's trunk,' says Flo. 'Come on. Grab some boxes and let's take them downstairs.'

'But why now?' says Evie. 'She hasn't done Christmas since she and Daddy broke up. Not a bauble, not a candle, nothing. These must have been sitting in that trunk for over twenty years.'

'She said it was time,' I say.

My sisters and I stare at each other, and then, without speaking, pick up an armload of boxes each and make our way downstairs.

And now there's a Christmas tree in the middle of the courtyard. A huge, twenty-odd-foot Christmas tree, sitting upright in a beaten copper pot. It wasn't there ten minutes ago, and now it is. I feel like rubbing my eyes.

'Marvelous,' says Kate to the couple of sweating men who must have dragged it in. 'Thanks so much. How much do I owe you? Is that all? It doesn't sound nearly enough. Here you go, much more like it. *Au revoir, au revoir. Joyeux Noël!*'

'Kate?' I say. It comes out quite strangulated. 'You got us *a tree*?'

'Holmesian powers of deduction,' says Kate. 'Let no one say my daughter is unobservant. Do you like it?'

'It's beautiful. But . . . But how?'

'I had it shipped,' says Kate. 'Well, flown in, actually.'

'But it's enormous.'

'It's twenty-five foot,' says Kate. 'Like they all were. Handsome, isn't it? I'm rather pleased with it. You never know, with trees, until you see them. But this one is a lovely shape, though the branches need to drop a little. I was worried it would look too sort of poignant, you know, tragically out of place, but actually it looks rather at home.'

'But how did it get here?'

'Clara! You are drearily obsessed with logistics. I put my considerable wealth to good use.'

'How long have you been planning all this, Kate?' asks Flo.

'A fortnight or so,' says Kate. 'Now – we need the crepe paper from the trunk to wrap around the base, even though that copper pot's quite pretty. Moustafa's getting more ladders. I can't bear heights these days as you know, so you're going to have to do the upper bits of the tree, girls. He'll help you. I'll be the stylist and the stage director – both jobs I'd have excelled at, incidentally. How clever I was to only ever use red baubles – old but timeless, so classic and chic.'

It's amazing how fast you can work when you put your mind to it. Within two hours, the courtyard (no slouch in the aesthetics stakes in the first place) is transformed into – well, I don't want to over-egg it, but honestly, into the most magical thing I have ever seen: it's half glittering grotto, half *Thousand and One Nights*. It is dusk now, and the tree, surreal and beautiful, rises upward, reaching for the sky, blazing with Christmas lights and heavy with baubles. Kate is right: it looks oddly at home. Everything else is candle-lit; the flickering light bounces off the glinting brass tables and onto the glazed tiles; the glass lanterns shimmer high above us; the little green pool sparkles in the half-light, and beautiful old rugs have been laid on the stone floor.

Moustafa and his helpers have dragged in an enormously long table and Fatima has set it for supper (it has been decided that the courtyard looks so spectacular that we want to eat in it). The table is blazing too, with crockery, silverware and an abundance of pearlescent, pastel-colored glass. Fatima goes to her kitchen and comes back with Maisy and Cassie, both grinning with delight and both equipped with large paper bags; these contain rose petals, which the girls scatter in lavish quantities all down the dining table and all around our feet, bouncing with excitement as they do so. When Ed comes down with the twins, Ava makes enormous eyes and says, 'Is it real, Daddy?', which I think is how we all feel. Even Robert stands there with his mouth slightly open.

'It's stunning,' he says. 'Really beautiful.'

'You don't mind, do you, Clara?' Kate asks. 'I hope it doesn't feel like I've hijacked Christmas. That wasn't the intention.'

'Mind? Of course not,' I say. 'It's the most wonderful thing ever. And I can't tell you how happy I am that you've . . . come out of retirement on the Christmas front.'

'Well, it's just this once. We'll be back at your house next year, though I'm thinking I might lift the ban on a tree in my own house. They just made me so sad, for so long. But you've changed that, you know. Your Christmases are lovely, Clara.'

'I learned from you,' I say, leaning on her shoulder.

'You learned well, my child,' she says, leaning back on mine. And then: 'Oh my God, I nearly forgot. Fatima! Fatima! THE TRUFFLE.'

I'll say one thing for my family: we can eat. Man, can we eat. Even the small children are like human Hoovers. I'm always perplexed by people who claim children hate vegetables, I think as I watch Flo's twins chow down on some puréed egg-plant and flatbread. ('A few little things,' said Fatima, arriving with plateful after plateful of amazing appetizers. 'Not the real food.') Maisy and Cassie are chomping on roasted red peppers with cumin ('We cooked the seeds!'), looking like illustrations from one of those bossy volumes about healthy eating. Mind you, child vegetable-hate is one of those supposed 'facts' that only becomes real because of people's mindless repeating of it. Pretty much the first solid things that babies ever eat are mashed-up vegetables, and they don't have any difficulty doing that, and I've always found it weird that it should be universally believed that, somehow – by magic – they then start shunning the things they loved eating two years before. It's just not true. But then, so many of the things people say about children aren't true either: see also 'children are cruel'. Mine aren't, and neither are the children of anybody I know. I'm sure children can be *made* cruel, just as they can subtly be encouraged to hate vegetables by a parent making a hysterical fuss of a piece of broccoli, but otherwise I see no evidence of epidemic veg-loathing. Maybe it's a British thing, like doing the washing-up in the sink and 'rinsing' the clean dishes in soapy water that's gray with dirt. The question of children hating vegetables wouldn't occur to any Moroccan person, for example; you might as well hate bread, or water.

On cue, Pat says, 'They're good at eating their vegetables, those wee 'uns. Mine wouldn't touch them.'

'That's because we *had* no vegetables, Ma,' says Sam. 'Other than potatoes.' Sam is one of those people who never met an avocado until he came to London, and who is still secretly suspicious of the more exotic fruits.

'Yes, we did,' says Pat. 'We had plenty of vegetables. And of course, everything we ate was organic, in those days. You never ate any chemicals.'

'Vegetables? Organic?' splutters Sam. 'Where? How do you mean?'

'It just was,' Pat says serenely. 'Organic. Back in the day.'

'Because pesticides hadn't been invented in the 1970s?' Sam says, laughing.

'Leave it,' I say to him.

'I was brought up on fries and mayonnaise,' he quietly says to me. 'And canned pies. And Angel Delight for treats. I didn't see anything green or leafy during my entire childhood. She's joked about it before. What does she mean, "Everything was organic"? Our cans of own-brand Spam?'

'She wants your childhood to have been lovely,' I say, 'and so she's reinventing bits of it. It doesn't matter if she contradicts herself. They all do it. We'll do it too, I expect, when the children are grown up. And she wants to fit in with us – the rest of us I mean. She's feeling quite defensive. Don't call her out on it.'

Pat is now chatting enthusiastically to Flo about the eating habits of babies she has known, and about the marvelous biodiversity of her own children's diets.

'I guess. But I don't like it,' says Sam. 'It makes me feel argumentative.'

'Nobody likes the rewriting of history,' I say. 'But it's just what people do. Kate's always telling us that our childhoods were "idyllic", which is true up to a point but kind of bypasses the bit where she and Julian split up and everybody went mad and Evie and Flo were completely traumatized for years.'

'Fucking families,' says Sam with feeling.

'I know,' I say. 'You have to force yourself to remember that you have your recollection, and she has her recollection, and it's okay if they aren't the same. Here, have some of these little crispy things. They're called *briouats*. They're delicious.'

'There's an incredible amount of food on this table and dinner hasn't even really kicked off properly,' Sam observes, biting into the pastry.

'It's Christmas Eve. Don't do your weird foody freak-out. The "we are all bourgeois pigs" thing. Now's not the time.'

'No, it's nice,' says Sam. 'God, these are good. I don't mind it tonight, for some reason.'

'Did you have a nice walk this afternoon?'

'It was fantastic. The boys were mesmerized by everything. My ma loved it. She wanted to have a tooth taken out by some filthy street dentist. It took ten minutes to convince her that it wasn't a good idea.'

'Really? Doesn't sound like her.'

'Yes. She was staring and staring at him – you know those blokes in the main square, they basically have a pair of pliers and a couple of cloths?'

'But didn't she think the set-up was too dirty?'

'She didn't, oddly. Or, she may have done, but then she asked me how much it would cost and when I said "about 20p" she became very keen. She only has two real teeth left and apparently one of them is sore. I thought it would be a sad way for it to go.'

'She loves a bargain, your mother.'

'Anyway, after that she wanted to buy some tortoises, so then I had to be the bad guy again and try to convince her not to. And then we went into the souks – I took her to the jewelry one, and at that point she really cheered up.'

'I'd have thought most of the stuff was too big and heavy for her, no? Too Eastern?'

'Yeah, a lot of it was.' He laughs. 'Though I like the idea of her going to her OAP nights completely bedecked in Marrakesh's finest.'

'Well, so, what – did you get her anything?'

'Mm.'

'Spit it out, Sam. What?'

'There was a gold curly necklace she took a real shine to.'

'Curly, how?'

'It was writing.'

I can suddenly see exactly what happened.

'In Arabic?' I say.

'Yes,' says Sam. 'She wouldn't be deterred. Mum. Mum! Show Clara the necklace I got you.'

'It's that nice,' says Pat. 'I'm that absolutely delighted with it. I love it, son.'

'Let's have a look, then,' I say, getting up and walking around to where Pat is sitting.

I've seen the necklaces before.

'Lovely,' I say, which it is. 'Beautiful.'

'Aye,' says Pat. 'What's it say again, Sam?'

'Allah,' says Sam.

'The merciful, the compassionate,' murmurs Moustafa, who has just deposited more flatbreads on the table. He looks at Pat, and then at Sam, and then at me, shakes his head very faintly and walks back to the kitchen.

'Thankee, Mooza,' Pat says to his departing form. 'Thankee kind. That's right,' she adds happily. 'Allah. They didn't have one that said Pat. Or Patricia.'

'It means "God", Ma,' says Sam. 'Remember? The guy in the shop explained it.'

'Aye, God,' Pat repeats. 'That's lovely, isn't it? Everybody likes God. And the wee baby Jesus.'

'We are all His children,' says Evie.

'Charming,' says Kate. 'Very nice, Pat. Quite right. Why shouldn't you wear a Muslim necklace? All monotheistic religions are basically the same.'

'Aye,' says Pat, who comes from Northern Ireland and lives in Eire. 'I love my necklace. But I wish Sam had let me buy a couple of wee tortoises.'

'I bought some when we came here when I was little, do you remember, Kate?' says Evie. 'I felt so sorry for them. They pack them into those awful tiny cages, all stacked on top of each other.'

'I remember having to smuggle them into Britain,' says Kate. 'In my handbag. I think they were illegal at the time, tortoises.'

'And Daddy was furious,' says Flo. 'And you said fine, you were going to take them out of your handbag and leave them to roam about the airport. Do you remember? And then he refused to sit with us.'

'He feared arrest, the fool. Anyway, they absolutely loved Notting Hill, those tortoises,' says Kate. 'They *thrived* on west London soil.'

'What happened to them?' I ask.

'They wandered off to hibernate and we never saw them again,' says Kate. 'Such is the way of tortoises. They have wild, ancient souls. Very spiritual beasts.'

'Aye,' says Pat. 'You're not wrong. They're that wise. You can tell by their faces.'

Dinner now starts arriving in earnest, dish after dish of it in enormous quantities, not least because half the table is vegetarian and half isn't and so the already generous quantities of food are doubled.

'This is the most food I've ever seen in my life,' says Pat. 'It's like a foreign wedding.'

'Please don't sniff it all,' I say, trying to make my voice sound pleasant and amused, but tormenting my napkin at the very thought of it.

'It smells nice,' Pat concedes, mercifully sniffing the air rather than the table. 'But I'll just be having some plain chicken for my main. Your mum organized it for me. Thanks for that, Kate,' she says.

'You're welcome, but you're really missing out,' says Kate. 'And I don't know how good your mashed potatoes will be – they're hardly the national dish. That *méchoui* smells so fantastic that even I'm tempted to try it. Are you sure you wouldn't like a taste? It's roast lamb, except over charcoals, and cooked for hours and hours. There's nothing overwhelmingly . . . *complicated* about it.'

'Ooh, no,' says Pat. 'I wouldn't fancy that. You don't know where the lamb's come from, do you?'

'Its mother the sheep, one expects,' says Kate.

'Imagine it's barbecued,' says Sam. 'Which it kind of is.'

'No thank you,' says Pat.

'Imagine the barbecue is at home, in someone's back garden,' says Kate.

'Oh,' Pat laughs. 'You'd never get anything like this back home.'

'But that's precisely why we'd all love you to try it,' Kate persists. 'And the tajines . . . try the tajines. They're just meat and vegetables, Pat. Stew. Barbecued lamb and stew and some salads. Perhaps if you imagined them being carried to the barbecue by overweight ladies with ham-like arms, clutching Tupperware and speaking English? Do you see? It's perfectly normal food, except nicer. Live a little.'

'I don't like the look of those wee yellow seeds,' Pat says, eying up a bowl of couscous with mistrust.

'They're grains,' says Flo. 'Like rice, but not.'

'And anyway,' Pat says, looking coyly down at her abdomen, 'I have a delicate stomach. I don't want to be getting diarrhea from foreign food. Tumtum ow,' she adds for the benefit of Fatima, who is hovering nearby with more plates. 'Bad lavvy.'

'How absolutely revolting,' says Kate. 'Please don't update us on your gastric anxieties while we're eating, Pat.'

'I just like plain food,' says Pat, patting her stomach. 'Plain food is best, for me.'

'I despair of you,' says Kate, but she says it in such a way that Pat smiles at her companionably. I don't. It really irritates the crap out of me, this food thing – not just the sniffing (though, *God*, the sniffing) but the reluctance to try anything new. Is that wrong of me? Is it culturally insensitive, unattractively prejudiced toward the simple, plain foods of the British Isles? I don't know. But it gets on my nerves. I want to shout 'IT'S NOT MADE OF POO!' about every dish Pat refuses with a wince and an unintelligible phrase in her weird new language ('Mercy no, yucka eat'). The food spread out before us on the table is so appetizing – and so delicious – that it would test the mettle of a gastric-banded hunger-striker. And she literally won't try a single mouthful of it. Her loss, but it's pretty maddening; also she's a woman in her sixties.

Actually I think that deep down Pat would probably like to try it, or some of it, but the 'your food versus my food' thing has become such an issue over the years, such a significant statement about herself – it basically means 'I'll go along with your middle-class lifestyle, but only up to a point' – that she couldn't even if she wanted to. It's a line that she's drawn in the sand. At least she's stopped turning up at my house with a whole suitcase of 'her' food – fizzy drinks, canned pies, crinkled oven fries stacked in a giant cool-bag, plastic bread, chips, cans of ground beef. She did this for three years, until she could be sure that I wasn't going to make her eat anything 'weird' or, God forbid, 'foreign' (curries are considered British), and that I was familiar with the concept of the chip. Imagine it the other way around: me going up to her house with a couple of bottles of Sauvignon Blanc, some vegetables, pasta, yogurt, salad, all because I considered her food so alarming that I didn't want to put it in my mouth over the few days I was staying. I mean, rude to the nth degree. But maybe I'm wrong. Maybe she wouldn't be offended at all. And at least with the chicken and mashed potatoes that's now placed before her by saintly Fatima, there is only one plate to be sniffed. Pat duly raises it to her nose, inhales deeply and sets in down again.

'No spices, nothing,' says Fatima, looking a bit baffled. 'Like Madame ask.' I wonder if she maybe thinks Pat is a tragic, and possibly insane, invalid.

'Lovely fresh smell,' says Pat.

'How's everyone back home, Ma? Did you get a chance to speak to them?' asks Sam.

'I had a quick word,' says Pat. 'I'll call again in the morning to wish them a merry Christmas.'

'Are they all okay?' I ask.

'They're fine,' says Pat. 'Tony's a bit down, you know, because of the time of year, but he'll be all right.'

'Oh God, is that still not sorted?' I say, not altogether kindly. But I know what conversation we're about to have next and I don't much care for it: it makes me feel like the late Michael

Jackson, tearing at my clothing with misery and wailing about how we must all think of the Earth's children. The problem is that, where Pat comes from, if men and women separate acrimoniously and they have children together, it is an accepted fact that one of them will behave like a bastard: there's no attempt made at imagining what things would be like if both people behaved – or could be persuaded to behave – well. What drives me mad about it is that it's so resigned: all the platitudes come out – 'He lives for that kid,' and so on – but no one ever seems interested in helping to nudge things in the right direction. So for instance if the father – Sam's brother Tony, in this case – is denied access to said child by a still-angry wife and for no good reason, it is taken as a given that that's quite simply that: the unhappy status quo is now how things are, and nothing can be done to challenge it.

'It's a shame, so it is,' says Pat. 'You should see the presents Tony's got for him. Trucks and everything. Lego.'

Every time we have this conversation, I tell myself that I need to keep my mouth shut next time. And every time I fail, because I say:

'Why doesn't he just take them round?'

'He's tried for the past two years. She wouldn't let him in,' says Pat.

'He'll never know if he doesn't try again,' I say. 'This might be the year she regains her sanity.'

'It's not that simple,' Sam says. 'She wants to punish him.'

'Actually, it *is* that simple. It is unbelievably simple. If she's behaving that badly, he goes back to court. I bet you even a lawyer's letter would do it.'

'He doesn't want to go to court,' Pat says. 'All that fuss. And they never believe the dad,' she adds, as though she were, in fact, an expert in family law.

'I think he's prematurely defeated,' I say, immediately

resolving to keep my mouth shut next time. 'I think you all are. Sorry, Pat. But you know how I feel about all this.'

I am, tonight, particularly incensed by the idea of Tony's little boy being deprived of his dad's company over Christmas just because his mother is antagonistic. I turn toward Tamsin and Jake, who are engrossed in a shopping conversation with Flo and organizing a visit to the leather souk, where the tanneries stink to high heaven. Pat has turned away and is already tucking into her chicken with gusto and telling Evie about the tortoises.

'Don't wind yourself up,' says Sam.

'I'm sorry,' I tell him. 'It's not fair on her. Or on Tony. Or on anyone. But it pushes all the wrong buttons. Does it really not occur to a single one of them that this little boy is growing up thinking "Where on earth is my daddy?" – to which the answer is "About a mile down the road"? Or that he's going to start thinking – if he doesn't already – "Why doesn't my daddy want me?" I mean, you know. It's so demeaningly simple-minded, their approach. It could all be avoided so easily.'

'You over-identify with this,' says Sam. 'Calm down.'

'Too bloody right I do,' I say. 'I can't help it. It's very much my . . . territory, as you know, but that's not the reason. The reason is that it just sucks and everybody sits around going "Oh dear" and doing nothing about it. They're not stupid people. What's the matter with them?'

'I don't know,' says Sam a little bit sadly. 'Or maybe I do. Patterns. The past. Not doing things differently. They all find it remarkable that you and I still talk. Let's not go there. Anyway – what about your dad?'

'My dead dad or my live ex-step-one?'

'Your dead one.'

'Well, he died, as you know,' I say, heaving a sigh. 'Not long after I had that conversation with Kate about him last Christmas.'

'Yes, I know *that* – I mean, where does it leave you?'

'It leaves me being half an orphan,' I say. 'Which is weird. I don't want to go on about it because it makes me feel a bit fraudulent. It was such a strange situation – us not actually knowing each other. Obviously it would be a million times worse if we had. But I still felt . . . a bit churned up. Half my DNA, you know? My genetic material. Half of what made me, gone. Never to return. We were destined never to run toward each other in slow motion, weeping with emotion.'

'I'm sorry.'

'I know. Thanks. Kate has this stuff – paperwork, something to do with probate coming through – that she's been trying to show me for a few weeks. But I don't know that I have the stomach for it. Every time I start thinking about it I feel angry and sad all at the same time.'

'With Kate?'

'Not so much anymore. Just with things generally. With him, I suppose, for never wanting to even meet me for a drink. With myself, for thinking it didn't matter.'

'Perhaps it doesn't,' says Robert, who's swapped places with Pat.

'I didn't think it did,' I say, 'but I liked the idea of having my options open in case I changed my mind.'

'Doesn't work, at our age,' says Robert.

'How do you mean?'

'We're too old to keep our options open,' says Robert. 'We need to *act*.'

'Rob! We're in our early forties. We're in our *prime*. What's got into you?'

'Yeah. Like I said, too old. We're at the age where you seriously have to seize the day. Carpe diem and all that. People think it's a young person's motto, but they're wrong. This – now – is when people die, buses knock you over, people get ill, parents go gaga, things go wrong . . .'

'Happy Christmas,' says Sam.

'Yes, happy Christmas, cheery-chops,' I say. 'Have some more food. Have a drink. Quiet your Voice of Doom.'

'I'm being factual. There is absolutely no point in "wait and see" or "I might do it some day" anymore. As you've just discovered in relation to your own dear papa.'

'God, how depressing. Do you really think so?'

'I really do, Clara. If I want to do something, I do it. If I don't, I don't. Same thing with people: if I want to see them, I see them. If I don't, I disappear. And I only see radiators these days – you know, people who give out heat and warmth. Might make me a selfish cunt, but I'm much happier. No more procrastination. It's too late.'

'Blimey. What brought this on?'

'Oh, the usual. I cocked up a love affair. It was my fault. I thought I'd bide my time because I wasn't sure. And then of course, something – or more accurately somebody – else turned up in the picture, and that was that. I know you're going to say it can happen at any age, but my powers of recovery aren't what they were. Plus,' he adds, sounding more like his usual self, 'I suddenly know too many ill people, and it's freaking me out. Cancer and stuff. Headaches that turn out to be tumors. Bits being hacked off them. Remember Rosie from our art department? She got breast cancer. She had a mastectomy. We're not as young as we used to be. Listen to your Uncle Robert, for he is wise.'

'No, I am listening,' I say. 'I always listen when you talk like a normal person. And I suppose you're right. Is Rosie okay?'

'She will be in about six months' time, I hope. But, you know – she's our age. Couple of years younger, actually. She'd prefer to have her own hair and her old face back.'

'Oh God. I'm so sorry,' I say.

'My point is: no point in delaying anything at this stage. No procrastination. Life's too short. Anyway. I've finished now. I'm depressing myself,' says Robert. 'Let's have some more wine. What's up with you, Clara?'

'I'm in Marrakesh. It's Christmas Eve. I went to buy herbal Viagra with my ex-husband earlier. He is you.'

'How hilarious you are. I meant generally. In your little life.'

'Oh,' I say. 'I don't really know.'

'Do you mean *"pas devant les Sams"*?'

'Oi,' says Sam. 'I'm not, like, deaf. Or an idiot.'

'No,' I say. 'I mean, I don't really know. Everything's fine. Work's good. Children are good. You know. It's all fine.'

'Oh,' says Robert. 'I see. Has your future third husband vanished before you could drag him up the aisle? Done a runner? Met the folks, perhaps?'

Robert and I haven't lived together for nearly a decade, but he retains the fantastically irritating ability to read me quite well.

'I don't know that, either,' I say. 'He hasn't been in touch for two weeks, which seems a bit weird. I mean, it was always an elastic and sporadic arrangement – there was no aisle, it was more –'

'Fuck buddies,' says Robert matter-of-factly. 'You said on the phone.'

'Well,' says Sam. 'Isn't that nice.'

'Well, no, it wasn't quite fuck buddies by the end. I mean, it's been going on for a year and a bit, on and off. It wasn't Aisle but it wasn't just Fuck, either. Not strictly just Fuck.'

'Fuck Plus,' says Robert.

'Yes, I suppose so. Fuck Plus Plus.'

'Lovely,' says Sam. 'How *gorgeous*.'

'Are you sure you didn't think it was Aisle?'

'Positive.'

'Clara!' says Robert. 'Come on. If it wasn't Aisle, why are you looking so bothered by it?'

'It wasn't Aisle! Why do you want me to say it was Aisle, you weirdo? No more Aisle for me, thanks. But . . . Maybe it was Fuck Plus with Like Squared.'

'You know TMI, too much information?' says Sam. 'Well, that. Happening right here, right now.' He points both index fingers at himself. 'In this chair. Live and direct.'

'You don't have to listen,' I say. 'It's nothing to do with you. *You* culled *me*, remember? And if you do listen, you don't have to sit there twitching like an old nan. Go and talk to Max.'

'Oh God, I can't,' says Sam. 'Don't make me. He's so posh that I literally don't understand what he's saying. Maybe one word in five. It's like radio waves – you have to be English, I think, to be able to tune in.'

'Max doesn't need anyone to talk to,' Robert says. 'He just likes watching us and smiling to himself. He treats it all like a trip to the circus. And anyway, he's got his BlackBerry and Kate next to him – he's fine.'

'And don't call me an old nan,' says Sam. 'Fuck's sake, Clara.'

'I'm sorry for you, if it was Fuck Plus with Like Squared,' says Robert. 'You should have seized the day. I'm never wrong. You'll know for next time. Pass the eggplant, would you?'

At times like these, sitting around and getting on and loving the children you have together, you sometimes wonder whether the hassle of separation was worth it. I know: it's an outré thought. Nobody's supposed to think, 'I wonder if we made a terrible mistake': you're supposed to carry on instead, onward and upward and saying to yourself, 'Phew, I'm glad that's over.' Which I broadly do.

Not that I had much choice in the matter, separation-wise: Sam huffed out. I'm guessing, though, that he merely precipitated the inevitable: I was feeling intolerably huffy myself by that point, and I expect I'd have huffed if he hadn't helpfully taken the huffing initiative (annoying, though, to be out-huffed). Was this the right decision, to huff? This is my constant question, and I don't mean merely in relation to Sam: is it worth putting up with stuff you really don't go a bundle on in exchange for a superficially easy life? Is it somehow *spoiled* to stamp your foot and say, 'Ew, I'm really not liking it' – is it something you're supposed to stop doing in your twenties? Is it folly to assume that beyond a certain point things can't be fixed? People fix the most seemingly unfixable things, after all – addiction, chronic illness, serial infidelity. In that context, you think maybe it's a bit silly to huff out because you look at the face next to yours on the pillow and think, 'Oh. It's you. Well, whoop-de-do.'

To me, the idea of hanging in there having a miserable time is a monstrous one, but then I can't take my own word for it, boringly, given that I have some difficulties with this whole kind of thing anyway. Toward the end of my relationship with Sam, I started waking up in the night spluttering, unable to breathe, desperately gasping for air, as though I were being choked. Sam and I both decided that I had – weirdly and out of the blue – suddenly developed asthma. I went to the doctor – it was becoming a nightly occurrence, and debilitating – who ran tests and said, 'No asthma here.' I never believed I had asthma in the first place. Call me Clara Freud and have a stroke of my beard, but I knew exactly what it was: I was metaphorically suffocating, and my refusal to confront it in my waking life made me literally suffocate in my sleep. (To add insult to injury, I used to have to gulp down huge, dramatic breaths of air in between chokes when it happened, so that I didn't actually pass out. When the choking was more or less over, I would then burp – buuuuuurp – like the burpiest freak in the history of burping. Sexy, eh? Pure fucking sizzling, that. Marriage-mendingly hot. And because I was embarrassed by the burpage – I've never gone a bundle on the companionable sharing of parp-honk bodily functions – I'd start laughing before I'd got my breath back fully, which of course would made me choke again. One night Sam turned over and said, 'I think the mystique's died, babe.' That made me laugh too, and then want to punch him. I mean, *he* was the one causing me to choke in the first place.)

I started sleeping like a baby the night Sam left – a sad baby at first, waking up and crying a lot, though cleverly managing to remain fully continent. I was sleeping blissfully through the night within a couple of months. I've never had a repeat of the choking weirdness since. That's got to mean something, surely? On the other hand, look at us. The fathers of my children are my two greatest friends, the people I can talk to in shorthand, the people whom I can guarantee I won't bore if my conversation turns to the domestic, to my children's school reports, to the question of pocket money, to the dodgy boiler (maybe not so much with Robert, re. the dodgy boiler. If I try to share the pain of white goods malfunction with him, he literally yawns in my face with his mouth wide open. It was ever thus). Maybe we should all live together in a kind of commune.

We are not troubled by oppressive, throbbing, promise-heavy waves of sexual tension, I'll grant you. But then, who is, as the years go by? Most couples have a sex life, a good sex life even, but I don't know anyone so overcome with lust that they drag their husband or wife of several decades into the undergrowth for an impromptu quickie anymore. Does this matter? The undergrowth plays havoc with your hair and there might be dog poos lurking, or the weirder bugs. And you don't need undergrowth for ecstatic rumpo, obviously (Flo, I noticed earlier, has taken to calling sex 'riding the Ninky Nonk', after *In the Night Garden*. Small children will do that to you).

I don't know the answers to any of this. There are few more

depressing things than not being desired anymore, I would say, but perhaps that's not the universal view. I mean, the old people who make me cry in supermarkets have presumably not pottered out to buy snacks to fortify themselves before their next epic, bed-breaking shagathon. Have they? Maybe they have. I don't know. It's awful to get to middle age and know so little.

The thing I'd really like to know is whether everybody thinks this, or whether it's just me. Also, I'd like to know if I've got some terrible rogue gene that disables me from contemplating long-term domesticity with anything other than horror and panic (maybe it's genetic. Maybe I got it from Felix, like my ear. Or from Kate. Or from both my bolting parents, yay). Or perhaps everyone has the rogue gene and they just butch it out, crash through the horror, leap over the panic and end their days buying ham together, all happy and content. It's complicated by the fact that in my case the horror and panic coexist with a subsumed longing for things not to change, a deep love of routine and an overdeveloped domestic streak. Part of me wants to cook supper for the same person forever, and part of me wants to whack myself in the face with a frying pan at the very idea. It's unhelpfully schizoid.

But then, look at the alternative. The man from the Connaught, say. I like the man from the Connaught, whom I've now been 'seeing' on and off for just over a year. The man from the Connaught and I have a very good time. I really liked the idea of the man from the Connaught existing in the background and then materializing every now and then, and then retreating. It was romantic and sexy and it kept one on one's toes. But, woe. The man from the Connaught has vanished – I've no idea why or how – in the past fortnight. There is radio silence, and now I'm annoyed. Where *is* the man from the Connaught? I'm too old for people to vanish for no rhyme or reason. I mean, what if the man from the Connaught is *dead*?

It's possible, if not probable. I wouldn't really like him to be dead. Maybe he's had both arms amputated and hasn't trained himself to text using his nose yet. I'd forgive him, but I can't contact him to find out, because when you're forty-two you don't send plaintive little texts to people who have, for whatever reason, vanished into thin air. So that's very trying too, the alternative to wedded bliss. It's not as easy as it looks. I could always find another man from the Connaught (don't believe anyone who tells you men from the Connaught are thin on the ground if you're over thirty and not a size four. In my wilder moments, I sometimes think it's a lie designed to keep women in their place, unhappy but grateful for the company). But what if the original rises again, like Jesus, and then I have *two* men from the Connaught to worry about? You see? It's complicated. It's more complicated than I really have the time or the emotional energy for.

Option three is to turn my back on what Robert's mother likes to call 'bedroom unpleasantness'. I could be like Pat. I could chuckle comfortably and tell people that 'my cuddling days are over'. When Maisy's grown up, I could reinvent myself as a spinster and take a postgraduate course in anthropology, like somebody in a Barbara Pym novel, and invite curates to tea (why don't I know any curates? It's irritating, though not half as irritating as not knowing Madonna. It's so crashingly *obvious* that my girlfriends and I should know Madonna, and hang out with her. She'd love it. What a waste). Oddly, this Pym-plan isn't as wholly unattractive as it might be: there's something very appealing about the idea of living in 'rooms' with a spinster friend and having cups of tea and never bleaching your moustache and preoccupying yourself with matters of the intellect rather than matters of the flesh or kitchen. The thing is, I think the charms of such a lifestyle would pall after a while. The issue is that the charms of all the lifestyles seem to pall after a while. It seems a pity. I am, after all, in my prime. Where is the lifestyle for me?

Plus, obviously, the children. To be perfectly honest, I'm not overly troubled – though I know that every single newspaper or magazine article I read tells me I should be – over the question of 'what's best for the children'. I know perfectly well what's best for the children: me, demonstrably. I moan about them all day, but they're extremely nice children. Add the fact that they have permanent access to their loving fathers and to an equally loving, if lunatic, extended family made up of both relatives and friends, and I don't think there's a problem. The only way of introducing a problem at this stage would be to produce an impermanent stepfather, or – God – a series of 'uncles'. ('Why are you walking like that, Mum, and wincing when you sit down?' 'Hoo, son, it's been *quite a night.*') I think that's probably a scenario that's best avoided. They've met the man from the Connaught, fleetingly, because I don't want them to think that I am in fact a nun: it's not a healthy thing for children to view their mother as a sexless being with a cobwebbed 'gina. But I'm not overly keen on them meeting a quick-fire succession of his successors – if he has indeed perished or suffered the indignity of a double amputation. Which I do hope he hasn't. I liked him more than I let on to Robert. I liked him enough to feel sad about his absence.

Is it different for men? Robert shags anything that moves, though perhaps his new carpe diem attitude will change that. I thought he was doing pretty well at carping every diem that he came across, but who knows? I have no idea at all of whom Sam shags, partly because he's discreet and partly because I don't particularly want to know (why not? Is that weird?). I don't want his penis to atrophy and drop off, obviously, but I don't need to know the particulars of its nocturnal activities, either.

'Are you okay, Clara?' says Tamsin, who's appeared in the chair next to mine. 'You look like you're daydreaming. Lovely, lovely dinner, wasn't it? Just glorious. It's so fantastic, being here.'

'Happy as a clam,' I say, which is true. When I was younger and the boys were small, I used to count my blessings, and I've never fallen out of the habit. My blessings are many. They are legion. That's the thing to remember. You know: nobody died. Well, apart from my dad, and possibly the man from the Connaught. Aside from that, though: all alive, wahoo.

'So am I,' Tam sighs. 'Who'd have thought, ten years ago?'

'You know,' I say, 'I thought for ages that you were with Jake because you thought anything was better than being alone.'

'I know you did,' says Tam. 'It's okay.'

'I apologize for thinking it,' I say, squeezing her hand. 'I always think I'm so right and so insightful, and just now – before you came over – I was musing on the fact that actually I know nothing at all.'

'You do,' says Tam. 'You know tons.'

'Well, there's a massive gap in my knowledge, let's say. I'm like somebody who seems to function but doesn't actually know how to count, or their world capitals, or the names of animals.'

'But you have experience,' says Tam.

'Yes,' I laugh. 'That's one way of putting it.'

'No, I mean it,' says Tamsin. 'Remember the pain theory?'

'Oh yes,' I say. 'I'd forgotten about it. We used to be obsessed with the pain theory. When was it – when you had Cassie?'

'When that awful Boden woman I met at my NCT classes was giving me advice,' says Tamsin. 'That's when we came up with it. The pain theory is absolutely true. It still holds.'

The pain theory is: you know those people who seem to have charmed lives? Idyllic childhoods, parents totally compos and healthy and still together fifty years later, lovely time at school, not an iota of heartbreak before meeting their delightful husband/wife, gorgeous children, zero illness anywhere, no financial worries, professionally successful, wonderful houses, no doubt or panic or dark thoughts in the middle of the night. Most of us have been broken at some point, and we're walking around with a few bits superglued back in place, with varying degrees of effectiveness. Not them: the most terrible or saddest things to happen to them are mildly tiresome, like painful wisdom teeth or having a flight cancelled. I'm pleased for them, and long may their joyous existence continue. But there's one caveat: they're not allowed to express any serious opinions. They can have them, obviously, but they're not allowed to say them out loud. They're allowed to say that roses are their favorite flower, or that they prefer bicycling to walking or Devon to Dorset, but that's it. I don't want to hear their opinions on single mothers, or on assisted suicide, or on the rights and wrongs of placing an aged parent in a residential home. I don't care what they think about the public health care they never use. I particularly don't wish to be lectured by them on things – the complexity of relationships, the pain of separation, the best way of ensuring children stay sane and happy when things go wrong – that they *literally* know nothing, zero, zilch, about. On these topics, such people are not allowed to talk: it would be like me lecturing people about nuclear physics, i.e. utterly absurd. That is the pain theory. And using the pain theory's criteria, both Tamsin and I have required superglue, which means we know stuff. So has everyone around this table, actually: like tends to stick with like, artfully patched broken pot with artfully patched broken pot. I wonder if that's why we were so instinctively hostile to poor Sophie and Tim two Christmases ago – whether it's because they were so full of opinions and so seemingly unburdened. They're happy now, by the way. Sophie is pregnant again. They've observed – rightly – that that's what people like them do: keep on banging them out and try to make everything about their life like a double-spread from the pages of a parenting magazine. It's not my definition of happiness, but it seems to work for them, and so I've never pointed out to Sophie, who has become quite a good friend, that I secretly think she's just given in.

There's no Christmas pudding in Morocco – well, there's no Christmas at all, if we're going to be exact. We've all imported puddings, but they're for tomorrow. Tonight, Fatima has made us a traditional French *bûche de Noël*, a chocolate sponge filled and iced with chocolate buttercream and rolled into the shape of a wooden log. She has decorated this with red berries and green holly leaves made of marzipan, and scattered confectioners' sugar over the top to look like snow. The icing has been scored with a fork, so the chocolate looks like wood. A tiny plastic squirrel is perched jauntily on the cake's edge, and I smile at her dedication: God knows where you find small plastic animals among the souks of Marrakesh. The *bûche* looks enchanting, both familiar and exotic, and even Pat volunteers that she wouldn't mind a little taste. Then she stands up and clears her throat.

'Cheers,' she says, raising her glass, which tonight contains cherry brandy and a dash of advocaat (I often wonder whether I could persuade Pat to co-author a book of cocktails with me). 'To everybody that's here. To all of us at Christmas. I'll never forget you.'

'We're not dead, Ma,' says Sam. 'Nobody's going anywhere.'

'I always want to spend Christmas with you,' Pat continues. 'If that's okay, like. I know we're not the same, but . . .'

'I'm going to cry,' says Evie.

My own throat has gone a little bit tight. I love annoying, plate-sniffing, food-denying Pat. I always want to spend Christmas with her, too. I want these people – my family and the remnants of my attempts at marriage – to stay with me always.

'We have such a nice time together. You're all that unusual. So thank you. For having me here and for . . . for everything.' She sits down again and looks around her in a slightly dazed way. 'I've never made a speech before,' she says as we all clap and cheer.

'I'm glad you did. But there's no need to thank anybody, Pat,' says Kate.

'You're part of the family,' I say. 'And you always will be. Thank you, Pat. That was lovely.'

'Aye,' says Pat. 'I know I'm not good with words, but I wanted to say a wee something. I was thinking about it for ages in the bath.'

'That was nice, Mum,' says Sam, giving her a hug.

'We're sorry that there are no pig latrines,' says Evie. 'We love you, Pat.'

6

25 December 2011, 7 a.m.

Christmas morning starts early in Marrakesh: we are woken at what feels like the crack of dawn by the muezzin's call to prayer. We all went to bed late last night, aside from the small children, who despite the excitement had conked out by 8 p.m., felled by their early start. For the rest of us, there were post-prandial cocktails, much conversation, a boisterous couple of rounds of the Name Game, a little bit of singing (by Pat, tipsy and in fine voice), a late-night dip in the pool (by Jake and Tamsin) and then a collective dash to get the presents under the tree and organize the positioning of the children's stockings. All glorious, but what was especially amazing to me was the lack of tidying up required. At home I barely have enough crockery or kitchen utensils, so that once you're allocated a glass as you arrive you have to hold on to it for dear life throughout the day. We have to quickly wash some of the plates between our turkey and pudding because I don't have enough dessert plates to go round; and all of this takes place in my hot, overcrowded kitchen, with everybody shoehorned into place. Here, we were stopped from even attempting to clear up by Fatima and, we were pleased to note, three other women who'd appeared from nowhere. I felt a bit guilty, but I was so tired by that point that I mostly felt nearly tearful with gratitude.

What's surprising to me about this whole Christmas-not-at-home malarkey is how comfortable it feels, considering it was conceived in a moment of madness. Maisy and the boys came into my room this morning to open their stockings, and if they did so in the pale Moroccan sunlight rather than in the London gloom – well, so what, really? It's odd, me thinking this, because Christmas at home is so part of my being – the one family tradition that still exists to be passed on – that I feel I'm somehow being unfaithful to myself just by being here. It's like Pat suddenly discovering that she not only likes all 'foreign' food but that her utter favorite is manioc, or sheep's eyes. Previously I'd believed that geographical location – my house, specifically – was what was holding the whole thing together: children, family, husbands, me. Today, I'm not so sure. The idea that we are holding *ourselves* together flits through my brain, only to be dismissed: we need foundations, and Christmas at home is the best foundation of all. Still, this isn't bad.

'Do you miss being at home at all?' I ask the children. The boys look at me as though I were mad, but they and Maisy eventually agree, after some discussion, that they wouldn't want to be away *every* year, 'because then we'd be used to it, and if we're going to be used to it we might as well be at home'.

After breakfast of tea and fruit – hard to see how any of us can countenance any more food after last night's extravaganza, but we're now all bracing ourselves for lunch in a few hours' time, imported giganto-turkey and all – Kate asks if I'd like to go for a stroll with her. And I would, partly to take a measure of exercise (there's an awful lot of pastry in Moroccan food) and partly because I know she wants to talk to me about Felix's probate, and I've been putting the conversation off for weeks. Christmas Day wouldn't be my number-one choice, but Robert's words last night about procrastination are fresh in my mind.

'Also,' says Kate, 'there's a shop in the new town, a saddler's originally, that is described in one of my guidebooks as "the Hermès of Africa".'

'I don't need bait,' I say. Then I think about it for a bit and say, 'But bait doesn't hurt.'

'They're only open for a couple of hours today,' says Kate, 'so we'd better step to it. And then we can be back for about eleven and do presents then.'

We walk through the streets, already crowded, of the medina, and are touched and delighted to note that our European aspect causes a dozen complete strangers to smile and wish us a happy Christmas.

'Fundamental difference,' says Kate, 'between the eastern and the western mindset. How many times have you walked around London and wished people you didn't know happy Eid or happy Ramadan or happy Hannukah?'

'Never,' I say, 'but it would be much trickier. You can't randomly assume all brown people are Muslims, and the Hannukah thing is even worse – look for anyone vaguely-Jewish-looking and be ready with your cheery greeting?'

'I suppose,' says Kate. 'I still think there's a generosity of spirit here that we would do well to emulate. You can tell by the food.'

'You can tell everything about people by the food,' I agree. 'Though let's try not to have some for a couple of hours.'

Twenty minutes later – stared at but unhassled, which is very different from how it was the last time I was here with Sam; sixty-year-old Kate claims this is because 'I am old, and they *revere* the old' – we are outside the old city walls. We walk a little more and find a horse-drawn carriage rank, and within minutes we are trip-trapping into the new town, with its Frenchified buildings and wide avenues. The Hermès of Africa hasn't quite opened yet, so we sit in a café opposite.

'I am resisting the urge to order those divine almond pastries,' says Kate, 'and I suggest you do the same.'

'Just coffee,' I say. 'I feel practically pregnant.'

'I hope you're not,' says Kate. 'I was almost a grandmother at your age.'

'No, Kate, of course I'm not pregnant! It was a figure of speech.'

'Good. The fashion for middle-aged women having babies is not an attractive one for anyone concerned, if you ask me. How's your friend Hope, speaking of which?'

'Probably contemplating pregnancy as we speak, knowing her,' I say. 'She's got a boyfriend, much younger – I don't remember if you ever saw him on Facebook, this time last year?'

'I don't remember either. I remember her cruising, though. Isn't it funny – well, not *hilarious* as such – but when I was in my late thirties, all I wanted to do was be someone like Hope, doing interesting work and having my own company and being in business. Julian was against it, and I was for anything Julian was for, and so that was that.'

'I know. Rather atypically doormat-ish of you, Kate, I always thought.'

'The Third World War in the background, darling. Raging away for years.'

'I had no idea.'

'Well, no. Nobody does. The only people who ever have *any* idea of what goes on inside a marriage are the two people in it, as surely you know by now, Clara. Everything else is just gossip and conjecture. When Julian and I divorced, I kept bumping into people for years afterward – good friends – who'd say, "Oh my goodness, I had no idea, you seemed so blissfully happy." The fact is, unless you go spewing your guts all over the place, nobody has a clue. And I don't like spewing.'

'But that was what started the rot? That he didn't want you to have a job?'

'Among other things. But yes, it was the catalyst. When Flo and Evie were older, you know. And I sat there looking pretty and twiddling my thumbs and organizing nice dinners for years on end. His point was that I didn't need to work, what with us having money. Rather missing the point. And of course ghastly waste of my excellent brain. That was what drove one *loopy*. The utter waste of brain.'

We sit and sip our coffees. Across the road, somebody from the Hermès of Africa is pulling up the shop's metal shutters.

'Go on, then,' I say. 'I know you want to tell me about the Felix stuff.'

'I don't know why you've made such a fuss about it, Clara.'

'Well. You know. It still kind of messes slightly with my head.'

'I do wish you'd be more robust. What if you were an Afghan peasant, struggling daily against the Taliban and the lure of opium?'

'I, er. I'm not, Kate, is the thing.'

'Or a Moroccan womanfolk who had to slaughter her own fowl?'

'But Kate. I'm from Notting Hill.'

'No excuse. One should always be prepared and vigilant and *capable*. There is zero point in sticking one's head in the sand about anything at all. I, for instance, would resist the poppy and slaughter the fowl.'

'You sound like Robert. Anyway, I'm here. I volunteered the question. Go on, shoot.'

'There's actually very little to report,' Kate says, 'which is partly why your ducking away is so annoying. So,' she continues, rootling through her bag and pulling out a thin folder, 'here we are. Probate.'

'Why was this sent to you, by the way?'

'What? Oh, because they didn't have your address.'

'Right. Great. Well, come on. What's it say?'

'I can't find the bit about the money. Ah yes, here we are. There's a tiny bit of money – about ten thousand dollars.'

'Oh,' I say, pleased. 'That's nice. And unexpected.'

'God knows what he did with the rest, he used to be terribly well-off. Still, not our concern.'

'No.'

'Now,' says Kate. 'The thing is. There isn't much money, but what you have is a fraction of it. Do you follow?'

'Not at all. What do you mean?'

'I mean, darling, that there's a wife.'

'Fair enough,' I say. 'Hardly surprising. I wouldn't have wanted him to die alone, in his Mexican eyrie.'

'And children. Rather a lot of them. You, obviously, and then two more with wife number one, two others with wife number two, and one with the current wife, whom he in fact wasn't married to. Common-law. Six in total, I believe.'

'Children?' I say. For some bizarre reason, the idea of Felix having other children has simply never entered my head. 'Wow. God. Weird.'

'Your half-siblings,' says Kate. 'Five of them. And they are – hang on, let me find the dates of birth – they are, yes, here we go: they are thirty-eight, thirty-six, thirty-two, twenty-nine and fifteen. Do you want the names?'

'I don't know. Not yet, no. This is so strange, Kate. I'm five people I've never met's older sister.'

'I know. Came as a surprise to me too; he never mentioned them. Rather have the feeling he was *fairly breezy* in his approach to fatherhood, old Felix. But here we have it: three boys, two girls. Or three men, two women, I suppose. They all have his surname. Well, aside from you.'

'I see.'

'One other thing: there's a letter. Here,' she says, pushing an envelope across the table at me. 'You don't have to open it now. It's from him. He sent one to each of his children, apparently.'

'From beyond the grave. This is really, really strange, Kate.

I don't know what to say. Shall we go and look at the shop? I'd like to think it through while looking at small leather goods, if you don't mind. I think I'd find it soothing.'

I stick the envelope in my handbag, noting first that Felix – my father – has rather adolescent handwriting.

'I quite understand,' says Kate, waving for the bill.

I am entirely able to focus on the Hermès of Africa. You'd think my mind might wander, but you'd be wrong. The work on the bags and cases we admire is outstanding: immaculate stitching, exquisite finishes and the softest, butteriest leather you could imagine. We're in the shop for about an hour, examining everything with forensic attention. Kate points out, rightly, that these are the perfect holiday souvenirs: you'd still love them back in London and would carry them happily without feeling they didn't look quite right outside their native country ('Unlike the lightweight hooded cloak I got here once, years ago, and which I wore to Glyndebourne for warmth until I realized I looked *exactly* like Satan'). I buy a satchel-style bag with a long strap and Kate buys two wallets, and then we carriage it all back to our house in the medina, where preparations for lunch are afoot and where it's time for us all to open our presents. I haven't lifted a finger all morning. I have five new brothers and sisters and God knows how many new nieces and nephews. This is the oddest Christmas I've ever had.

I read the letter as soon as we get home, of course I do. I take it up to my bedroom while everyone's downstairs gearing up for the marathon that is present-opening. I put it on the bed and stare at it for a bit. I've already noted the adolescent handwriting on the envelope. It's odd because Kate is rather fussy about calligraphy: she disliked a friend I had throughout my teenage years purely because of the rounded, loopy way she formed her Ws – 'Like bottoms,' Kate had sniffed, 'or breasts:

awful beyond belief' – and dotted her Is with a happy face. Perhaps the writing reminded her unpleasantly of Felix's and of teenage single motherhood. Who knows? Anyway, here we are, and here is my late father's missive, the only letter he has ever written to me. I open the envelope carefully, wondering in passing at the oddness of his saliva having been on the licky bit. If this were a crime program on television, we could run a DNA test. Except we don't need one.

Oaxaca, Mexico

9 March 2011

Dear Clara,

I have been no father to you. It seems trite to apologize and I shan't attempt to.

I have been a hopeless father to all of my children, with the exception of Aurelio, the youngest, whose mother and I have lived together for these past sixteen years.

I am sending variants of this letter to all of you – to you, Clara, and to your half-siblings. Their names are Jorge, Elias, Katherine, Isabel and Aurelio. Katherine and Isabel live in San Francisco, California. Jorge, Elias and Aurelio are here in Mexico. If any of you are curious about each other, my lawyers will be able to assist with addresses.

Your mother is a great woman and spoke very highly of your stepfather.

With all good wishes,
Felix Maddox

I sit on the edge of the bed and try to take this all in. I don't quite know what I was expecting, but this perhaps wasn't it. Couldn't he have lied a bit? Said, 'Sorry I was so crap, it must have felt horrid'? Said, 'Sorry I had absolutely zero interest in you at any stage of your existence – that sucks, and I apologize'? Said, 'I'm sorry I never met my grandchildren'? He doesn't sound very nice. It's not what you'd call warm, that letter.

And I'm née Maddox. That's weird. I quite like it. Maybe I'll reverse the deed poll Kate filled out on my behalf nearly forty years ago. Clara Maddox: rather smarter than Clara Dunphy, formerly Clara Hutt.

Well, there we go. That's that. Line drawn under chapter. Except, I think as I wash my face – I'm not crying, just hot and a bit dusty from my walk with Kate – that maybe I should look them up, old Jorge and Elias and the rest of them. Send them a letter or something. An e-mail. They're my family, after all – they're no more or no less Of The Blood than my beloved sisters Evie and Flo and a great deal more Of The Blood than, say, Julian or Pat. Oh, I don't know.

'Are you okay, love?' Pat asks as I arrive back downstairs and sit myself down among the banquettes and floor cushions.

'I'm fine, Pat,' I say. 'Kate and I were just going through some stuff from my dad's probate – my real dad, the one I never knew. All done now.'

'Ooh, that's a horrible thing, that probate,' says Pat.

'It was more strange than horrible,' I say. 'But anyway, it's done now.'

'So humiliating,' muses Pat.

'Well – yes, I suppose so,' I say, rather startled by her insight and empathy. 'Sort of. I mean, you really can't be humiliated by something so absolutely outside your control, but it does feel a little . . .'

'Aye, that's the thing,' says Pat. 'You're that powerless.'

'Thanks for your concern,' I say, giving her hand a squeeze. 'It's all done now. Let's enjoy Christmas.'

'It's an awful spot, the arse,' says Pat. 'Of all the places to be getting something like that.'

'The arse? How do you . . .? Oh, I see. Prostate.'

'My friend's husband had it,' says Pat, shaking her head. 'Sad business, that was. Terrible trouble with his waterworks. The build-up, you know. The pressure.'

I close my eyes, because I think that if I keep them open and focused on Pat's sweet, round, concerned face, I might just explode with laughter. I take a couple of deep breaths.

'Come on, Pat,' I say. 'Let's get these presents open.'

I don't know whether being in Morocco has focused the mind, or whether it's pure coincidence, but I am the delighted recipient of the best presents I've been given in years: presents that actually remind me of the absolute, pure pleasure of receiving. It's almost as though everyone has been mindful of my Christmas fixation and has sweetly gone out of their way to make things extra-nice for me. Kate, along with the dinner service she tells me she bought me at the shop we went to yesterday and is having shipped back to London ('so that we have enough plates next year'), has made me an album of photographs. I have hundreds – thousands, probably – of photographs of my own children, but only a handful from my own childhood: they were another casualty of separations and house-moves and rented flats and my general carelessness. Whenever I wondered aloud to Kate whether she had any she could give me, she'd go all vague and mutter about attics, and eventually I stopped asking. Now she hands me a sumptuously bound cornflower-blue leather album. The photograph on the first page is tattered and faded; it is of Kate and a man wearing jeans and a duffel coat, laughing in what looks like an Oxford quad.

'Is that him?' I say, squinting at the picture.

'Yes,' says Kate. 'Terrible photo, but the only one I had. It's literally taken me six months to find it.'

'He looks nice,' I say.

'He *was* quite nice,' says Kate. 'In his day. Carry on.'

There's a photograph of me as a toddler, wearing a turquoise velour playsuit and with a daisy chain on my head, perched on Kate's hip and smiling at Julian, and then all the familiar ones of home, a deluge of them: birthday parties and Christmases and school holidays, and us in the garden, and us in France, and us in restaurants and in bed and on the sofa. There are Evie and Flo, tiny babies at first and then little children and then grown-up girls. There's me in a succession of appalling teenage haircuts, including – the horror – a mullet dyed ginger. There are friends and relatives and lunches and suppers and teas, and, on the last page, a formal portrait of my sisters and me standing on either side of Kate that someone took as the basis for a painting, if I remember rightly. I have no recollection of the painting at all, but the photograph is beautiful.

I go to kiss my mother. 'It's the best thing you've ever given me. The best present, I mean. Ever. Better than my Sony Walkman. I love it.'

'Pleasure,' says Kate. 'You seemed to be going a little bit doolally on the families front. I thought you might find it grounding.'

'That's gorgeous. Lovely photies. But now my turn,' says Pat. 'Open mine.'

'Thanks,' I say, 'but you all open some too. I don't want to be the only grown-up who's opening presents.'

Pat's present to me, wrapped in paper featuring bare-buttocked, mooning Santas, is a white porcelain mug lavishly embellished with gold paint around the rim and handle.

'Thank you,' I say. 'It's lovely.'

'Turn it round,' Pat says. 'There's writing on it.'

I turn the mug round. *World's Best Daughter-in-Law*, it says, in curlicued writing.

'Oh, Pat. I don't know what to say. That's so nice. It's so nice of you. So incredibly nice that I . . .' It's useless: my eyes have filled with tears.

'Have a tissue,' says Pat, pulling one out of the sleeve of her cardigan. 'You don't have to thank me. It's a pleasure, love. And I mean it,' she adds, grinning at me. 'So I do.'

I hug her very vigorously and get up for a bit to distribute the usual piles of presents to everybody else and also, to be honest, to take a few surreptitious deep breaths. When I sit down again, my own presents keep coming. There's a handwritten invitation from Robert, on thick cream-colored card, asking me to be his companion on a press trip to Zanzibar, which he knows I've wanted to go to since I was twenty.

'This is fantastic,' I tell him. 'Are you sure?'

'No one I'd rather go with.' He smiles. 'You have to swear to keep your hands off me, though. No funny business, Clara.'

'Challenging. I can't promise I'll manage to control myself . . .' I say.

'Who could?' says Robert.

'. . . but I'll try my hardest.'

'Here,' says Evie, shoving a parcel into my hand. 'I got you other stuff, but this is my best present to you.'

'It's Christmas Hamster!' I say, as soon as I've torn off the first inch of paper. 'Christmas Hamster! He was your favorite thing in the whole world!'

'You taught me how to knit, when we were little. I thought you'd like him. I'm quite cut up about losing him again so soon,' she says. 'But I can come and see him every year at your house, at the Christmi. So it's okay.'

The next hour goes on in this vein: meaningful present after meaningful present. Sam gives me a picture made out of shells he and Maisy have gathered on the beach in Ireland. 'We've been making it for weeks,' he says. 'I hope you like it. Sorry about the glue smears.'

'I love it,' I say truthfully, covering Maisy, who is pink and beaming with pride, in kisses.

'Rather puts the small leather goods into perspective,' says Kate.

'Doesn't it just?' I go to kiss Sam, and find he kisses me back like a normal person.

We sit there, all together, and wade through our gifts. The champagne is flowing, Jack and Charlie are bickering, the little girls are squealing at everything they open.

Later, just before lunch, I ask the boys to go and get their laptop and to log into one of their Facebook accounts. This Charlie does.

'What are we doing, Mum?' he asks.

'We're seeing if we can find some people,' I say.

'Okay – well, what are they called? I need names.'

'Try looking for Isabel Maddox,' I say.

'There are seventeen of them,' Charlie says a moment later. 'Look – here they all are.'

'See if there are any in San Francisco,' I say.

'Yep, two.'

'Let me see.'

It's obvious immediately: Isabel Maddox, though bearing very little physical resemblance to me, has my ear – my Maddox ear, with its little pointy bit. She looks nice. She works in television production. She has two children. She lives near a park, by the look of things.

'Look up Katherine, also Maddox. Actually, no – that's quite a common name. Look up Elias Maddox.'

Another minute, and there's my half-brother. He lives in Mexico City and is a doctor. He has two big dogs. He's handsome, actually, Elias. And he has my ear too. So does Jorge, who is a tree surgeon.

'Do you know who they are?' I ask the boys. 'They're your uncles and aunts.'

'How . . . oh, from your real dad,' says Charlie.

'Except he wasn't really your dad,' says Jack. 'Julian was more your dad, wasn't he?'

'Yes,' I say. 'He was.'

'They look okay,' says Charlie with a shrug. 'Oh God, Mum – you're not going to ask them to Christmas next year, are you?'

'Oh man,' says Jack. 'Not *more* of us. We don't *need* more of us.'

'Yeah,' says Charlie. 'We're good as we are.'

I could meet them all. It would be so easy. A few messages exchanged on Facebook, a couple of plane tickets . . . My family: my blood, my DNA, my genetic inheritance. A whole new sort of life. And a whole new sort of Christmas.

I look over at the seating area. At my mother, my lovely, loopy, fantastic Kate, my force of nature, mad as a bat and brave as a lion. I look at my technically half-sisters, whom I love in ways I can't even express. I look at my children, the apples of my eyes, and at their fathers, their fabulous, funny, talented fathers, whom I'll never stop loving either, in a different way. I look at Jake and at Tamsin, my oldest friend, and at little Cassie. I look at my adorable nieces and at my dear brother-in-law. I look at Pat, who's not even related to me anymore and whom I bitch about in my head and whom I love, and who made me cry with a mug. I'm so busy looking that at first I don't notice my phone beeping, and when it beeps again I look down at a text from the man from the Connaught.

Kate was right. Water *is* thicker than blood. Love is what matters, and love is what I have, and who cares where it comes from?

I close the laptop lid.

'Come on,' I say. 'Lunchtime.'

THE END

MERRY CHRISTMAS!

Acknowledgements

Thanks to my publisher, Juliet Annan, for bearing once again with my unauthorly approach to deadlines. I'm a journalist – the idea of writing something eighteen months in advance is absurd to me, but I do see that it's not remotely absurd to publishers, and I'm very grateful that my dear Mrs. Penguin didn't get her feathers in a flap and peck me to death with her beak while awaiting delivery of my manuscript.

Thanks to Jenny Lord and Ellie Smith at Penguin, who didn't peck me to death either.

Thanks, as ever, to the incomparable Georgia Garrett, my agent and beloved friend. (She's not my friend because she's my agent – I hate that 'how gloriously you love me, person whose job it is to do well by me'. She's my friend because we've known each other since we were eighteen.)

Thanks to the wonderful Leanne Shapton for making me my favorite book jacket, ever.

Thanks to Patricia McVeigh for help with the Irish.

Thanks to Jenny McIvor for 'Mr. Penis'. That must have been a fun night.

Thanks to my family, blood and extended, for their love and support. Special thanks to the fathers of my children.

And thanks to my mother for being my mother. Any other mother would be the most hideous comedown. Any small talent I may have, I owe to her.